IRON & STEEL

WILLIAM ABRAMS

authorHOUSE®

AuthorHouse™
1663 Liberty Drive
Bloomington, IN 47403
www.authorhouse.com
Phone: 1 (800) 839-8640

Published by AuthorHouse   06/15/2016

ISBN: 978-1-5246-0895-8 (sc)
ISBN: 978-1-5246-0893-4 (hc)
ISBN: 978-1-5246-0894-1 (e)

Library of Congress Control Number: 2016907837

Print information available on the last page.

This book is printed on acid-free paper.

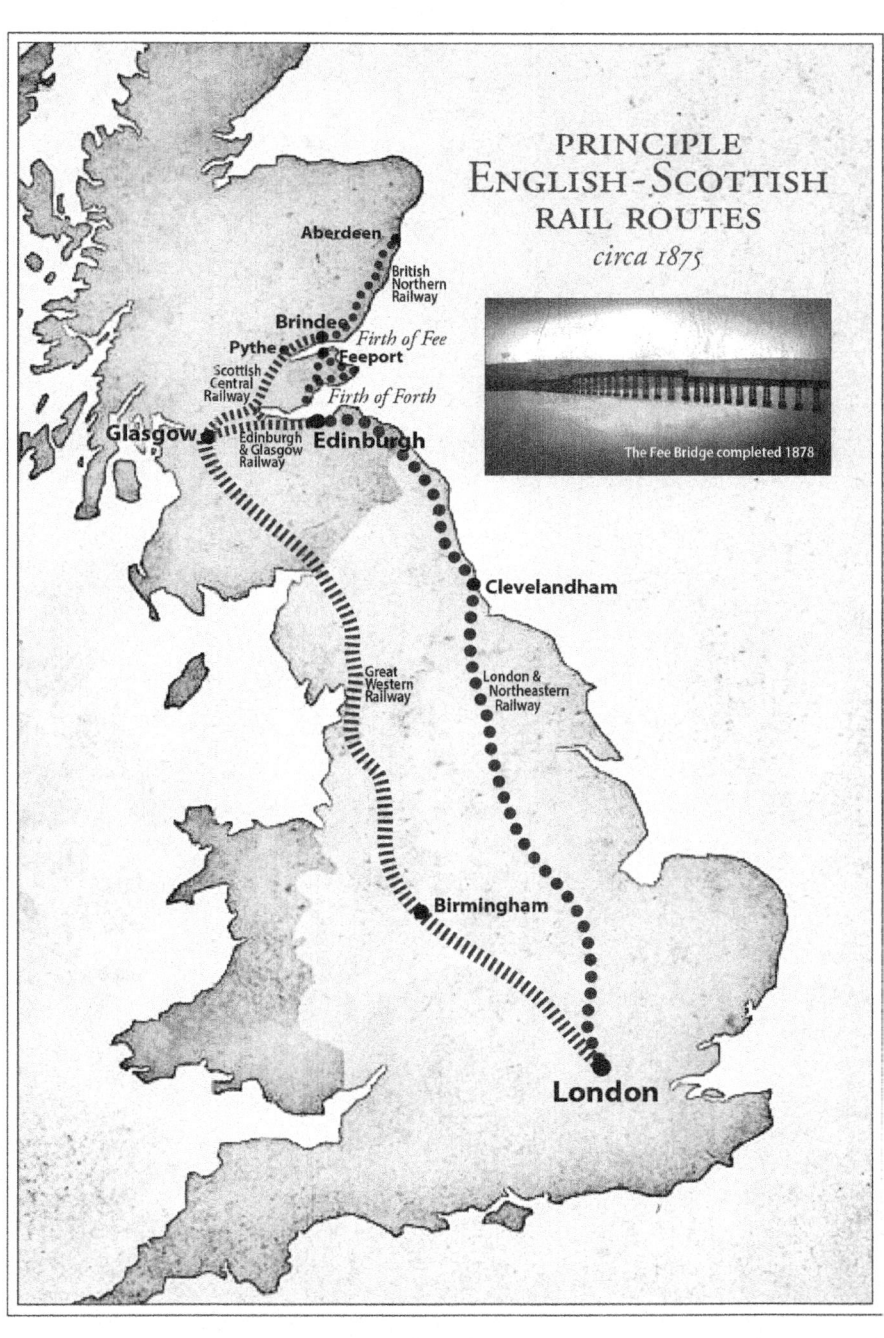

PRINCIPLE
ENGLISH-SCOTTISH
RAIL ROUTES
circa 1875

Aberdeen

British
Northern
Railway

Brindee
Pythe *Firth of Fee*
Feeport
Scottish
Central
Railway *Firth of Forth*
Glasgow Edinburgh **Edinburgh**
& Glasgow
Railway

The Fee Bridge completed 1878

Clevelandham

Great
Western
Railway

London &
Northeastern
Railway

Birmingham

London

It was a stormy night, the final Sunday of the year, and the evening train to Aberdeen was more crowded than usual because of the upcoming New Year holiday. Many were making the trip for the first time, and inside the coaches, a number of passengers jerked in their seats, startled by the sudden ferocity with which the windows began to rattle as the train started onto the new bridge. Nearly two miles in length, the bridge was a vast viaduct extending across one of the broad estuaries, known as firths, that cut like gashes into the Scottish coastline.

Up front in the locomotive, the driver peered into the night through a small porthole, one of two such windows cut into the front of the locomotive's cab. Opposite the driver, the fireman grimaced through the other. Although covered, the cab offered little protection: It was open on the sides and rear, and while the men faced the searing heat of the firebox and boiler, their backs were soaked with cold rain.

The driver tightened his grasp on the throttle as the train reached the highest section of the bridge, which stood nearly ninety feet above the firth. Down below, the frigid water thrashed against the bridge's supports, pelting the cast-iron columns with foam and spray. In the distance, he could see the lights on the far shore, blurred by the driving rain. The lights were still more than a mile away when the cab was engulfed by a tremendous rush of wind. Sparks flew from the coach's iron wheels, and the driver held fast to the throttle as the storm seemed to focus itself directly on the train.

Edinburgh, Scotland

1871

The directors of the British Northern Railway sat together on one side of a long conference table in the company boardroom. Though once impressive, the room had long since lost its luster. It was more than ten years since the walls had been painted, and there wasn't a chair without a burn or gash, and most had both. On the wall behind the conference table was a yellowed print of the inaugural run of the *Coast Flier*, the line's premier train. Like the locomotive and coaches it depicted, the print was close to twenty years old.

Richard Taylor, the board's chairman, fiddled with the gold watch chain that curved along his stomach. The board member to Taylor's right did the same, while others pulled at their whiskers or tapped their cigars against the large pewter ashtrays that were evenly spaced along the length of the table. They were bored.

Tacked to the wall in front of them was a series of drawings for a bridge designed to connect the towns of Feeport and Brindee across the Firth of Fee in Scotland. When completed, it would be the longest bridge in the world, a fact one would have expected to inspire a certain enthusiasm. The board members, however, had seen the plans before, and in spite of the bridge's great length, there was nothing extraordinary about it. Moreover, the engineer to whom the plans belonged had been speaking for close to an hour, putting the men to sleep with details about girders and expansion joints; more than anything, they looked forward to the meeting's end.

Two consulting engineers sat to the right of the board members, along with an observer from the Royal Navy. They, too, grew impatient, as did Charles Jenkins, a fourth engineer, who sat on a low bench in the corridor just outside the boardroom.

Charles was tall and lean and, at twenty-eight, was the youngest of seven men who had submitted plans for the bridge. Like the board's two consulting engineers, Charles wore a long beard, a fashion common within the profession. His suit, however, was of a different cut, and its heavy wool bore the dark-green plaid of the provincial style.

Two weeks before, Charles had made what should have been his final presentation, but he knew the board was leaning toward the design then being presented, a decidedly conservative plan consisting of a series of standard wrought-iron trusses supported on brick columns. In stark contrast, Charles had put forth an extremely daring proposal—a cantilever scheme in which the bridge's spans were to extend from the supporting towers like huge metal arms. Moreover, they were to be built of steel, a material the British railroad establishment had yet to adopt, relying instead on a combination of cast iron and wrought iron, as well as brick and stone.

Charles, however, was not prepared to concede the competition. Throughout the proceedings, several of the board members had expressed considerable interest in his plan, and he came this day hoping to make one last plea on his own behalf. To that end, he'd commissioned a painting, a six-foot canvas that rested by his side, barely dry, in a leather canister case.

Still, Charles knew his chances were slim, and as he sat waiting, his thoughts returned to a notice he'd seen that morning, inviting trained engineers to Russia for the czar's Siberian rail project. There were other projects as well, in Egypt, Venezuela, and the Canadian Provinces. The thought of going abroad had been a persistent one of late, but there was his fiancée and their upcoming marriage to think about. This was no time for him to leave the country.

That being said, he was not at all looking forward to returning to work at his father's labeling shop, which is where Charles was scheduled to resume the following Monday. With no money coming in and no prospects on the horizon, he had little choice, but it certainly wasn't going to do anything to appease his future father-in-law. Charles's fiancée, Victoria Cooper, was the daughter of a prominent physician with a Harley Street practice. As far as he was concerned, engineers, even those few like Charles who had received their training in school, were little more than mechanics, a view Charles's working at the labeling shop was only going to reinforce.

There was some irony in this, Charles knew, in that it was only because of the shop that he and Victoria had met at all. After nearly two decades of effort, his father's business had become remarkably successful over the past few years, so Charles's mother, looking to put some of that newfound wealth to good use, had sent his younger sister, Celia, away to school. It was there that she met Victoria. The two girls had been roommates their first year together and were in the midst of trading weekends at one another's homes when Charles returned to London two summers before.

His thoughts were interrupted when next to him, the door opened. Charles glanced up, expecting to see one of the board members. Instead, it was Darrs, the engineer who had been giving his presentation. Although the two men had never been introduced, they had seen each other before, and Darrs nodded in acknowledgment.

Charles bowed his head in response, thinking that would be the end of it, but Darrs continued.

"Jenkins, isn't it?"

"Yes," Charles said.

"You are the one proposing to build the bridge of steel. I saw the plans—very interesting. I've employed the cantilever myself, though never in metal . . . Oh, do forgive me," Darrs interrupted himself. "I haven't introduced myself. Stewart Darrs," he said, extending his arm.

Charles stood up to shake hands. "You're referring to the adjustable ramps used to move the trains on and off the ferries here in Edinburgh and on the Fee?"

Darrs nodded. "Those here on the Forth are due for replacement. As I'm sure you noticed, the present ones are timber. I was already thinking of wrought iron, but I think I will look into steel as well."

Again Darrs extended his arm to shake hands, after which he continued down the hall. Charles watched after him, surprised by the fact that Darrs would know his name. Charles also took encouragement in Darrs's comments about steel.

Charles waited until Darrs turned the corner and was out of sight, then knocked on the boardroom door. He'd come of his own accord and had no guarantee the board members would even let him speak. Knowing that Darrs's presentation had gone on for more than an hour, Charles questioned the board members' patience to sit through another one.

"Come," Charles heard from behind the door. He knew the voice. It was Taylor, the board chairman, who again spoke as Charles stepped into the room.

"Yes, Mr. Jenkins, what is it?"

"Excuse me, Mr. Chairman. I was wondering if the board would be so kind as to allow me a few more minutes of its time?"

"Mr. Jenkins, you know the rules of the competition," Taylor said.

"I realize my request is irregular, but I have something I believe will be of great interest to the board." Charles shifted his glance from the chairman to the other members.

"Irregular indeed," Taylor said. "Mr. Jenkins, you have had your chance like all the rest. If you feel you've made your case poorly, I'm sorry, but in fairness to the others, I cannot allow it."

"Oh, let the man speak."

Taylor glanced to his left. The remark had come from Robert Kern, the board member who had been Charles's most outspoken supporter throughout the proceedings.

"Mr. Chairman," Kern said, "as we are all aware, Mr. Darrs is the clear favorite. If a challenge does exist, it comes from Mr. Jenkins. At least we can take a few minutes to hear him out."

"Yes, let him speak," another board member said.

Taylor grimaced. He would have preferred to say no, and would have, had no one other than Kern spoken up. "Very well, Mr. Jenkins. But please keep it brief."

Charles nodded and stepped to the front of the room, where he removed the canvas from the canister. Darrs's drawings remained tacked to the wall, and Charles unfurled his painting directly on top of them. The effect was stunning, and several of the board members shifted forward in their seats. Rendered in oil, the treacherous waters of the Fee suddenly stretched before them, glistening beneath what would be two miles of cantilevered steel. The difference could not have been more striking: Where Darrs's plan required eighty-nine spans of varying lengths, Charles's completed the crossing using only seventeen, each of them three times longer than even the longest spans in Darrs's design.

"Mr. Jenkins, we are all well aware of your design from the linens you displayed at previous meetings," the chairman said.

"I thought a painting would allow the board members to more easily imagine the bridge as it would actually appear."

"Mr. Jenkins, we are not here to enhance the imagination of this board."

Charles's eyes brightened in defiance. Despite the chairman's remonstrations, the expressions of several board members indicated the painting had done its work.

"As you all can see, what I propose is a bridge of such distinction that its fame would be certain to surpass even that of Roebling's Brooklyn Bridge."

Again, the board members stirred. Although just under way, the suspension bridge being built in New York was already creating something of a sensation. Its main span would be a third again as long as any bridge then in existence, and engravings of it as it would appear when finished were already circulating in the press.

For his part, however, Chairman Taylor remained unmoved. He was not sure the company stockholders really cared about having a bridge more famous than the one in New York. Actually, it was he who did not care. Nor did he wish to tolerate what he perceived as Charles's growing impudence.

"Gentlemen," he said, addressing the entire room, "the dramatic nature of Mr. Jenkins's painting changes nothing. The fact remains that we have no guarantee that such a bridge can even be built. And even then, by Mr. Jenkins's own estimate, the steel for his design would cost nearly twice as much as the iron for Mr. Darrs's. What possible reason can we have for spending twice as much on a material whose strength and durability have yet to be proved?"

"It has been proved," Charles said. "As we speak, the Germans and the Americans both are building in steel."

"What they do in other countries is of no concern to this board," Taylor said, his voice stern.

Charles pulled up on the bottom of the painting, revealing the drawings underneath. "Don't you see what Mr. Darrs has done? He's simply taken a standard form, one that is now being used to bridge creeks and streams around the world, and here intends to repeat it eighty-nine times."

"And what of it?" Taylor asked. "As Mr. Darrs himself points out, the repetitive nature of the design will aid in its construction."

"Excuse me, Mr. Chairman," Kern said.

Taylor turned abruptly. "Yes, Mr. Kern, what is it?" he asked with obvious annoyance.

"I apologize for the interruption, but might I make an observation?"

Taylor hesitated, his expression growing somewhat scornful, before he gestured his consent.

Kern nodded and took a moment to clear his throat. "Mr. Chairman, although I appreciate your concern, I must point out that the men who come forth to work on this project will not only be constructing a bridge, but be playing a part in history, building what has never been built before."

"Please, Mr. Kern, not another one of your speeches."

"Bridges are not factory objects," Kern said. "They are today's equivalent to the ancient cathedrals, monuments by which a nation and its people are judged."

"Mr. Kern, my interest here is not with cathedrals. It is with keeping this railroad in operation, and to that end, we need a bridge.

A very long bridge. What it looks like is of no concern to me, nor should it be to you."

It was no secret that the British Northern was on the verge of bankruptcy. Ten months before, two railroads, the Edinburgh & Glasgow and the Scottish Central signed an agreement creating a route that made it faster to zigzag from Edinburgh to Brindee via Glasgow than it was to travel in a straight line. Overnight, there was competition where there never had been before, and the price of British Northern shares plummeted.

The British Northern's sphere of operation was confined to the east coast of Scotland. The line ran up the coast from Edinburgh to Brindee and then to Aberdeen. It was less than 100 miles but was an arduous trip, involving multiple ferries, that often took in excess of six hours. Two broad estuaries—the Firth of Fee and the Firth of Forth—cut the company's rails into three distinct sections. The line offered connecting service, but delays and cancellations were frequent. Gale-force winds were common in winter, and even in good weather, passengers and freight twice had to be transferred from land to ferry and then back again.

It was a burdensome process, and one that could be remedied only by the construction of two enormous bridges, the second of which, that across the Forth, was not yet even in the planning stage. They were bridges on a scale never before attempted, and with that in mind, Taylor was interested in only two things: that they be feasible to construct, and that they not fall down, a matter of no small importance, given recent history.

"Mr. Kern, I have no intention of risking this undertaking because of your misplaced notion of glory, when hardly a month goes by without some new story about a bridge collapsing."

"Those stories are about iron bridges," Charles said.

"Mr. Jenkins, no fewer than three experts have sat before this board detailing steel's tendency to give way without warning," Taylor responded.

"Three *iron* men is more like it," Charles scoffed. "Twenty years ago you had stonemasons spreading the same fears about iron."

"And what of steel's propensity to rust?" Taylor asked. "This railroad is not about to spend a quarter of a million pounds for a bridge that will need replacing in less than twenty years."

"Properly maintained, the bridge will last forever," Charles said.

"And who will maintain it? By the time it's painted once, the work will have to start all over again," Taylor said.

"Mr. Chairman, everyone knows maintenance costs are figured into passenger and freight charges. No one is planning to cut into the railroad's profits," Kern replied.

Taylor's expression hardened. He took a deep breath and leaned forward, the edge of the table cutting a crease across his stomach.

"Gentleman, with all that we have just heard, might I remind you that in its design and choice of materials, Mr. Darrs's bridge relies on what has been tried and tested. We are running a railroad," he said sternly. "We are not here to construct monuments."

Chapter 2

All along the street, carts and wagons were parked two and three deep. Horse manure, dampened by a drizzling rain, littered the coarse layer of rubble that surfaced the roadway. The street was in a warehouse district a few blocks from the Thames, but a number of the buildings had been converted to other uses. Some were supply houses for the construction trade; others made specialized parts and machinery, while in large, fading letters their facades proclaimed the names and wares of previous tenants. Inside a building that bore the words *Herrold & Sons, Imports* in peeling black letters, Charles stood before a mechanical press, placing bottles onto a leather-cushioned cradle at the heart of the machine. He watched as a central arm positioned a label on the bottle just as two other arms descended to sweep it smooth on the glass.

Around him, dust swirled in the meager bands of light penetrating the shop through a row of soot-coated windows. There was a steam engine in one corner, and an intense glow emanated from the open hatch of the firebox, into which a man shoveled coal. Overhead, four iron rods secured an iron driveshaft to the ceiling. They trembled intermittently, while leather drive belts waffled on their way from the shaft to the flywheels of three presses. Each of the presses, like the one at which Charles worked, was specially designed to affix labels. Stacked against the walls were crates of *Mohegan Health Tonic*, London's best-selling patent medicine.

Once the bottle was labeled, Charles returned it to the table from which he'd taken it with one hand, while with his other he positioned another bottle on the cradle. It was a procedure he had known for years, but his father had recently installed a new, more powerful steam engine, and when Charles returned to the shop two weeks before, he'd needed several days to adjust to the increased speed. Now he waited, growing impatient with what he perceived as the machine's increasingly inadequate pace. Time and time again, he was ready with another bottle before the arms completed their cycle.

Here he was at the shop, exactly where he'd been twelve months before. It was going on a year and a half since Charles had returned to London, and still he hadn't secured a single contract. No doubt his desire to build in steel had worked against him, but it was not the only obstacle he faced. Open design competitions were extremely rare. Most railroads maintained engineering departments of their own. Except for the largest projects, the railroads had no need to look beyond their own personnel, and when they did, they tended to confine their dealings to the most established firms. The Fee had been something of a last chance.

Charles had an engineering degree from London's recently founded School of Technology. Unlike most of his classmates, who, following graduation, had gotten jobs with the railroads or the many firms that catered to them, Charles had also completed a six-year apprenticeship at the Barrol Steel Mill outside Birmingham. In spite of his expertise, however, the six years had worked against him. He had no professional experience, while his classmates were already rising to positions of prominence.

It was a risk Charles had known going to Birmingham. His mother had questioned him about it, and therefore his father as well, but Charles had been determined. Still, with the Fee project all but lost to him, over the past month he'd sent letters of introduction to five of the city's top engineering firms, not one of which had responded. No doubt he could have found something as a surveyor or a draftsman, which he wouldn't have minded, but that would hardly satisfy his future father-in-law.

In front of Charles, the central arm of the press started up with a label still hanging from the bottom, having failed to attach to the bottle. He waited for the machine to complete another cycle, and this time the label remained attached, but it happened again with the next bottle, and he reached for the main lever to take the press out of gear.

Of all the obstacles his father had encountered building his labeling machines, none had proved more difficult than that of regulating the flow of glue to the labels. As it stood, the labels were stacked in a four-pronged claw that moved up and down on tracks in the center of the press. The glue was contained in a shallow pan attached to the rear of the machine and was applied by a moving roller that swept underneath the claw as it descended toward the cradle on which the bottles were placed. With each pass, the underside of the bottom label was coated with glue, and it was actually the adherence of the paper—moistened by the glue—to the surface of the bottle that would draw the label from the stack as the claw began its ascent.

The mechanism, however, was sensitive. When too much glue coated the roller, the labels would pull from the stack two or three at a time. If too little glue coated the roller, labels that appeared firmly attached would peel from the bottles as the glue dried. To deal with the problem, his father installed a strip of metal across the front of the pan to regulate the flow of glue. Later, he added a second strip, and then a third one, made of cork, to sweep the excess glue from the roller. Still the problem persisted, and eventually his father realized the problem had as much to do with the glue he'd been using as with the machine itself. The glue flowed too rapidly to control with any kind of precision, and his father's next step was to add corn flour, something he continued to do to this day. Thickened as it was, however, the glue would coagulate in the pan, which meant that every seventy-five bottles or so, the pressman was forced to stop what he was doing to remove the pan and stir the glue.

Generally, a few swift turns would get the glue moving, but Charles lingered, scraping the sides of the pan with a flat wooden stick as one might a mixing bowl. With all that was going on in his life, right at that moment Charles's focus was far more immediate. He was glancing toward his father's office, where, for more than an hour, his father had been meeting with two men Charles had never seen before. The men were well dressed and clearly of some importance, and Charles believed it was a meeting in which he should have been included. He even considered joining it on his own, but then hesitated at the thought of the stains on his sleeves and the workman's apron tied around his neck. Had he known the men were coming, he would have dressed more appropriately, and he was angry for not having been informed of the meeting beforehand.

Charles's self-consciousness with regard to his attire had grown acute since returning to work. Whether it was grease or the jagged edge of one of the machines, the shop took its toll on clothing, and Charles took care in what he wore to work. Dressed as he was, however, there was nothing to distinguish him from the common laborer, a fact he was daily reminded of as he walked the crowded streets to and from the shop. He could hardly fail to notice the parade of men with top hats and umbrellas who streamed past without so much as a glint of acknowledgment, and though outwardly Charles responded with a countenance of disdain, inwardly he felt compelled to see himself through their eyes, not as the engineer and expert in metallurgy he imagined himself to be, but as the press operator he was.

Suddenly, the door to his father's office opened. Charles couldn't hear what was being said, but he could see his father pointing out various pieces of equipment around the shop. The press at which Charles was working was some distance from his father's office, and he watched as the men moved toward the press closest to them, where another man, a few years younger than Charles, worked a table of bottles. For a moment, Charles thought his father was going to call him over. He appeared to be looking in his direction, but then turned away.

The men stayed for another few minutes, during which Charles's anger only intensified. He should have been the one to demonstrate the machinery, not Tim, the man at the other press. Tim had been with his father the past six years, but it was Charles who had been involved in the original design of the machines, and once the men were gone, he watched his father return to his office and then followed him inside.

"Father, I have to talk to you."

His father was at his desk, scribbling some numbers on a piece of paper. "Just a minute," he said, without looking up.

"Who were those men?"

"Charles, I'm in the middle of something."

"I want to know who those men were."

His father glanced up at him. "They make furniture polish," he said with some irritation.

"What were they doing here?"

"They'd heard about the presses and wanted to see them for themselves."

"Are they planning to use our services?"

"Possibly," his father replied, still trying to concentrate on his figures.

"You should have told me they'd be coming."

"I didn't know."

"How could you not have known?" Charles asked with an expression of disbelief.

"I didn't know. What do you think, I'm keeping things from you?" His father put down his pencil and looked up at Charles. "Son, I don't know what it is, but since you've been back, I can't say you've been the most pleasant person to be around. Something's gnawing at you. Is it tonight with the Coopers? Are you nervous?" he asked, knowing Charles would be having dinner with his fiancée and future in-laws.

Charles looked at his father. "The way things are around here, you'd think Tim was your son."

His father made a face. "That's ridiculous."

"He was the one you had demonstrating the presses," Charles said.

"Not by choice. Tim's machine just happens to be nearest to the office."

"Which is why I should be working there," Charles said.

"So that's what this is all about," his father said. He sat forward in his chair, which, like everything else he'd done since his son had come into the room, was to some extent calculated for effect. He knew Charles would be upset that he hadn't been the one to demonstrate the presses. He also knew the shop's current success had as much to do with work Charles had done early on as anything he or Tim had done in the years since he'd left. No one knew the extent of Charles's abilities better than he did, having come to rely on them when Charles was still a boy. By the same token, he also understood

Charles's disappointment. Charles had shown him his plans for the Fee, and though no expert himself, he knew enough to recognize their brilliance. At the same time, it was right about then that Charles had asked Victoria to marry him, and the elder Jenkins could only imagine what his son might be feeling.

Still, since returning to the shop, Charles had been moody and ill-tempered. He'd made little effort to fit in, and Jenkins also didn't like the way Charles had been handling the machinery. That morning in particular, Charles had engaged the piston on the steam engine before the oil had had a chance to properly coat the cylinder wall. Jenkins had heard the squeal from his office, and while Charles would have argued the significance, as it was, in fact, only a short squeal, it had been bothering Charles's father all day. In his mind, mistreating a machine was no different from mistreating an animal. Charles, of all people, knew better. And so, perhaps, he should have called Charles over to help with the demonstration. But it was also true that he hadn't known the men would be coming, and it wasn't as if he'd led them to Tim's machine, so he wasn't going to apologize for it now.

"Charles, the truth is I don't know how long you'll be here. Last year, what was it, a month or two before you were off to Scotland?"

"How often do you think a chance like that comes along?"

"I'm not saying you didn't have reason."

"Reason!" Charles exclaimed. "I can't believe you're even saying this. You know what it would have meant to get the contract for the Fee."

"I do know," Jenkins said emphatically. "But I've got a business to run, and a responsibility to the men working for me. There's nothing I'd like more than to have you working with me on a permanent basis, but it doesn't seem that's what you want, and I can't be asking Tim to step aside if I can't depend on your being here for more than a month or two."

Chapter 3

Charles moved hurriedly, pulling hard on the large brass handle of an entry door to the Chestwick Street Station of the London & North Eastern Railway. Together with its train shed, the building occupied a full city block and, though smaller than the line's main terminal in the city, it had the same turreted facade. Inside, too, patrons were treated to the same marble floors, brass handrails, and crystal chandeliers that had become virtual trademarks of the company, each bearing the LNE monogram. The grandest building in the area, the station earned even further distinction by housing an array of shops and restaurants that could not be found anywhere else in that part of town.

It was evening, but many of the shops were still open for business. Passing one of the shoe-shine stations, Charles hesitated briefly. Had he more time, he would have stopped. He was wearing a new suit, similar to the suits worn by Dr. Cooper, and for full effect, Charles thought to get his shoes shined, but he didn't want to be late.

Charles had entered the building through a side entry and walked quickly toward the main entrance, where he knew there would be a line of hansom cabs waiting at the curb. They were the reason he'd come. He was due at Victoria's house in less than half an hour and didn't have time to take the trolley.

"Yes, sir," the driver said as Charles climbed into a cab.

"The West End. High Street Gardens."

Charles sank back against the cushioned seat as the cab started off. Before returning to the shop, his finances had deteriorated to such a point that he never even considered taking a cab or having his shoes shined, and although he wasn't thrilled to be spending the extra money now, there was a certain pleasure in it, just as there was in giving Victoria's address as his destination.

In sharp contrast to earlier in the day, Charles was feeling rather well and looking forward to the evening. Thinking back on the day, he was sorry he and his father had quarreled. Whatever Charles's complaints, his father certainly paid him well enough. And there was the shop itself to think about. There wasn't another one like it, and the visit by the men from the polish company could only speak of larger things to come.

The cab arrived and Charles stepped down. It was misty, but no longer drizzling. The Coopers lived on one of the finest blocks in the city, and he stood for a moment, looking up at the house, before climbing the steps to the front door.

The butler showed Charles into the sitting room, where Victoria sat by her mother on the sofa. Both women were wearing dresses with puffed sleeves and lace collars, and both looked up from their magazines when Charles entered.

From the moment he'd met Victoria, Charles had been captivated. Like a damsel in a picture book, Victoria had long blond hair and the most beautiful white teeth. But it wasn't her beauty alone that was so alluring. She had a refinement, an elegance that seemed to embody all Charles aspired to. One could see it in the way she carried herself and hear it in her voice.

"Charles, would you like a drink?" Mrs. Cooper asked, setting aside her magazine.

Victoria did the same as Charles took her hand and leaned down to kiss her cheek.

"My husband has just gotten home and won't be down for a few minutes yet," Mrs. Cooper added.

Charles glanced at his future mother-in-law, thinking a moment before nodding his acceptance. "Thank you."

Mrs. Cooper looked at the butler. "Please pour Mr. Jenkins a drink," she said as Charles took a seat across from the two women. He watched as the man went to the cabinet where the alcohol was kept.

"You know, I did so enjoy meeting your parents," Mrs. Cooper went on. "Your father has a wonderful quality about him. I felt so at ease, as if we'd known each other a long time."

"People have said similar things before," Charles replied, receiving his drink.

He was gladdened to hear Mrs. Cooper speak so. The parents had met for the first time at a dinner hosted by his parents two and half weeks before. At one point, the talk between his father and Dr. Cooper had become quite heated, and, in Charles's mind at least, the meeting had been something of a disaster.

There was a large fire burning in the fireplace, and Charles tugged at his collar.

"You can take off your jacket if you like," Mrs. Cooper said.

"That's quite all right."

"Really, go right ahead. Everyone complains about how warm I keep the house, but I've developed a touch of rheumatism, and I ache terribly when I'm cold."

"Really, I'm fine," Charles said, not wanting to be in shirtsleeves when the doctor came in.

"Charles, you know Victoria and I were talking, and as a relief from all the wedding planning, I thought it might be nice if one Sunday you were to escort us to the Crystal Palace."

"Crystal Palace? I thought it was still closed."

"They're planning to reopen after the New Year," Victoria said somewhat coolly.

Charles looked at her. She'd hardly glanced at him since he'd arrived, and he wondered what the matter was. Working at the shop made it difficult to get together, and while he and Victoria had corresponded, they had not actually seen each other since the dinner held by his parents.

"I've just been reading an article on all the new exhibits," Mrs. Cooper went on. "Did you know that, before the renovation, nearly half the displays were the very same ones they'd had when the hall first opened twenty-five years ago?"

"I can believe it," Charles said. "I haven't been since I was a boy, ten or fifteen years ago, and even then it was more a museum than anything else."

"As I remember, right as you walked in, there was a locomotive with big black wheels and red spokes."

"That's right," Charles said, smiling.

"Oh, I do hope they keep that."

"I'm sure they will. They'll probably put it alongside one of our current locomotives in one of those 'then and now' comparisons the magazines love so much."

"Charles, I can't tell you how I'm looking forward to having someone in the family who knows how things work."

"That's very kind of you," Charles said. He smiled and again looked at Victoria, thinking she, too, might be pleased.

"As I'm sure you'll find out," Mrs. Cooper continued, "when it comes to things mechanical, my husband is as lost as I."

"I'm sure he must know something."

"I suppose he knows something about medicine, but the truth is he can't even put in a nail."

"Mother, don't exaggerate," Victoria said.

"What's that?" Dr. Cooper said, coming into the room.

"I was just telling Charles how, after we'd had the room re-papered last year, one of the men had to re-hang all the pictures."

Dr. Cooper cocked his head, considering his wife's remark. Her voice was audible from the hallway, and he'd entered the room prepared to defend himself. The words, however, seemed benign, and he approached Charles with his arm outstretched.

"I told him I didn't want the house falling down, and that you weren't to be trusted with a hammer," Mrs. Cooper added.

Dr. Cooper stopped short to look at his wife. Charles, having risen from his chair, extended his hand somewhat awkwardly.

"The men had a good laugh over that," Mrs. Cooper said.

"Yes, I'm sure they did," the doctor responded with a frown. He turned to Charles and took his hand. "A drink?" he asked.

Charles gestured at the glass in front of him on the table, suddenly worried that it had been disrespectful to have started without his host.

"What else has my wife been telling you?" the doctor asked, going to pour himself a drink.

"We were talking about the new exhibits at Crystal Palace."

"That's right. I've asked Charles to accompany Victoria and me when it reopens." Mrs. Cooper looked at Charles. "I know it will be terribly boring for you, but you've no idea how these things interest me, and I'm sure I'll learn much more if there's someone there to answer my questions."

"The way you flatter me, I don't see how I can refuse," Charles said, still feeling a certain anxiousness.

"Dear, perhaps you should come along. You could stand to learn something as well," Mrs. Cooper said to her husband.

"Yes. I imagine we all could," Dr. Cooper said, returning with his drink. "Victoria tells me you've been working for your father."

"That's right. He has been retooling some of the machinery and asked if I would help out." Charles took a sip of whiskey. It was true. Now that he'd installed the new steam engine, his father was planning to overhaul the equipment.

"Then it's only temporary."

"Of course," Charles replied, "although the changes my father has in mind are rather extensive. I want to stay until all the kinks are worked out."

"I see," Dr. Cooper said.

Charles could hear the disappointment in the doctor's voice, and it was not the first time. Charles had been somewhat grand in his initial description of his father's business, depicting it more along the lines of a factory. Dr. Cooper had been surprised to learn it was merely a labeling shop. It also didn't help when Charles's father told Dr. Cooper that the shop's only customer to that point was the maker of *Mohegan Health Tonic*. The so-called tonic, a combination of alcohol, opium, and cocaine, was advertised on billboards all over town, though as far as Dr. Cooper was concerned, it was nothing but quackery and preyed on the public's ignorance.

"And after that, what are your plans going forward?" Dr. Cooper asked.

"I'll continue to look for other projects."

"It's over with the Fee then?"

"It seems so."

"No chance at all of getting the contract?" Dr. Cooper pressed.

"I did have some supporters, but in the end, I believe they will go with the more traditional design. I think it was my idea of using steel that most frightened them."

"Then why not use iron?"

"Unfortunately, that wasn't possible."

"No?" the doctor questioned.

"The plan I proposed was designed specifically with steel in mind. Iron simply couldn't handle the stresses involved."

Again, Dr. Cooper nodded his head. "Perhaps next time you might be wise to choose a different design. If it's iron they want, then give them iron. There's no sense beating your head against the wall."

"Yes, Charles, the secret is to give them what they want," Mrs. Cooper said. "In no time at all, you'll have as many clients as my husband has patients," she said, smiling wryly.

Charles realized the comment was offered on his behalf, but he didn't want to get caught between the doctor and his wife and looked to Victoria to intervene.

Victoria looked back at Charles. Their wedding was only a few months off, and she did not at all feel as she'd imagined when Charles first proposed. She remembered the day they'd first met. It was afternoon, and they were walking along the Thames. He was telling her how the entire history of London could be seen in its bridges. He said anyone could lay down rails or cobblestones with hardly a thought, but eventually one would come to a river, or valley, or something else that had to be crossed, and it was there that the true extent of a man's abilities were revealed.

Charles was nearly eight years Victoria's senior, for which reason alone she might have taken his interest more seriously than that of the schoolboys she had met to that point. At the same time, no one had ever spoken to her so, and while she herself had no interest in bridges, the passion with which Charles spoke of them convinced her of their importance. She was also worldly enough to have heard of Robert Stephenson and Isambard Brunel. They were engineers, and their names were famous throughout the world. Stephenson and his father had even been knighted by the queen.

Victoria knew the disparity in backgrounds was sure to cause some awkwardness, but when she thought of Charles, it was them she was thinking of, and at the time Charles proposed, he was in fact competing to build the longest bridge in the world.

Charles, however, had not won the contract for the Fee—though that alone was not responsible for her current feelings. Early on, Charles made a point of telling her just how slight his chances were. Still, it made it harder for her to stand up to her father, who by that point was dead set against the marriage. To make matters worse, there was her mother, apparently determined to defend Charles to the end. Victoria knew her mother prided herself on speaking frankly, but recently her candor had taken on an extremely sharp edge. This was especially true where Victoria's father was concerned, and Victoria couldn't be sure if what her mother said was meant in earnest or simply as a jab at her father.

Victoria looked at Charles. "It seems to me that what Father says is perfectly sound advice."

"Of course it is," the doctor concurred.

The comment was not at all what Charles had expected. He had hoped Victoria would defend him in some manner, though he now realized he should have expected no different. It was only right that she defer to her father.

Charles turned to the doctor. "Dr. Cooper, with regard to giving people what they want, I have no doubt that in the near future steel will be the engineering material of choice. And not only for bridges but for everything else as well."

"That may be, but what about right now? You have your own ideas, your own way of doing things. I understand that. God knows it's that very spirit that's built the Empire. In Africa, they are naming countries after Englishmen. But tell me, what good are your ideas if you can't put them to use? What if it's ten years before steel is accepted? What then?"

"As a matter of fact, there are many places where steel is already in use. The Germans and the Americans can't get enough of it."

"Unless you're planning to move, I suggest you concentrate on the situation here at home. That is, of course, unless you want to spend the rest of your life labeling bottles at your father's shop."

Dr. Cooper finished his drink and went to pour another. His words were harsh, but it was his daughter's future he was thinking about. As far as he was concerned, other than a few well-known exceptions, engineers were nothing but glorified mechanics. And Charles wasn't even that. He labeled bottles in the East End.

Chapter 4

Four weeks had passed since their previous meeting, and the members of the British Northern's board of directors once again sat in the company boardroom. The two consulting engineers were also present, as was Rear Admiral Jonathan Stashard, the observer from the Royal Navy. Again, Stewart Darrs stood before them, explaining a series of structural renderings.

The plans were fundamentally the same as the ones he'd displayed at the previous meeting, except for the fact that he'd inverted fourteen of the bridge's eighty-nine spans to satisfy a demand from the navy for increased clearance under the bridge.

"Mr. Chairman, before we hear anymore, might I take the liberty of making an observation?"

Taylor glanced to his left. "Very well, Mr. Kern, say what you must."

"Gentlemen, as you know, I have been opposed to Mr. Darrs's bridge from the start. It has struck me as a work without imagination or distinction of any kind. Still, if it deserved any praise, it was for its simplicity of aspect. Even that will be lost, given the changes he now proposes. The thing is no longer even symmetrical."

"Are you suggesting the entire bridge be turned upside down to satisfy your sense of aesthetics?" Taylor asked.

"I am merely pointing out that providence has presented us with this opportunity to reconsider our decision, and it so happens, without any modification, Mr. Jenkins's design would very nearly achieve the necessary height as it is."

"It is not providence that has us here again, Mr. Kern, but the navy. However high your regard, let us not confuse the two."

Taylor was angry. He'd already been through this once, two months before, with the town council in Pythe. Pythe lay to the west of Brindee, and only twenty years before, it had been the most important port on the Fee. West of Brindee, however, the channel grew too shallow for the newest ships, and Brindee had surpassed Pythe both in population and commerce. What was left of Pythe's shipping consisted mainly of barges and small steamers, not one of which was more than thirty feet in height. But that meant little to the Pythe council members, who feared an even greater decline if Brindee were to become an important rail center as well. They'd gone to Parliament to block construction of the bridge, at which time a compromise resulted, requiring the railroad to add fifteen feet of clearance to the forty-five feet stipulated in the original bill. As far as Taylor was concerned, if the navy had an objection, Stashard should have said something then.

The chairman pointed to the drawings. "Admiral, there you have eighty-eight feet. Enough headroom for anything you damn well please. Or do you suppose it may be necessary to send a flotilla of square-riggers up the Fee to quell a Scottish rebellion?"

Around Taylor, the other board members laughed.

"Enjoy your sarcasm if you like," Stashard said, "but it is the fleet that makes the Empire what it is, and should our ships grow larger..."

"For God's sake, we are talking about a gunboat garrison. West of Brindee, the water is too shallow for it to be anything else," Taylor interrupted. The navy did maintain a base on the Fee, but as he said, it was merely a gunboat garrison used as a training facility for cadets.

"If necessary, a channel can be dredged," Stashard said.

"Admiral, even if the government were to build a fleet of 500-foot battleships, with your base on the Forth only fifty miles to the south, I see no reason why the navy would suddenly decide to station heavy warships on the Fee."

"Where Her Majesty chooses to station her warships is not my concern. My responsibility is simply to see that her waterways are kept free from obstruction," Stashard said.

"And so we are here," Taylor said wearily.

At the front of the room, Darrs stood silently. He'd recently turned fifty, and though he had a full head of hair, it was mostly gray, as was his beard, which he wore in the manner of his father, who had been a captain in the Merchant Marine. For some time, Darrs looked at the floor, not wanting to intrude on the exchange, though he was listening. As he'd originally designed the bridge, trains were to have made the entire crossing in the open, on top of the bridgework. Now, in this one section, trains would run inside the bridge rather than on top of it. The spans in question were twenty-eight feet tall, so that by inverting them, Darrs was able to increase clearance under the bridge nearly thirty feet. It was a simple solution, and one that did not affect the rest of the structure, an important consideration so late in the process.

There was a pause in the conversation and Darrs looked up. "Gentlemen," he said, "we are all familiar with the sight of a train running across the top of a lengthy bridge or viaduct. It is a pleasing sight, I agree, but with regard to the structure, it is equally practical to have the trains run within the bridgework."

Kern looked at Darrs. He realized Darrs was an engineer, a man of facts and figures. Even so, Kern was startled by Darrs's apparent literalness, and it wasn't the first time.

"Mr. Chairman."

"What is it, Mr. Kern?" Taylor asked impatiently.

"I merely wish to say that I don't think Mr. Darrs quite grasps the issue at hand."

"Oh, do be quiet," Taylor said.

"Mr. Chairman, I only . . ."

"Mr. Kern, I rather think it is you who doesn't grasp the issue at hand. It is less than fifty miles from Edinburgh to Brindee. With our present steam engines, that trip should be made in little more than an hour. Unfortunately, this company has two very big problems."

"Yes, yes," Kern nodded, unmoved by the chairman's admonishment. "The Fee and the Forth."

"The way it stands now," Taylor continued, "the run takes nearly three and a half hours, and that's in good weather. In winter, the firths might as well be oceans, the way they divide our tracks."

"Mr. Chairman, might I point out the ferries you now find so insufficient are in fact the handiwork of Mr. Darrs."

"Mr. Kern, our problem is not the ferries. Our problem is the fact that eleven months ago the Edinburgh & Glasgow formed an alliance with the Scottish Central. However out of the way it may seem, it is now faster to travel from Edinburgh to Brindee via Glasgow than it is to travel in a straight line. What we need is a bridge—a very long bridge. I don't give a damn what it looks like, so long as trains can run across it and it doesn't fall down." Taylor turned to the board's two consulting engineers. "Is there anything of significance this board should know regarding the changes being suggested?

The two men looked at each other, surprised to suddenly be the focus of attention.

"I'm waiting," Taylor said sternly.

"The track needn't be anywhere in particular," one of the men said. "Inside the bridgework or on top of it."

"Then it will stand?" Taylor questioned.

"If it would stand before."

"Is that a yes or a no?" Taylor demanded.

"Yes, it will stand."

"Then as far as I'm concerned, the matter is settled."

Chapter 5

It was after eight o'clock when Darrs arrived home. Following the board meeting, he'd returned to his office, where he spent the rest of the day.

"Good evening, sir," Mary, the maid, said with a welcoming smile.

Darrs had been in Brindee the past two weeks, having returned to Edinburgh only that morning for his meeting with the British Northern. He had a newspaper in one hand, which he shifted to the other as the girl worked with considerable care to relieve him of his coat. Darrs was a large man, six feet, with a strong build, and while his movements could be stiff, there was also a gentleness to them, unusual in a man of his size.

Once free, Darrs thanked the maid and turned into the drawing room, where his wife was doing needlepoint in the light of a lamp from which she'd removed the shade.

"How is Mr. Taylor?" she asked, glancing up from her pattern as her husband crossed the room to in a winged-back chair by the fireplace.

"There was some division among the board members, which is the reason I went to the office afterward. There are still a few things to take care of."

"Albert is still at the office, I imagine," Mrs. Darrs said, referring to her husband's chief assistant.

"I sent him home as well. There's nothing left to be done today."

Mrs. Darrs watched as their cocker spaniel, Matilda, took up position alongside her husband's chair. His hand hung over the side and he scratched absently at the top of her head, which the dog tolerated for a few moments before sinking to the floor to lick her paws.

Mrs. Darrs looked at her husband. He'd been working hard and she could see it. As a rule, he took considerable care with his appearance, but it looked to her as if it had been a week or more since he'd last been to the barber. His hair was somewhat unruly in the back, and his beard could have used a trim. He was a quiet man. He seldom spoke except when addressed directly, but there was something reassuring in his presence, and though she did little to show it, she was excited to have him home.

Darrs was born in Monsby, a small town on England's northwest coast. When he was sixteen, his father apprenticed him to a local engineer, and once qualified, Darrs left home for Scotland to take a position he'd seen advertised in the newspaper. He was twenty-two. By twenty-seven, he was chief engineer of the Edinburgh & Brindee Railway, one of the lines that would eventually be combined to form the British Northern. It was then that he'd designed his so-called floating bridges, the system of adjustable ramps and railed ferryboats that currently carried the line's trains across the Fee and the Forth. When they were built, there wasn't another system like it anywhere in the world, and Darrs made quite a stir with it, so much so that, soon afterward, he left his job with the railroad to set up on his own engineering practice.

The year was 1859, and in the three decades since the railroads first came into existence, their growth had been stupendous. By that time, all the country's major cities had been linked. Railroads, however, were expensive to build, and many towns and villages had yet to be reached by the system. This was particularly true in Scotland and northern England, where local businessmen and civic leaders were getting together to promote railroads of their own. The projects were limited in scope. Some were no more than five- or ten-mile runs between market towns or coastal villages. The projects lacked capital, and many went bankrupt before they ever opened. Others were actually elaborate swindles, feeding on the frenzied imagination of people opening their newspapers each morning to new stories of the fortunes being made on the railroads.

Most, however, were proposed in earnest, and Darrs set himself the task of designing railways at prices promoters could afford. He did not bother with great masonry creations. For bridges and trestles, Darrs relied on modest structures of iron or wood. In particular, he favored the wrought-iron truss, a new type of metal bridge that enlarged upon earlier timber designs. It had yet to gain wide acceptance and was considered lacking in both appearance and strength, compared with the massive stone and brick arches that were then the norm on the larger lines. The new trusses were, however, inexpensive and easy to build, and Darrs would erect dozens of them.

It was a time when engineers like Brunel and Stephenson were achieving a level of celebrity once reserved for poets and war heroes, but the work Darrs was doing carried little in the way of prestige. There also were charges of recklessness. Railroad-related deaths were highly publicized in the press, and while accidents were common even on the larger lines, nowhere were they so frequent as on the small independent lines then springing up across the countryside.

Darrs, though, had no shortage of clients among the rural merchants and farmers who saw themselves being passed by. He gained a reputation for planning railroads that were both inexpensive to construct and profitable to operate, and, though he continued to live rather modestly, he had amassed a fortune that would have impressed even the wealthiest nobleman.

Matilda rose to her feet again as the maid entered the room with a tray of food, which she placed on a table in front of Mrs. Darrs, who put down her needlepoint. She arranged a plate for her husband, then tore off a piece of bread for the dog, who was staring fixedly at the food.

The maid took the plate across the room to Darrs, who nodded his thanks.

"Will there be anything else?" she asked, looking back at Mrs. Darrs.

"Thank you, Mary. That will be all," Mrs. Darrs replied with a smile.

The maid offered a slight curtsy and turned to Darrs. "Goodnight, sir. Good to have you home."

Darrs, who had just taken a bite of food, worked to swallow his mouthful but finally just raised his hand in response.

The girl smiled and again curtsied, after which she took her leave.

Mrs. Darrs reached for her needlepoint and returned to her stitching, though she made a point of glancing up every few seconds to look at her husband as he was eating.

"There's a nice pie in the kitchen," she said as Darrs was finishing his plate. "I could serve it with some brandy."

"And you—will you join me?" Darrs asked, before putting the last bite of food into his mouth.

Mrs. Darrs smiled and again set her needlework aside. She stood up, as did the dog, who was soon following her down the hall to the kitchen.

Chapter 6

Charles gazed through the curtained window, his body swaying with the motion of the coach as the train steamed north toward Birmingham, a two-hour ride. It was Tuesday morning, and there were three other passengers in the compartment, all of whom, like Charles, had boarded the train in London. In the seat opposite him, an older woman worked at her crochet, making what looked to be a purse. There were also two men, both wearing suits, both reading the newspaper. Charles also wore a suit, but he did not have a newspaper. In his lap, he had the most recent issue of the professional journal *Engineering*, though at that moment he lacked the concentration to read. He was thinking of Birmingham and in many ways regretting he'd ever left. Barrol had offered Charles a permanent position, but he hadn't wanted to spend the rest of his life working in a steel mill. Neither, though, had he intended to work as a pressman in his father's labeling shop.

Charles thought of the day he'd proposed to Victoria. She had just returned from her last year at school. He hadn't seen her since the previous Christmas, and she looked even more exquisite than he remembered. By that point, with his sister urging him on, Charles had been writing Victoria long letters, in which he included drawings—sketches of his favorite bridges, and those he would build himself. Only a few weeks before, he'd sent her a rather large drawing of his final design for the Fee, and flush with enthusiasm, he'd asked her to marry him. That was a little more than five months before, and now he wondered if he'd made a terrible mistake.

Charles glanced at the woman across from him, with whom he'd shared a smile when they first boarded. She, however, was engrossed in her crochet, as the men were in their newspapers. Charles glanced down at the journal on his lap, the cover of which carried an engraving of a timber trestle in California. Inside the journal were other illustrations as well, a whole series of them from places with names such as Colorado, Nevada, and Wyoming. The journal featured the railroads of the American West, and the images remained etched in Charles's imagination. As far as he was concerned, a wood span of fifty feet could be as remarkable as one five times its length in wrought iron or steel. Wood did not leave the same margin for error. Every beam, every strut pitted the engineer against the limitations of the material, and though he would never have thought to use wood where steel was readily available, he could not help but admire the ingenuity of those who were forced to out of necessity.

More than once, Charles had envisioned such heroics for himself. Most often it was in the tropics, an idyllic landscape from which he would carve a paradise. Over the years, he had developed highly elaborate scenarios, planning everything down to the supplies he would need. Though only daydreams, Charles's mind was such that he did not indulge in the purely fantastic. It would inevitably occur to him that even building in wood, he would need nuts and bolts and screws. They were things he could bring with him, but items he was eventually sure to run out of, and he'd imagined the process of creating them from scratch—finding and digging-out the ore, melting it down into iron bars that he would then heat and reheat, beating the softened metal flat, folding it over and beating it again, until it was hard enough to carve into. In his mind, Charles determined that he could do it, but it would not be easy, and over time his imaginings had come to include a nearby town or port, from which, on occasion, he could send for nuts, bolts, and other provisions.

When the train reached Birmingham, Charles hired a cab to take him to the Barrol Mill, which was on the outskirts of the city. The property had once been an estate, and the original manor house was still standing, though much of the interior had been gutted. It served as the entrance to the mill, a massive brick structure extending in both directions behind the house.

During his apprenticeship, Charles had overseen construction of a rail siding leading to the loading docks in the rear of the mill. It wrapped around the grounds of the estate and enabled the finished steel to be taken by train to the Great Western rail yard for shipping. Looking out from the cab, Charles could see a pair of half-loaded flatcars.

He had the driver stop when they reached the front of the old estate house, and after paying his fare, Charles went inside to find Barrol, who was usually somewhere in the mill. This day, however, he was in his office, a huge room that had once been a formal dining room.

"Charles! Come in, come in. I was just showing Mr. Boxworth the pamphlet we're planning to circulate at tomorrow night's meeting of the Institute," Barrol said, gesturing to the company bookkeeper.

Charles took the pamphlet from the bookkeeper's outstretched hand and glanced at the title: "Proclamation of Independence."

"Who's we? You and Prestwick?"

"No, it's not just the two of us," Barrol replied, hearing the skepticism in Charles's tone. "This time we've gotten several others to sign on as well."

The others Barrol referred to were steelmakers, and the meeting, Charles assumed, was the next gathering of the Iron & Steel Institute, a trade society supposedly dedicated to the interests of the nation's metal manufacturers. In reality, it was a lobbying organization for the nation's ironmakers that until recently had been known simply as the Iron Institute. In that guise, the organization had pushed through Parliament a series of statutes that actually made it illegal to use steel in any work "affecting the public safety." Known collectively as the Iron Laws, they had effectively barred the use of steel altogether, until the last few years.

"You really think it will do any good?" Charles asked.

"Laws or no laws, they're still spreading the same lies."

"So long as they refuse to modernize themselves, they have no choice."

"Well, they do a good job of it. I think someone is interested and the next thing they have all sorts of worries about rusting."

"That, and its suddenly giving way without warning," Charles added.

Barrol nodded. "I'd love it if you were to come to the meeting."

"It's here in Birmingham?"

"Yes, tomorrow," Barrol said with some enthusiasm.

Charles thought for a moment. He would like to attend, but after a moment started to shake his head. "I'd like to, but I've started work at my father's shop."

"The labels again?"

"Yes," Charles replied a bit dispiritedly.

"If you ever want a change, you know you're always welcome here."

"Yes, sir, I know that. Thank you."

"In any case, you might as well get over to the house," Barrol said.

"I'll come by before I leave."

"You're not staying for supper?"

Charles shook his head. "I have to get back."

"Go on then. Elizabeth will kill me if I keep you here talking to me."

The bookkeeper let out a small laugh, in response to which Charles also forced a bit of smile.

Still, for Charles it was no laughing matter. Barrol's comment merely highlighted the difficulty of his position. Although there was never any formal engagement as he now had with Victoria, Charles had spent his last three years in Birmingham openly courting Barrol's eldest daughter. Indeed, when Charles first returned to London, his plan was to establish himself as an engineer and then send for her, a plan to which Elizabeth, knowing nothing of Victoria, was still fully committed. It was more than five months since Charles had become engaged, and he had still been unable to tell Elizabeth. She would be devastated. He could picture the color draining from her cheeks. And the questions—Who? Why? How long? Anything he said would only make it worse.

Beyond the mill stood the Barrol house, which is where Charles found Elizabeth, in the kitchen with her two younger sisters.

"Charles, how can you be so thoughtless?" asked Kate, the youngest, who was fourteen.

"Kate, you keep quiet," Elizabeth said sharply. Elizabeth was twenty, the same age as Victoria, though her hair and eyes were dark.

"Thoughtless?" Charles asked, though he could tell Kate was just being playful.

"Talking so long with father. I saw you turn into the driveway half an hour ago."

Charles cocked his head. "Half an hour?" he questioned as he approached the table at which the three girls were shucking peas.

"Twenty minutes for sure," Kate said.

Elizabeth stood up. "Oh, Charles, don't pay any attention. She's just trying to cause trouble," she said, fixing her sister with a look of considerable wrath. "Wait here. I'll get my coat."

"You know mother didn't want you going for a walk. I heard her saying it was too cold," Kate said.

"Hello, Charles," Elizabeth's middle sister, Sara, said in a much more mature tone.

Charles smiled. "Hello, Sara," he replied.

"Isn't she even going to help us finish the peas?" Kate asked.

"No, Kate, you and I will do it ourselves," Sara answered. "So just keep working and stop bothering Charles."

"I'm not bothering Charles. Am I Charles?"

"No, of course not, but you might be a bit more respectful. And not just to Elizabeth but to both of your sisters," he added, again smiling at Sara.

Elizabeth returned with her coat and, without saying a word, headed straight for the back door.

Charles excused himself and followed her outside.

"I realize she's my sister, but sometimes I simply want to strangle her," Elizabeth said when Charles caught up to her.

"You know she doesn't mean anything," he said.

"I'm not so sure. She knows how I've been feeling."

"And how is that?"

"Charles! It's been two months since you were last here, and you've barely written."

"I did write."

"Yes, three times to tell me you were thinking of me. If you were really thinking of me, you would have written more than that."

Charles made no reply. He merely kept pace as Elizabeth made her way around the side of the mill toward the back of the property. For much of its distance, the rail siding Charles designed followed the bank of a wide stream. The two paralleled each other for close to a quarter mile, at which point the stream turned off, winding through a wooded valley that stretched for several miles behind the mill. It was there that Charles and Elizabeth went to be alone, heading down a dirt path that followed the bank of the stream. Most of the trees were bare, which was something of a blessing in that, despite the cold, the sun beat down strongly where it could. They walked for several hundred yards to a spot where a number of large rocks provided a place to sit at the water's edge. There, Elizabeth stopped, although she did not sit down. She simply turned to Charles, her expression demanding some sort of explanation.

Charles looked at her in silence for several moments before finally speaking. "I don't know what to say."

"Charles!" she exclaimed, expressing a combination of exasperation and disbelief.

"I have been thinking of you. You don't know. It's just that it's been a very difficult time."

"The Fee," Elizabeth said, her tone suddenly more understanding. He'd actually written her four notes, the last to inform her that he had not gotten the contract for the Fee. "I know it must be hard. There was a point at which you seemed so optimistic."

"I don't know why," Charles said, walking toward the stream. "The truth is, I never stood a chance. How I ever thought there was a possibility of the British Northern using steel—I must have been out of my mind. It's just that the plans are so good."

Charles had a coat on over his suit, but it was not buttoned, and with his hands in the pockets, he half sat, half leaned against one of the larger rocks. It was a coat Elizabeth had never seen; the same was true of his suit, and he looked quite well. She was still angry, but she was glad he was there. Over the last two months, she had come to question whether she would ever see him again, and she walked over to him.

"What are you going to do now?" she asked.

She was standing right in front of him, glancing up. Charles glanced down at her, a mass of thoughts in his head. "I've started working with my father," he said.

Charles had no desire to hurt Elizabeth. He loved her as he always had. It was the reason he'd been unable to tell her of Victoria. Now, however, he'd come to question whether he'd ever truly been in love with Victoria. On the contrary, it seemed what he'd been so taken with was merely a vision of what he'd imagined her to be, attributing to her a kind of perfection. At the same time, Charles had come to realize that the only reason he and Victoria were together in the first place was the difficulty he had had in finding work. If he'd landed a contract or other suitable employment, he would have sent for Elizabeth, in which case his courtship with Victoria would never even have begun.

These were not insights of which Charles was in any way proud. They demonstrated a susceptibility to circumstance, to which he'd always believed himself immune, something he again sensed as he gazed down at Elizabeth.

For some time now, she had allowed him to hold her and kiss her quite freely, and while they had never done anything that could prove irreversible, they were quite skillful at satisfying their desires. They were so adept, in fact, that they did not even have to remove or loosen any of their clothing. Fully dressed, they could wrap themselves in each others arms with an intensity so great that one or both was moved to sigh. It was a practice they often resorted to on days such as this, and it was one of the reasons Charles had stayed away. The last time he'd been to Birmingham, he'd been unable to contain himself, and in spite of the fact that he had been unable to tell Elizabeth of his impending marriage, he had been attempting to conduct himself in as honorable a manner as possible. Still, Elizabeth continued to look up at him. He knew she was angry with him and had every reason to be, but he sensed that if he put his arms around her and pulled her to him, she would not resist.

Chapter 7

Darrs's office was only a few blocks from his house and offered an excellent view of the Edinburgh waterfront, including the British Northern wharf, home port to the *Leviathan*. The *Leviathan* was the largest of the railed ferries currently used to carry trains across the firths, and though Darrs was not looking, he knew the sound of her horn. Even with the windows closed he could hear her docking as he got up from his desk to open the door.

Having settled on the bridge's design, the British Northern sent out letters inviting bids from more than a dozen construction firms. Only six replied, just as only seven men had answered the call to submit plans for the bridge the previous year. Despite the fact that the Fee would be the longest bridge in the world, the issues surrounding the railroad's finances were common knowledge.

Still, for those who did respond, there was a shared desire to have a hand in the largest venture of its kind ever attempted, and among them was Bass & Company, one of the nation's best-known builders. Much to Darrs's liking, Bass was also one of the few firms experienced in the use of caissons, a new construction technique developed specifically for underwater excavation.

"Mr. Bass's reputation is very well known to me," Darrs said, welcoming a representative from the firm into his office.

"Thank you. Mr. Bass is extremely intrigued by the project and would have come himself if not previously engaged."

Darrs withdrew a set of linens from a case and unrolled them on the desk.

"The trusswork appears quite standard, but I see you've chosen to build the supports of brick rather than cast iron. That will slow construction," the man said.

"It will," Darrs concurred, "and I did consider cast iron. Ultimately, though, I believe the British Northern will be grateful for not having to paint and maintain so many supports over water."

The man nodded and continued to look at the plans.

"Have you given any thought to the staging? The spans will have to be assembled on shore, I assume," the man said.

"Yes. They'll be erected on shore and then floated into position," Darrs replied.

"As Brunel did for the *Royal Albert* at Saltashe. The story is he had a terrible time of it."

Darrs pointed to the drawings. "The spans here are less than half the length of those at Saltashe."

"Yes, but at Saltashe, Brunel had only two spans to position. Here there are eighty-nine," the man replied.

"Which is the reason I am anticipating three years for completion."

"Three years," the man repeated, showing some skepticism. "I would say that's fairly ambitious."

"Are you familiar with the Birkendale viaduct?" Darrs asked.

The man shook his head.

"Completed three years ago for the Scottish Central. We raised sixteen spans in four months," Darrs said.

"The same design as those for the Fee?" the man asked, clearly impressed.

"The same—although not as long."

"And Birkendale? That was over water as well?"

"There is a river at the bottom of the glen, but no. Most of the work was over land."

The man tilted his head with skepticism. "And you really believe you can match that pace over water?"

Darrs went to the door, which opened onto an outer room; there sat three men: two at drafting tables, and a third, the secretary, at a desk.

"Mr. Stevens, will you come in, please," Darrs said to the man closest to the door.

Stevens nodded and got up from his table.

"Mr. Albert Stevens, my principal assistant and chief mathematician," Darrs said by way of introduction.

"A pleasure to meet you," Stevens said, shaking hands with the man.

"Mr. Stevens is a Cambridge graduate," Darrs added, in response to which Stevens lowered his eyes.

The man, though, was clearly impressed. "Cambridge—really?"

"Mr. Stevens has suggested an excellent plan for taking advantage of the tides. I'll let him explain," Darrs said.

Stevens's plan was to build a railed platform on which the spans could be assembled and then rolled to the end of a construction pier for launching. The spans would be positioned crosswise on the end of the pier, with barges under the overhanging ends. In that way, when the tide rose, the barges would lift the span free so that it could be towed out to take its place on the bridge.

"It's a good plan," the man said, "but still, that's an awful lot of spans to launch. Not to mention the cofferdams for the foundations."

"Cofferdams won't be necessary," Darrs said. Motioning Stevens aside, Darrs turned to a second page of drawings. "Excavation is to be conducted by means of caissons, which, if I'm not mistaken, is a technique Bass & Company has used in some of its projects."

"It is true; we do have some experience," the man said warily.

While there was nothing unusual about either the bridge's spans or its supports, caissons were far from standard. Bass & Company's experience with caissons was limited to a few relatively small projects involving docks and wharves. Even more worrisome were the stories coming from America, where caissons were being used to found the towers of the new bridge linking Brooklyn and Manhattan.

"You are aware of the reports coming from New York? Men doubling over and collapsing only minutes after coming up from the riverbed."

"You are referring to Caisson disease," Darrs said, "and I share your concern. Still, Mr. Stevens and I have given the matter considerable study, and we believe the men will not fare nearly so badly on the Fee. We've gone over all the published materials from New York and also those from St. Louis, where caissons are being used on a new bridge going up across the Mississippi River. In both cases, excavation has proceeded to depths of seventy feet or more. Bedrock on the Fee lies a mere twenty-five feet beneath the river bottom, at which depth there were no reports of injury."

"That may be. I have not examined the matter myself, but when word gets out, I'm not sure it will be so easy to find men willing to take the chance."

"The work won't be for everyone," Darrs said. "Still, if the matter is properly explained and the pay is reasonable, I'm sure there will be men ready to do the job."

The man looked at Darrs. "I've read reports that even the chief engineer in New York, Mr. Roebling is suffering the effects."

Darrs nodded. "Mr. Stevens and I will be making regular descents into the caissons, if that is your question."

Chapter 8

Like many parts of London, Westminster had seen its skyline transformed in recent years. Big Ben and the new Parliament building were not yet twenty years old. Buckingham Palace was only thirty. Throughout the area, four- and five-story buildings lined broad thoroughfares that had once been the site of crooked alleyways. It was in such a building that many of the city's better-known engineering firms had their offices, including Denney & Farlow, in whose reception area Charles now sat. Earlier in the week, he'd received a reply to one of his letters of introduction, though because it was going on two months since he'd first written, he imagined it was more a courtesy than anything else.

Right at that moment, he was thinking of Elizabeth. Not only had he failed to tell her of his plans to marry someone else, but he'd also ended up making love to her, at least so far as was their fashion. Victoria's parents were preparing to send out wedding invitations, and he was no closer to ending things with Elizabeth than he had been before. Before though, it had been fear alone that kept him from telling. Now, it wasn't just fear. It was increasingly clear that Elizabeth was the one with whom he truly belonged. Indeed, the image he now held of her was so powerful, was so flooded with emotion, he had a notion to forget everything—Victoria, his father's shop, London—and board a train back to Birmingham that very afternoon. He could see her with hair pinned tightly to the back of her head. It was a style prescribed by her father as a safety measure for women seeking entrance to the mill, and one that Charles had always found less than flattering. In his thoughts, however, it now took on new meaning. No longer did he see it simply as a safeguard against the sparks and hot ash of the furnace, but as a sign of her love for him, of her desire to be with him even in the heat and grime of the mill.

Charles glanced up. A bell had rung, and a man was standing before him.

"Mr. Farlow will see you now," the receptionist said.

Charles followed the man down a hallway that led to a large room with windows on both sides, where there were several rows of drafting tables. Like Charles, most of the men in the room had long beards. Some worked alone. Others stood together in small groups, discussing a variety of project plans tacked to the walls.

They reached Farlow's office, where the receptionist turned Charles over to Farlow's personal secretary. It was he who showed Charles inside. Farlow sat at his desk, puffing on a long, curved pipe. He was a distinguished-looking man, with a thick gray mustache and a full head of gray hair. Charles walked toward him, surveying the office as he approached. One wall contained a large library of technical manuals and handsomely bound journals. The others were paneled in dark wood and adorned with large daguerreotypes and photographs of some of the firm's major projects.

Farlow rose to his feet, extending his arm to shake hands. "Mr. Jenkins, it is a pleasure to meet you."

"Thank you. Likewise."

"I do hope you'll forgive me for taking so long to respond to your letter. It can get extremely hectic around here, and I needed some time to consider the matter."

"That's quite all right."

Farlow gestured for Charles to take a seat; he sat down, a little surprised by Farlow's manner, which was more congenial than expected.

"I've had a chance to go over your drawings and I must tell you, the precision with which you are able to calculate loads is remarkable."

In writing to offer his services, Charles had included his plans for the Fee, as well as a brief paper on the cantilever principle he'd published while in Birmingham. "You can thank the material for that," he said. "Steel allows for a much more precise knowledge than iron."

"You mentioned in your letter that, after receiving your engineering degree, you did an apprenticeship at the Barrol Steel Mill, in Birmingham."

"Correct."

"An unusual decision for a man planning to build bridges." Farlow spoke between clenched teeth, having returned his pipe to his mouth.

"To do what I wanted, I felt a firsthand knowledge of the material was needed."

"One shouldn't propose to allow 1,000 feet of metal to support itself without knowing something of its character."

"Exactly," Charles said, astonished by Farlow's understanding.

"I haven't yet had the chance to read your paper in its entirety, but I was able to glance at it and was interested to read that you trace the cantilever principle to an ancient construction technique practiced by the Chinese."

"Yes, there are any number of what could be termed cantilever bridges in China and other parts of Asia. You often see them depicted on the vases and Chinese prints so popular these days. Of course, in China they're made of wood."

"I take it that you already had the cantilever in mind when you left for Birmingham."

"Actually, no. Even then, I was looking to develop a long-span bridge suitable for railroads; but at the time, I was still thinking in terms of the standard truss, supported on both ends. I didn't realize steel could take its own shape." Charles himself had first seen one of the wooden bridges he spoke of depicted on a platter in a sideboard in the Barrol home.

"In terms of steel," Farlow said, "its superior strength has been established, but as you know, there are questions concerning its consistency."

"I do know, but the reality is, ton for ton, steel is even more consistent than iron—certainly cast iron and, in most cases, wrought iron as well."

"I have heard the opposite," Farlow said.

"I'm sure you have, and five or ten years ago, what you heard might have had validity. To make a consistent steel, you need a furnace that will reach 2,700 to 2,800 degrees. That's almost 1,000 degrees hotter than what's needed for wrought iron and almost 2,000 degrees hotter than what's needed for simple cast iron. Just as important, though, you have to be able to keep that heat long enough for everything inside to reach the same temperature. Ten years ago, we didn't have the furnaces to do the job right, so what you were getting was a lot of half-cooked metal. That's the reason it was so susceptible to fracture."

"But you're saying that's no longer the case?"

"I am."

"And the cost?" Farlow asked. "If I'm not mistaken, the price of steel is still nearly twice that of iron."

"Of cast iron, yes. But not top-quality wrought iron. It might only be half again as much, and given its greater strength, you don't need as much."

"Is that true only for your cantilever designs?"

"That would be true for any bridge."

"What of suspension bridges?" Farlow asked. "Tell me your opinion there?"

"In my opinion, suspension bridges lack the necessary rigidity for use by the railroads."

"Even when trusswork is used to stiffen the road deck as Roebling is doing in New York?"

"It's one thing if all you intend to carry are trolleys. Trains are another matter. To handle the kind of forces involved, you need a bridge that supports itself with fixed members. Otherwise, it's almost certain to shake itself apart within a few years."

"You are quite sure of yourself, Mr. Jenkins," Farlow said.

Farlow's expression was rather stern. Charles, whose excitement had brought him forward in his chair, slid back.

"You needn't worry. I meant that as a compliment," Farlow said. "Confidence is important. People respect it. Although I must tell you, the railroads are not likely to give up on iron anytime soon. I have no doubt steel will win out in the end, but it is a stubborn world in which we live. One must be prepared to go the distance. In the meantime, steel will have to struggle against iron, just as iron had to struggle against stone and brick."

"Certainly my desire to build in steel did little to help my cause with the British Northern," Charles said.

"Though I hear you made quite a stir with your painting."

"You know about the painting?" Charles asked. Again Farlow impressed with his knowledge.

"I doubt there's an engineer in all of London, or Edinburgh for that matter, who doesn't know. Personally, I think it was a brilliant idea, though if you're planning to offer your services elsewhere, I should warn you not everyone feels as I do. There are still those who believe a project's plans should speak for themselves, without any sort of ballyhoo, as they call it. Myself, I don't see it that way. The profession has changed, and we must accept that."

"How do you mean?"

"Take the Fee. Ten or fifteen years ago, there would have been a real question as to whether or not such a bridge was even possible. That's no longer the case. Right now, as we speak, there are probably 100 men in London alone who could draw up plans for the Fee, the majority of which would most likely prove quite feasible. The question is no longer can a thing be done, but who will do it, and with that in mind, a painting that seizes the attention of a board of directors or a Parliamentary committee might be just the thing to make the difference."

"I had hoped so," Charles said.

"Still, a painting is not going to do it on its own. Many factors come into play, often the least of which is the quality of the engineering itself." Farlow drew on his pipe. "You were in Birmingham for six years. What about since then? Other than your involvement with the Fee competition, you don't mention anything in your letter."

"My father owns a small industrial shop here in London. I'm responsible for maintaining the machinery."

"I see," Farlow said, sounding less than impressed. "Mr. Jenkins, let me be frank. I have no doubts as to your expertise with metals, but your lack of practical experience does concern me. Designing bridges on paper is not the same as actually building them."

"I am aware of that, but in my own defense, I am not entirely without practical experience."

"How's that?"

"While my primary purpose in going to Birmingham was to learn about steel, Mr. Barrol was free to employ my services as he saw fit. At one point, I designed and oversaw the construction of a new loading dock and rail siding to connect with the Great Western's main line. I realize that, compared with the kind of work you do here, that may not sound very impressive, but it did involve grading a roadbed and laying track as one would do on any rail project." Although Charles had begun the interview with few expectations, he suddenly found himself very much wanting a position at the firm.

"Anything else?" Farlow asked.

"On that scale, no, but I did install a system of tracked dollies for delivering coal from the storage bins to the furnaces. Power was supplied by a steel cable running between the rails. It was something I was rather proud of."

"I imagine Robert Barrol must have been sorry to see you go."

"You know Mr. Barrol?" Charles asked with surprise.

"Only by reputation. Still, it can't be every day he's approached by a trained engineer looking to apprentice himself."

"No, I imagine that is so."

Farlow sat back in his chair. "In any case, Mr. Jenkins, the nation's steelmakers are beginning to show some strength, and I am willing to give you a chance. I'm sure you've heard about the pamphlet they circulated at the recent meeting of the Iron & Steel Institute."

"I have," Charles said, suddenly realizing why Farlow had contacted him after all this time.

"As I said before, I don't think the railroads will be switching anytime soon. But if there is movement in that direction, I want to be prepared. Tell me, when can you start?"

Charles left Denney & Farlow with a feeling of elation. He was dressed in his new suit, and he walked the streets with a self-assurance he had not felt in the longest time. Around him, the city itself seemed different. Charles sensed the energy in the rush of traffic and marveled at the vast array of buildings that only the hour before had seemed to stand coldly at a distance.

Charles stopped to buy a paper at the newsstand before deciding what to do next. His first thought was to go to the shop. His father knew about the interview. He would want to know the outcome, and the news was certain to go a long way toward easing the tensions that had grown up between them. Charles knew that the main reason they hadn't been getting along was the frustration he himself had been feeling, but the shop was all the way across town, and he couldn't go there without first going home to change. He didn't want to do that. Instead, he glanced at the trolleys coming down the street, looking for one heading toward High Street Garden and Victoria's house.

Chapter 9

Five Years Later

The Firth of Fee stretched for nearly twenty-five miles from the North Sea in the east to the town of Pythe in the west, where it was fed by the Fee River. For most of its length, the firth was two to three miles wide, but it was not a haven from the elements. Open to the sea, it was the setting of frequent storms—gales and sudden squalls that would move in with little warning. Even in the best of weather the sky was mainly gray, though it was a gray of many casts. At times it could even appear a strangely radiant white, which, along with the surrounding hills and pastures, combined to produce a landscape that was both lush and bleak.

Feeport and Brindee stood opposite each other near the eastern end of the firth—Feeport to the south, Brindee to the north. In spite of their proximity, however, the two towns had little in common. Brindee was no longer even a town, but a thriving city of foundries and mills extending along the rails of the Scottish Central, which followed the northern bank of the Fee from Pythe to Brindee.

It was between the two that the British Northern was building its new bridge, which from the Feeport side now extended nearly half a mile from the top of the bluff that ran along the firth's southern shore.

From the Brindee side, the completed portion of the bridge was even longer. Close to a mile had been erected, and it was there that Darrs stood, some twenty feet from the end, along with several men from the Clevelandham Society of Engineers. They were as far they could go. Beyond them, the bridge workers were still laying planks for the temporary decking.

It was a blustery November day, and where they stood, nearly a mile from the shore, some ninety feet in the air, the wind swept through their hair and beards. Darrs did not wear a hat, but most of the men with him did, and they held them in their hands to keep them from blowing away.

Clevelandham was one of several industrial cities clustered along England's northeast coast, about 100 miles to the south of Edinburgh. It was home to Hodges & Pike, the company contracted to build the bridge, and at that moment, the firm's owner, Edgar Pike, was at the center of a second, larger group some fifty to seventy-five yards behind the one led by Darrs.

Darrs had barely looked up since starting onto the bridge and was surprised to see that Pike and the others had fallen so far behind, though, in fact, it was Darrs's gait that was responsible for the distance between the two groups. Darrs had walked the bridge many times. He was accustomed to the decking, the planks of which were set some eight to ten inches apart. This was not true of the other men, and while the openings between the boards did not appear large enough to fall through, it was nothing anyone wanted to test—just as no one wanted to test the strength of the temporary handrails running along the sides of the bridge.

Given the openings beneath their feet, the growing distance down to the water was also visible at every step. There was no bluff on the north shore. Beginning from the bank, the bridge rose to a height of nearly ninety feet, and the pace of the men slowed considerably as they approached the end of the completed portion, where gulls could be seen flying in the spaces between the slats. Together with the wind, the sight of the birds made the bridge feel a good deal narrower than its already slender fifteen feet.

For his part, Pike, though he'd also walked the bridge numerous times, would just as well have stayed on shore. He had no love of heights, and glancing at those around him, he imagined there were others who felt the same. No one suggested turning back, but he was sure that was only because they did not want to admit their fear, especially given the apparent nonchalance of the nearby workers, several of whom Pike saw sneering.

"Windy enough for you, gentleman?" one of the men with Darrs asked when Pike and the others finally reached them.

Their discomfort was visible, though it was Pike's expression that really concerned Darrs. The outing that day was far from strictly social. Pike himself was a past president of the Clevelandham Society, which, in addition to engineers, included a variety of fabricators and parts suppliers. Pike owed several of them substantial sums and was hoping to stir up their support.

Darrs had estimated three years for completion. It was going on five, and a gap of more than half a mile remained. No doubt the weather had been against him. The first two winters, storms had shut down operations altogether, but that was far from the only problem. The second summer, just when things finally seemed to be getting on track, Darrs had been forced to completely redesign the bridge's supports.

The survey of the riverbed on which he'd based his design was wrong. The bedrock that was said to lie some twenty-five feet beneath the bottom of the firth was nothing but a layer of hardened sediment.

It grew thinner the farther one got from shore, and the caisson crews broke through while at work on the foundation for the bridge's fifteenth support.

Whatever the reasons, the fact remained that the the project was two years behind schedule and still another year and a half to two years from completion. Pike was going to need real leniency on the part of his creditors, and Darrs could see the worry on his face. Worry wasn't even the word. It was fear. The fear of a man in danger of losing his business.

Chapter 10

Charles grabbed hold of the banister post and started up the stairs. "Victoria."

He took the steps two at a time, using his left hand to help pull himself up. In his right hand he held a listing of properties written on a sheet of embossed letterhead. He opened the door to the master bedroom, which was directly across from the staircase.

"Victoria," he called again, and then once more as he rounded the bed, heading for the dressing room.

It was Sunday morning. Victoria and he were having lunch at her parents' house, and he assumed she'd be getting ready. The dressing room was empty. He went to the bed, where he spent a few moments glancing through the papers on his nightstand. When he didn't find what he was looking for, he walked down the hall to his daughter's room, where he could hear Victoria's voice coming from inside.

"Have you seen the envelope in which this letter came?" Charles asked.

"Papa, Papa," his daughter called, as Charles entered the room.

"Miss Anne," Jenny, the nursemaid, called after the child as she raced across the room.

Victoria also called to her, but Anne, who was four years old, was undeterred and, reaching her father, wrapped her arms tightly around his legs.

"Have you seen the envelope in which this letter came?" Charles asked Victoria again, patting his daughter's head.

"Charles! Anne could have put out her eye rushing away like that."

Charles looked at Victoria, who was holding a pair of scissors in one hand and a silver comb in the other. "I'm sorry. If I had known you were cutting Anne's hair, I would have knocked before opening the door."

"You should have knocked anyway. You should always knock." Victoria looked at her daughter. "Now, young lady, come back here this instant."

Although the girl made no special effort to be quick about it, she did as her mother said, and Charles once more held out the letter.

"Have you seen the envelope in which this came?"

"What is it?"

"That list of properties we received from your father."

"It's not in your study?"

"No."

"What about the bedroom? Did you look on your nightstand?"

"I just looked. It's not there. Are you sure you haven't seen it?"

"You must keep still," Victoria said to her daughter, who, though once again in the clutches of the nursemaid, continued to squirm.

"Victoria," Charles said.

"Anne, I won't play this game with you. Be still so I can cut your hair."

"Victoria," Charles said again.

"You have the letter; why do you need the envelope?" Victoria asked, her eyes still focused on the child.

"It has some figures on the back—some calculations regarding one of my projects."

"Why would you do your calculations on the back of an envelope?"

For a moment Charles said nothing, watching as Victoria snipped a straight line across Anne's bangs. He didn't have an answer and was unlikely to come up with one, seeing as the calculations were not for one of his projects but were some figures he'd scribbled down regarding household expenses. He'd simply attributed the numbers to his work for added importance.

"Are you sure you haven't seen it?" he asked again.

"Where was the letter?"

"In my study. But the last time I saw the envelope was in the kitchen, which is why I'm afraid it might have been put in with the rubbish."

"Where are Anne's ribbons?" Victoria asked, addressing the maid.

"I was just cutting some new ones before you came upstairs. They're over there, on the dresser."

"Will you get them for me, please?" Victoria said, taking hold of the child.

"Yes, ma'am."

"Victoria," Charles said impatiently.

"Well, I certainly didn't put it in with the rubbish," she replied.

"I didn't say that you did. I was just wondering if you'd happened to see it or knew where it was."

Victoria looked at him. "Shall I stop what I'm doing and go searching this instant?"

So confronted, Charles realized the thoughtlessness of his behavior. At the same time, the question of the sort of house they could afford was a subject that concerned both of them, and as it was undoubtedly the first thing her father would want to discuss, Charles thought his concern ought to count for something. Having lied about what was on the envelope, however, he was in no position to say any of this without first admitting his dishonesty, something for which he was suddenly quite resentful. He would never have felt the need to lie if Victoria had only shown him a little consideration to begin with. Without saying another word, he turned to leave.

"Oh, very well," Victoria said, rising to her feet. "Jenny, will you finish with Anne's hair?"

"Yes, ma'am."

"Mama," Anne said, reaching up to her mother.

"Yes, dear, Mother will be right back."

Victoria leaned down to give her daughter a hug and then followed after Charles.

"Charles, as you know, we are due at my parents by noon, and I still haven't finished getting ready myself."

Charles, who was several paces ahead of her, took hold of the banister and started down the stairs. "Then perhaps this wasn't the best moment to set about cutting Anne's hair."

"I was simply clipping her bangs to keep them from falling in her eyes."

Charles said nothing in reply. He reached the bottom of the stairs and walked through the sitting room to his study. Since leaving Anne's room, his resentment toward Victoria had only deepened. It seemed typical of so many of their exchanges. Victoria had a talent for making his concerns seem inconsequential. Regardless of what they were, they could always wait, while her own concerns invariably required immediate attention. And while in this particular instance she might have had a point, seeing as he could probably have recreated the figures in the time he had now spent looking for them, it was her tone that truly irked him.

Charles would never have argued the fact that Victoria's speech was more refined than his own, but at times it seemed to take on an added emphasis. This was especially true whenever they were involved in a disagreement, the implication being the problem somehow had to do with him and the lowliness of his background. Or so it seemed to Charles, and her last few remarks had done little to alter the impression.

Once in his study, he began to search through the stack of papers on his desk.

"I still don't know why you would do your calculations on the back of an envelope," Victoria said.

"I thought you had to get ready."

"I'm here now, I may as well help you look for it. Tell me, which of your projects are the figures for?" She could see he was angry, and though she maintained a certain coolness, she thought it best to show some interest. Still, he did not answer.

"Charles, please. I'm sorry I was short with you, but I was thinking of what you'd said."

"What I'd said?"

"About my father. What you'd said about his movements being odd," Victoria replied.

Charles looked at her. The last time they'd seen Victoria's parents, he had noted something unusual in his father-in-law. Still, this was the first she'd said anything about it since, and what it had to do with anything then going on, Charles had no idea.

Chapter 11

What kind of fiend, not once to inquire over our circumstances in spite of the desperate state in which he knows we exist. Having wrung from us all there is to wring, including the blood of my husband, does he now expect us to go begging in the street?

Edgar Pike was not the bridge's first contractor. That man was Alfred de Forge, who died two years into the project. De Forge was the low bidder for the original contract. In fact, he submitted a bid a full 30,000 pounds less than Darrs's own estimate for the bridge, and the mistake became apparent almost from the start. Every month the project continued, de Forge was going further into debt, and the delay of the redesign was simply too much for him. He hadn't been in good health to start with and had died before work on the bridge ever resumed. The letter Darrs was reading was from de Forge's widow. It had come in the morning post—one of two or three such letters he'd been receiving each week for the past three years.

Following de Forge's death, his creditors had been merciless. They'd descended upon his widow while she was still at the cemetery, and Darrs, who was in attendance, felt compelled to intervene. He and his wife escorted Mrs. de Forge and her daughter home, where Mrs. de Forge showed Darrs the company books. At the time of his death, de Forge owed close to 70,000 pounds, more than two-thirds of which was for materials already in Feeport—cast-iron plates and brick for the caissons and supports as originally designed. They were items that could be put to other use or easily sold off, and Darrs convinced the railroad to assume the bulk of the debt. For several months, they also tried to continue the project with Mrs. de Forge in control, but it proved impossible and was in fact the primary reason Darrs had been able to convince Chairman Taylor to have the railroad assume the debt. Taylor was the "fiend" mentioned in the letter, and prior to assuming the debt, it was he who had been receiving Mrs. de Forge's correspondence—crazed telegrams, two and three a day.

The death of her husband had clearly unhinged the woman, and it continued to weigh heavily on Darrs as well, as did the situation with Pike. Darrs made a practice of investing in the companies with which he did business, and as Hodges & Pike was a publicly traded company, he owned 100 shares that were now worth a small fraction of what he'd paid for them.

Hodges & Pike was the firm that had built the Birkendale viaduct, and there was considerable optimism when Pike took over the contract following de Forge's death. That was no longer the case, and while Darrs was not concerned over the shares, it was a clear indication of the company's standing. Nor was Pike the only one facing bankruptcy. There was also Taylor and the British Northern. In the five years since the merger between the Scottish Central and the Edinburgh & Glasgow, the British Northern had lost more than a third of its business. Except for a few prime runs, its trains were operating at a loss. One of the few reasons it had any business at all was that even with the merger, there was no through connection south of Glasgow. To get to London and the rest of England, riders still had to make their way across town from the Scottish Central terminal to that of the Great Western.

All of that, however, was about to change. The two lines had recently started work on a rail connection between the terminals. Once completed, the Great Western would be able to run trains directly from London, all the way into Brindee. Depending on how the project went, the British Northern could be in bankruptcy before the bridge was ever finished, and here again Darrs felt at least partly responsible.

Although he had not been directly involved with the original survey of the riverbed, he was the one who had recommended the surveyor. The man, a local geologist, came highly recommended, but from what had since been learned, it seemed he'd drilled holes for about half a mile and satisfied himself it was the same all the way across.

Given the magnitude of the error, Darrs immediately stopped charging for his services. It was the least he could do, and it was the money he was working for. Darrs had been thinking of building a bridge across the Fee for years, as far back as when he'd designed his ferry system. Even then, he knew the ferries were only a temporary solution. He had no doubt the Fee would eventually be bridged, and he continued to believe in the value of what they were doing. As it stood, however, it was not going to be soon enough for either Pike or Taylor.

Chapter 12

Like the company boardroom, the offices of the British Northern had long since lost their luster. It was nearly twenty years since the floors had been stained, and there were well-worn paths in all the main corridors. Taylor had not given a great deal of attention to his office of late, but as he awaited the arrival of Walter Blackman, chairman of the London & North Eastern Railway, he was suddenly aware of just how shabby it had grown and wished he'd done more to prepare.

The London & North Eastern was the most powerful railroad in the nation. It headed a consortium that included most of the lines in the eastern half of the country, and given the company's holdings in everything from iron and coal to land, many people considered Blackman the most powerful man in Britain, more powerful even than the prime minister. Taylor had known Blackman was coming for more than a week, which was plenty of time if not to stain the floors, then at least to put on a fresh coat of paint and buy a few new chairs.

Then again, no amount of paint or stain was going to hide the fact that the British Northern was on the brink of bankruptcy. Taylor had little doubt that Blackman's purpose in coming that day was to settle the matter once and for all, and to a large extent, Taylor knew he had no one to blame but himself. The British Northern's troubles had not suddenly begun five years before with the merger of the Edinburgh & Glasgow and the Scottish Central. They started at least two years before that, when a series of mergers led to the formation of the Scottish Central itself. For the first time in its history, the British Northern faced real competition, and to anyone who'd ever doubted the need to bridge the firths, that need had become blatantly apparent. Still, Taylor had not acted.

The rivalry between the Great Western and the London & North Eastern, the country's two largest railroads, had become so heated that a drive into northern Scotland seemed virtually certain. The Great Western and its allied lines already controlled most of the rails between London and Glasgow. The London & North Eastern was only slightly behind in its push toward Edinburgh, and Taylor and the other board members watched with absolute glee as the company share price climbed for twelve straight months.

In the end, however, the London & North Eastern did not form an alliance with the British Northern. In a move seemingly designed to destroy the line instead, the London & North Eastern formed its own alliance with the Scottish Central, and shares in the British Northern plummeted. Within weeks, the company was trading for pennies, and it was only then, in desperation, that Taylor had launched his plan to bridge the Fee. By then, however, it was too late, and he knew that if he hadn't spent so much time envisioning his new estate and the white pebble drive leading to its entrance, he would have started on the bridge when he should have—two years earlier, in which case it would have been done by now, even with the delays.

There was a knock on the door, and Robert Kendall, the company treasurer, stepped into the room.

"They're here. The receptionist is just seeing to their coats and hats," he said.

Taylor sighed. "Very well,"

"Whatever he says, we must stress the fact that even in its present form the bridge represents an investment of more than 200,000 pounds."

"Mr. Kendall, you are free to say what you like, but, in its current form, the bridge does not so much represent an investment as a mounting debt."

"Then what do you suggest?"

"I don't suggest anything. I plan to sit here and listen to what he has to say."

"You are aware that whatever he offers, the board is likely to agree at this point," Kendall said.

Taylor nodded. He was fifty-seven and facing financial ruin. He didn't need anyone to remind him of just how pitiful his position was.

Again, there was a knock on the door.

"Yes?"

"Mr. Walter Blackman of the London & North Eastern," the secretary said.

"Very well. Show him in."

Blackman brought three others with him. In addition to his private secretary, he was accompanied by John Wembly, director of the Northumberland Railway; and Roger Kippen, director of the Stockton-Newcastle Line, both members of the East Coast consortium.

"Good day, gentlemen," Taylor greeted them. "Allow me to introduce Mr. Robert Kendall, treasurer of the British Northern."

"Mr. Kendall," Blackman said, bowing his head. "And allow me to introduce Mr. John Wembly and Mr. Roger Kippen, both of whom you may know."

"Yes, we've had occasion to meet," Taylor said.

Blackman reached into his jacket pocket for a pipe, and Taylor signaled to his secretary, who quickly brought an ashtray.

Blackman acknowledged the man and then glanced back at Taylor. "I imagine you have some notion as to why I've asked for this meeting."

"I have a notion."

"Then you won't be offended if I take the liberty of being direct?"

"As you like."

"Very well. Let me begin by saying the London & North Eastern and its associates have been interested in the British Northern for some time, though knowing the financial hardships your line has faced, we've charted a waiting course."

"So that you might end up buying it for pennies on the pound."

Blackman looked at Taylor, somewhat surprised by the remark.

"As long as we're being direct," Taylor said.

"Then yes, Mr. Taylor, that had been our intention. A number of developments, however, have caused us to reconsider our course of action."

"Is that right?"

Again Blackman was surprised, this time by the hostility in Taylor's voice, which made no sense, given the purpose of the meeting.

"Mr. Taylor, as I'm sure you are aware, commerce in and around Brindee has grown markedly in recent years. It has expanded with a swiftness we never anticipated, but in spite of the fact that Brindee is an East Coast city, it is the Great Western, by way of its affiliation with the Scottish Central, that has established itself as the region's predominant agent of trade and communication."

"Might I remind you the British Northern will soon be in a position to challenge that dominance."

"You are referring to your bridge, of course, which brings me to the next point. There is no denying the importance of your efforts on the Fee, and to your credit, it now appears as if you will likely succeed."

Taylor was stunned by the remark. Given what he'd assumed was the reason for Blackman's visit, it was a major admission. "Then you are no longer counting on the British Northern going under?" he asked in a tone that did little to hide his astonishment.

"We are aware that your position remains precarious and that, left to your own devices, the line could still fall into bankruptcy. We are also aware, however, that it could take two or three additional years for that to happen, during which time the Great Western's hold on the region will only grow firmer, especially with its new rail connection in Glasgow."

"Surely a bridge across the Fee will do much to break that hold," Taylor said, so beside himself with relief he was almost giddy.

Blackman, however, did not share Taylor's giddiness. "It is true that a bridge over the Fee will do much to secure your position in terms of passenger traffic on the coastal corridor. As for posing a serious challenge to the Great Western, you must think in terms of freight revenues, and your bridge by itself is unlikely to have a significant impact on the overall movement of goods and materials to and from Scotland."

Taylor, whose sense of giddiness had abruptly disappeared, suddenly felt like a fool. "By itself." The words seemed to echo in his ears as it finally dawned on him the reason Blackman was there. He wasn't there to make an offer for the British Northern. For that, he wouldn't have brought along Kippen and Wembly. He was there to propose some sort of joint venture regarding the Forth.

Taylor sat forward in his chair. "Mr. Blackman, sir, you must forgive me. I completely misunderstood the purpose of your visit."

"It would seem so."

"I do apologize for my confusion."

"But you now understand the purpose of my being here, and for having asked Mr. Kippen and Mr. Wembly to join us."

"You are here to discuss the Forth."

"Yes," Blackman said. "It, too, must be bridged if we are to have any hope of challenging the West Coast lines in the north of England and Scotland."

Chapter 13

It was a rainy Monday morning, and Charles sat in a staff meeting in the firm's conference room. The subject was a proposed extension to the London Metropolitan Railway, or LMR, a line three and a half miles long that ran under the heart of London. Completed the previous decade, the LMR was the world's first underground railway. Farlow was the line's chief engineer and also one of its biggest promoters, certain that the present tunnel was only the first in a series of underground lines that would eventually spread throughout the city. There was some talk in Parliament that this might be the time to begin that expansion, and while, for the moment, it was only talk, Farlow already had a dozen men working on the project, including surveyors and draftsmen.

Charles was charged with designing the extensions to either end of the existing tunnel, a role of considerable importance, although at that precise moment he was merely trying to keep from falling asleep. He was sitting near one end of the conference table, while Otto Fein, the project's manager, presided at the other end. The meeting had been going on for close to an hour, the last three-quarters of which had focused on the possibility of replacing the line's current steam locomotives with a pneumatic or electrical system. They were topics that had little to do with Charles's part in the project, so to keep from dozing off, he doodled in the margins of his notebook.

Since joining the firm, Charles had received several promotions, but as much progress as he'd made, he now viewed himself on something of a dead-end path. When it came to bridge projects, he was always second in line behind Roger Fielding, a partner. Even Charles's expertise with metals was no guarantee of future advancement. Other realms were coming to the fore, and in clear disregard of seniority, Farlow had entrusted the day-to-day running of the underground project to Fein, a German-born specialist in pneumatics who'd been hired only six months before. It was a point of considerable contention in the office, and while Charles continued to perform his duties with a fair amount of diligence, his thoughts of late had centered as much on rents and mortgages as anything to do with engineering.

The door opened, and Charles glanced up from his notebook as Farlow's personal secretary poked his head into the room.

"Excuse me, Mr. Fein."

"Yes, what is it?" Fein replied sharply.

"Mr. Farlow would like to see Mr. Jenkins."

"This moment?"

"Yes, sir."

Fein shook his head, clearly annoyed, before motioning for Charles to go.

Although Charles had sat up straight at the sound of his name, it was a reflexive response. He was still somewhat listless and did his best to shake the feeling as he followed the secretary down the hall.

"Jenkins, come in, come in," Farlow said, lighting his pipe and gesturing to a chair.

Charles sat down across the desk from Farlow.

"What do you know of the Forth?"

Charles looked at Farlow, not sure what he meant.

"The Firth of Forth. What do you know about it?" Farlow asked again.

"I know it's an estuary in Scotland—an extremely broad one, if that's what you mean. Edinburgh sits upon its southern shore."

"Have you ever given any thought to how best it might be bridged?" Farlow asked. "Knowing your plans for the Fee, I imagine you must have given it at least some consideration."

Charles met Farlow's glance head on. "I know the estuary narrows near Edinburgh, and that the most likely site for a bridge lies a few miles from the city, in the village of Queensferry."

"Anything else?"

"Yes. Compared to the Fee, the depth of the water poses a major obstacle, but at Queensferry there is a small island roughly halfway between the two shores that would allow for the crossing to be made in two spans—two spans of roughly 1,700 feet each," Charles said.

Farlow nodded, satisfied with what he'd heard. "I'm sure you know the Great Western recently entered into an agreement to run its trains on Scottish Central rails north of Glasgow."

Charles nodded. "When they complete the connection between the terminals, it will be possible to run trains directly from London all the way to Brindee."

"Giving the Great Western a virtual monopoly on the movement of goods to and from Scotland," Farlow added. "Not to be outdone, Walter Blackman, chairman of the London & North Eastern traveled to Edinburgh this past week to meet with the chairman of the British Northern."

"Richard Taylor."

"Correct," Farlow said, clenching his pipe between his teeth. "If my information is accurate, Blackman wants his own route into Brindee via the east coast, and his purpose was none other than to begin discussions for a bridge across the Forth." Farlow removed his pipe from his mouth and looked squarely at Charles. "The negotiations could take several months, but once a formal announcement is made, the competition will be fierce, and I want to be prepared. Two spans, both of them longer than Roebling's bridge in New York. You do realize what a project like this can mean? And not just for the firm but also for the individuals whose names appear on the plans?"

"I do," Charles said.

"Naturally, I've already spoken to Mr. Fielding," Farlow said, returning his pipe to his mouth. "But my intention is not that the two of you work together. There will be time enough for that. For the moment, I want both of you to work separately."

Charles nodded, feeling a certain disappointment. He should have assumed as much, but for an instant it seemed to Charles as if Farlow had been entrusting the work entirely to him.

"As for your work on the LMR extension," Farlow went on.

"I take it that you'll want to reassign my duties to someone else," Charles said.

"Not at all. The LMR project is far too important to take you away from it, even for this. You'll have to work on both."

"I understand," Charles said.

Farlow, who had been sitting quite erect, settled back in his chair. "By the way, I have no doubt you'll want to use steel in your design."

"For spans of that length, I'm not sure you could do it with any other material."

"You may have already considered this, but I have no doubt Robert Barrol would like to have a hand in this himself."

Charles looked at Farlow. He hadn't considered it, and he was more than a little surprised by the idea.

Farlow again took his pipe from his mouth. "I'm sure his involvement would also help when it comes to securing a good price on the metal."

Chapter 14

"Stewart, I thought you were coming to bed."

Darrs glanced up from his desk at his wife, who stood in the doorway to his study. She was wrapped in a robe, but had already been in bed, waiting for him to join her, when she realized he was not yet even upstairs.

"I was," he said, "but something occurred to me as I was locking up." Darrs reached down to pet Matilda, who had followed his wife downstairs from the bedroom.

"More to do with the Forth?"

"Yes," Darrs said, motioning to his desk. "An engraving I ordered of the new bridge in New York arrived today. I didn't expect it, but it's been hand-colored, and I wanted to have another look at it."

Mrs. Darrs moved closer so that she too could see the engraving, and realizing it was upside down from where she stood, Darrs turned it around.

"It is quite beautiful," she said.

"Suspension bridges do seem to have a special quality about them. Certainly they have a unique appeal among the public."

"They're just so graceful."

"Unfortunately, the engraving is a bit more decorative than I'd hoped."

Mrs. Darrs looked at her husband questioningly.

"While it does give a sense of the overall structure, it's not to scale," Darrs said, "so it's really not of any use to me."

"Does that mean you're planning to base your bridge on this one?"

"Of course the Forth will require two spans."

"Two spans! Two like this?" Mrs. Darrs asked, gesturing to the engraving.

Darrs looked at her. "I haven't had a chance to fully examine the matter, but I do know the only spans now in existence that even approach the length of those needed on the Forth are suspension spans. So, yes, I imagine something of the sort will be required."

Again Mrs. Darrs looked at the engraving. With its golden cables and cathedral-like towers, the bridge possessed a majesty that was instantly apparent, and she now gazed at it with new excitement, envisioning her husband's bridge with two such spans. She'd known her husband almost all her life. They'd grown up in the same town, and married after he'd completed his apprenticeship. That was more than thirty years before, and she'd always imagined him to be a very fine engineer. But this! This was something else entirely.

"Stewart, you will be the most famous engineer in the world."

"There's no guarantee I'll be the one to get the contract."

"If not you, who? Who else has your experience?" his wife asked.

"You are referring to the Fee, but as it is, the Fee remains something of a double-edged sword. So long as it goes unfinished, I'm not sure I'll even be considered. The project is sure to attract all the top firms in the country."

"That may be, but think of how Mr. Taylor depends on you. He would never entrust the work to anyone else."

Darrs looked at his wife, who was holding her robe closed at the neck and looking back at him with great resolution. It was a pose he'd seen many times and, for all of its firmness, one he found especially endearing. Moreover, as Taylor had wired him with the news the very day of his meeting with Blackman, she was likely correct. In this case, however, the choice would not be Taylor's.

Darrs stepped out from behind his desk. "My dear, this is a joint venture with the London & North Eastern. They are sure to have a say in it. The decision won't be Mr. Taylor's alone."

"Mark my words, Stewart. If Mr. Taylor has anything to say in the matter, the Forth contract will be yours."

Mrs. Darrs crossed the room to pick up Matilda, who had curled up in an armchair in the corner next to Darrs's desk.

Darrs waited for his wife by the door. "Again, I can only hope you are right," he said, as he turned off the gas and followed her out of the room.

Chapter 15

The sun glistened on the surface of the firth, casting streaks of light across the finished span, which sat crosswise on the end of the launching pier. A major structure in itself, the pier extended some 200 feet from shore and also served as a dock for the launches and tugs used to shuttle men and equipment back and forth between the shore and the foundations being sunk in the riverbed.

Darrs had just arrived. It was a cold morning. He wore gloves and a long coat as he watched the men prepare to launch the span. Underneath the overhanging ends of the span were the barges that would lift it from the pier. There was only an inch or two separating the span from the barges, which meant it wouldn't be long.

His assistant's plan to use the tides was a good one, and the assembling and floating of the spans was one of the few things that had gone smoothly from the start. The wrought-iron beams were being made to order at Pike's metalworks, in Clevelandham, and arrived in Brindee already sized and shaped. Even the rivet holes were being drilled in Clevelandham. All that was left was to assemble the parts, and among the sounds of the construction site was the near constant cracking of the sledges as the men hammered down the rivets, cinching the beams together.

Out on the water, a tug idled, ready to tow the span into position. Around Darrs, the workers hustled about making final preparations, though most of the men paused to offer a slight bow or a quick "Good morning, sir." Many had been there from the start, and Darrs knew the faces, if not the names, of the vast majority.

"Mr. Darrs, I was just told you were here. It must be bad news."

Darrs turned to Pike, who also wore a long coat. He was breathing hard, and in the cold his breath rose like a cloud of smoke before his face.

Although developments on the Forth had done much to reduce the pressure on Taylor and the railroad, they did nothing to help Pike. The British Northern had already advanced all the money due according to the contract, which left Pike to pay for the rest of the bridge out of his own pocket. And he was right: Darrs wasn't there with good news.

"As you know, I traveled to Edinburgh yesterday to meet with Chairman Taylor."

"And?" Pike questioned. "What did he say about the bonus? Did he make any concession with regard to the deadline?"

Darrs hesitated. "As would be expected, he is very interested in seeing what can be done to increase the rate of progress."

Pike sighed. "Again, the second pier Taylor and Mr. Stevens have been after me to build," he said, referring to Darrs's assistant, who was also the resident engineer.

"It would enable you to launch two spans at once," Darrs replied.

"You are aware of the costs involved in building another pier?" Pike replied.

Before them, the present pier squealed sharply. The tide was beginning to lift the span, and the planks groaned under the shifting load. Both men had turned at the sound, and then Pike glanced back at Darrs.

"And even with a second pier, by my calculations there is still no chance of meeting the deadline. Counting this one here, we have nineteen spans go, and fourteen of them are the inverted spans for the main channel. They're twice as long."

"They are longer, but there is nothing to say they'll be harder to erect."

"Other than the fact that they're longer," he said with some exasperation.

Darrs hesitated before responding, so Pike continued.

"Mr. Darrs, even with a second pier," he said, doing his best to speak calmly, "by my estimate, assuming the best, we won't be done until December or January. The contract calls for a train to cross the bridge on the first of September."

Darrs looked at Pike. This was not a conversation he'd been looking forward to, and Darrs imagined that was at least part of the reason he'd paused to watch the men as they worked to float the span. The bonus Pike spoke of was 50,000 pounds, a figure that would go a long way toward mending his accounts, and given the developments on the Forth, Darrs thought the chairman might be more amenable to modifying the terms. Taylor, however, was adamant in his refusal. The Forth had nothing to do with the Fee. Pike had signed the contract. He knew the terms and was bound to meet them, bonus or no bonus.

"We are still obliged to make our best effort," Darrs said.

"Best effort," Pike huffed. "At this point, what does it matter to me when the bridge is finished? As I said, at the current rate, there's not a chance it will be done before December, and that's assuming we're able to work through the winter. We've been all right this year, but who's to say what's to happen. Last fall's storms were some of the worst we faced—something Mr. Taylor seems entirely unwilling to acknowledge. Mr. Darrs, we have made every effort to keep to the schedule, but there must be some allowances." Pike tugged at his coat. "What, does he think I've squirreled the money away or used it to purchase a new wardrobe? Every penny that's come to me by way of this project has gone into the bridge, so that my best effort at this point is trying to have a company when all of this is said and done."

Darrs made a slight grimace. He was disappointed with Pike's response but knew what was behind it. Pike was a good man. At Birkendale, not only had they raised sixteen spans in four months, but they'd also done it without a single accident or injury. It was something almost unheard of at the time and owed much to Pike's organizational skills. On the Fee, too, despite the delays, the project had been remarkably free of injury. The one bad accident occurred before Pike was there. As Darrs predicted, they had not experienced any cases of Caisson disease, but early on, four men died in an explosion in one of the digging chambers. No one was certain of the cause, but the best explanation was that the flame from a kerosene lantern ignited the oxygen being pumped into caisson from the surface. It was something for which Darrs took full responsibility, and afterward, they'd stopped using pumped air altogether.

Since then, there had been no major incidents. Pike was a trained engineer with a long list of accomplishments of his own. It was one of the reasons Darrs had been so encouraged when he took over the contract. In fact, to some extent the project was now going as Darrs had always intended, having based many of his estimates on Birkendale. One of the foremen of the caisson crews had even devised a powered vacuum to suck loosened sediment from the riverbed, reducing by more than a third the time needed to sink the last foundation.

Even with the improvements, however, Pike was unlikely to meet the deadline. Darrs remembered similar circumstances at Birkendale. Like the Fee, the Birkendale project had gotten off to a slow start, and Pike was afraid he was going to end up losing money on the job. He'd had to lay out what he thought were enormous sums just to start operations, and they were nothing compared to the sums he now had invested in the Fee.

Ultimately, they'd finished more than a month ahead of schedule at Birkendale. By the end, they were raising spans at twice the rate initially planned. At Birkendale, however, they hadn't had to sink caissons. No degree of familiarity was going to result in that kind of improvement.

Chapter 16

It was late, and Charles sat alone in his study. Before him on his desk were some preliminary sketches for the Forth, and while they were far from complete, he was satisfied with what he'd done so far. In spite of being able to relate certain facts off the top of his head, Charles had not spent long hours contemplating the Forth. The basic dimensions at Queensferry were well known among engineers. But he did have ideas, and though he'd been at work only a few weeks, he believed he was on the right track.

Charles remembered his experience before the British Northern as an unknown. Though it had been low on his list of thoughts in recent months, Denney & Farlow was one of the most renowned engineering firms in the world. It possessed a history of innovation dating back nearly a century, to the pioneering use of cast iron, and Charles saw it as only fitting that the same firm should now be turning its sights to steel.

Right then, however, he wasn't thinking as much about the Forth as about the plans tacked to the wall in front of him. They were for a 1,200-foot cantilever bridge across the Devern River near Birmingham. Charles had created them while still apprenticing at the mill, and Barrol, seeing the bridge as an excellent opportunity to promote his new metal, agreed to supply the steel at cost. Together, Charles and he presented the plans to the Great Western, which seemed duly impressed. In the end, however, the railroad would not commit and, after a year of delays, ended up shelving the project altogether.

Though never built, it remained the longest span Charles had ever designed, and he'd gotten out the plans as a point of reference. It had been years since he'd last looked at them, and almost immediately he'd seen changes he would make, which was perhaps to be expected. It was ten years since he'd first started drafting the plans, and he had learned a great deal in the time since. Still, even with the plans before him, he found it hard to recall actually drafting them. For two years, they'd been everything to him. He'd labored over every detail, down to the smallest lettering, yet here in front of him, they seemed from another lifetime.

Charles thought of Elizabeth, which in itself was nothing unusual. Hardly a day went by without some thought of her coming into his head, and usually it was far more than a single thought. Charles had not forgotten the image of Elizabeth with her hair pinned to the back of her head or his plan to board a train for Birmingham that very day. Indeed, when it came to Elizabeth, Charles functioned under the belief that he had committed a terrible wrong. He hadn't even had the courage to face her. He'd written a letter. It was hateful. The only thing that softened it in any way at all was that he knew it had not come as a complete surprise. Elizabeth was too intelligent not to have sensed something. She'd asked him about it, once even suggesting she wouldn't have blamed him—his being in London and their being so far apart.

Charles had denied it vehemently, not wanting to hurt her—or at least not wanting to see her hurt. It was as if he'd betrayed her not once, but twice, and in so doing had lost any chance of his own at real happiness as well. This was not to say he was desperately forlorn. He was well aware that over the past few years his life had assumed a form he'd always hoped it would. But a deep-seated preoccupation with what might have been continued to impede his ability to take pleasure in things as they really were.

Charles glanced up at the ceiling. He could hear Victoria moving around their bedroom, which was directly above the study. Certainly his feelings for Elizabeth had done nothing to benefit his marriage. Whatever his complaints, they were no fault of Victoria. And at this point, who was to say he would have been any happier with Elizabeth? It was possible, of course, but he realized his feelings at this point had more to do with his own shame and regret than anything actually to do with Elizabeth. The fact was, he couldn't be sure of what they might have shared, whether more or less than he liked to suppose. As with the Devern plans, he was thinking it was a long time ago.

Much to Charles's discomfort, Farlow continued to press him about Barrol, and Charles had yet to figure out precisely how he planned to deal with the matter. It had been close to six years since he'd last seen Barrol, and given the way things ended, he couldn't be sure Barrol would even respond. Still, he was thinking that by now, Elizabeth was most likely married with a family of her own, something that would certainly make things easier. Charles could still hear Victoria moving about above him; putting his plans aside, he got up from his desk to join her.

Chapter 17

Darrs made two major changes to the bridge when it was discovered that the supports would not stand on bedrock, but clay and mud. He doubled the size of the caissons to spread the weight over a larger area, and he redesigned the bridge's supports. Instead of solid brick, the portion above the water was now being constructed of metal beams. Unlike the beams for the spans, which were made of wrought iron and being manufactured in Clevelandham, the beams for the supports were cast iron and were being poured on-site in a large shed near the start of the bridge on Brindee shore. The shed had a dirt floor, on which eight wooden molds lay in a row. Each of the molds was a little more than eight feet long and a little more than a foot wide. Each was also lined with several inches of wet sand, in which there were channels dug at the ends for the flanges and holes by which the beams would be bolted together. Next to the channels for the flanges, there were also notches for lugs, connection points for the wrought-iron bars that would be used to brace the beams together.

Behind the molds, five men stood by the forge, a brick encasement, which, other than the light coming through the entrance, was the only source of illumination in the shed.

"Do you see? The rubbish is all the way through," one of them said. "We could ladle till she was empty."

Darrs looked into the cauldron, the surface of which glowed a dull red. There were also patches of grayish-black impurities, known as slag. As it rose to the surface, two men worked to skim it off, though with each pass of the ladle, more came up.

The men were Scottish locals. They were used to working with Brindee iron, which they believed to be of much better quality than the iron that Pike was shipping them from his own Clevelandham region. The men had been grumbling about it from the start, and clearly there was a good deal of slag. Darrs had also seen brighter reds, which had to do with heat. The duller the red, the sooner the iron would begin to cool when removed from the fire. The iron could become sluggish in the molds, so that it didn't flow freely, especially into the small channels dug at the ends for the flanges and lugs. Early on, there had been instances when the bolt holes were misshapen. They were smaller on one end than the other, so the bolts didn't fit through the opening. The holes had to be bored true, but the flanges and lugs would often crack under the drill, in which case the beam had to be returned to the shed to have new lugs or flanges burned on.

At the time, Darrs gave orders to mix in the cast-iron plates left over from the original caissons. It was Welsh iron that de Forge had poured in his Cardiff metalworks. Darrs knew it was of good quality, and it alleviated the problem. Now, however, they'd run through all the plates, and according to his assistant, Stevens, the resident engineer, they were once again having the same problem.

"I want to see it in the mold," Darrs said.

"All right then. She's as ready as she'll ever be," one of the men said, setting down his ladle.

The cauldron was connected by chains to a winch with a double crank, which two of the men used to raise the cauldron from the fire. The winch was equipped with a rotating boom, and once the cauldron was clear of the forge, they directed it over the forms on the floor, into which the two men who had been skimming the slag were now inserting cylinders of hardened cement. The beams were being cast around cement cores, a common practice in the trade that offered costs savings without any compromise in strength.

The man closest to Darrs handed him a thick scarf, which Darrs wrapped around his nose and mouth. The others also covered their faces with mufflers or kerchiefs so that all that showed were the men's eyes. With a brief glance of acknowledgment, the two men at the crank tipped the cauldron over the first of the eight molds.

Immediately, a dense cloud of smoke began to fill the shed as the molten iron came into contact with the wet sand. The nearest supply of freshwater was more than two miles away and would have required the construction of a pipeline to access, as a result of which the water being used to dampen the molds was saltwater straight from the Fee.

Darrs watched as the mold filled, paying close attention to the channels at the ends for the lugs and flanges. With the first mold filled, the men moved to the second, where once again a noxious cloud hissed upward. Darrs stepped back, again watching as the metal filled the mold.

It was when they moved onto the third form that he began to see a difference. The iron no longer flowed as freely, and one of the men retrieved his ladle. He urged the metal around the mold, creating small swells to carry it into the cuts for the flanges and lugs, after which they moved onto the fourth form. Despite the muffler across his mouth, the man with the ladle was caught square in the face by the rising fumes, causing him to stagger back, coughing violently.

"Well, don't go on hacking in here. Get yourself some air," the man closest to him said, taking the ladle from his hand.

The coughing man started toward the door as the man who'd spoken took up position alongside the molds. Like the man before him, he needed to create small waves to carry the molten iron into the corners. Slag continued to rise to the surface, and even as he stirred and coaxed the metal about the form, he worked to skim off larger clumps.

There were still four forms to go, but at that point the foreman, who stood next to Darrs, gave orders to return the cauldron to the fire.

"Before we ran out of the plates, we could get through all eight before having to reheat," he said. "Now it's four or five at most, which does slow things down."

Darrs nodded, though it wasn't the time he was thinking of. Properly attached, a burned-on flange or lug could be as strong as, or stronger than, the original, but Darrs wasn't looking to take any chances. They were getting to the inverted spans, the supports for which were more than ten feet taller than those for the noninverted spans.

Chapter 18

In addition to assigning the project to both Charles and Fielding, Farlow intended to stage an internal competition to determine whose plan to submit for the Forth. He was looking for finished products and had given the men six months to complete their work. Charles had no illusions as to the difficulty of his position. Fielding was not only a partner, he was also sure to submit a suspension design, and Charles had come to question whether anyone would consider anything else. The project had been formally announced, and all the talk was of suspension bridges. One of the top journals had even weighed in on the subject, saying a suspension bridge was the "obvious choice."

At the same time, in spite of Charles's early optimism, he, himself, had come to have serious doubts about his cantilever plan. In fact, he was no longer certain it was feasible. The crossing was going to require two spans of at least 1,700 feet. Despite his best efforts, however, he had been unable able to produce a span beyond 1,500 feet—at least not one with any margin for error. As Charles now saw it, to build cantilevers of the size he needed, it wasn't simply a matter of enlarging his current design; he was going to have to modify the form of the beams themselves, something for which he needed help.

Along with this, Farlow continued to ask about Barrol. Every Monday morning, like clockwork, following their weekly staff meeting, Farlow approached Charles to ask if he had heard from Barrol. Eventually, uncomfortable as it was, Charles wired Birmingham. Much to his surprise, Barrol replied almost immediately, inviting Charles to the mill, which was the reason Charles sat on a Great Western's northbound train from London. Still, while Charles took the quick response as a good sign, he remained anxious. Along the lines of his recent thoughts, he was hoping Elizabeth was married and no longer living at home, as he knew seeing her at this point could only prove awkward.

The train reached Birmingham, and Charles took a cab from the station to the mill. It was nearly six years since he'd been there last, but little had changed. The rail siding he'd designed looked just as he remembered it, only he was surprised to see not just one or two half-loaded flatcars, but a fully loaded four-car train.

Charles paid the driver and walked into the mill through the old manor house. The door to Barrol's office was open, and he could see Barrol with his back to the door, glancing at some papers. Charles knocked.

"Charles! Come in, come in," he said, smiling broadly.

"That's quite a line of cars I saw on the siding," Charles replied.

"You won't hear me complaining," Barrol said as they shook hands, although his voice trailed off.

As he spoke, Elizabeth walked into the room through a side door. For a moment, she and Charles simply looked at each other.

"Hello, Charles," she finally said. She had a stack of papers in her hand, and she handed them to her father.

"Elizabeth," Charles replied.

"I'm Father's secretary now," she said.

"And a darn good one," Barrol said. "I couldn't get along without her."

"What about Mr. Boxworth?" Charles asked, speaking purely out of nervousness.

"Boxworth," Barrol repeated, suddenly remembering what he'd been doing before Charles arrived. "He moved into the office across the hall, and he's waiting for me right now. I wasn't sure what time you'd be getting here, so we started going over the books for last month." He turned to Elizabeth. "The figures on your desk, are those for this month or last?"

"This month."

"Then Boxworth has everything for last month?"

Elizabeth nodded and Barrol turned back to Charles. "In any case, you'll have to excuse me for a few minutes."

"You do know why I'm here? It's about the Forth," Charles said.

"Yes, yes. Don't worry, we'll have plenty of time to talk. In fact, why don't you stay for supper? That way there's no rush."

Charles glanced hesitantly at Elizabeth, who lowered her eyes.

Barrol reached into his pocket for his watch. "It's nearly one o'clock now. There's no sense coming all this way just to turn around and go home again. Besides, I won't take no for an answer. In the meantime, I have no doubt you'll want to look around. We've made a number of changes since you were here last. Elizabeth, why don't you take Charles back to see the new rolling equipment. That should impress him."

Again Charles looked at Elizabeth, who this time returned his glance.

"I won't be with Boxworth but fifteen or twenty minutes. I'll meet you in the mill," Barrol said. With that he was gone, leaving Charles and Elizabeth standing together in silence.

As before, for several moments they simply looked at each other. Charles didn't know what to think, and it wasn't just the shock of finding himself alone with Elizabeth. There was Barrol, as well. At best, Charles had hoped their dealings would be cordial. It never occurred to him that Barrol would be pleased to see him, and that was to say nothing of his nonchalance in leaving the two of them alone, as if it were the most natural thing in the world.

Unknown to Charles, over the years Elizabeth had shared very little with her parents about the end of her relationship with Charles. From the beginning, she did her best to hide her feelings, a practice she continued the previous Friday, when her father told her of the wire he'd received from Charles. She acted quite indifferently, even when her father went on to tell her that he was thinking of inviting Charles to Birmingham.

Of course, Charles had courted her for close to four years. Her father didn't have to be a genius to know there might be some awkwardness in their seeing each other again after so many years. For the life of her, she had no idea why he would suddenly go off, leaving the two of them alone together.

"Well, if I am going to show you the new equipment, we might as well get started," Elizabeth eventually said.

Charles followed her down the hall to the back of the house, where a large wooden door led to the mill proper. Elizabeth paused to pin up her hair, at which point she noticed Charles looking at her intently. She remembered he'd never been especially fond of her with her hair up, and she was suddenly self-conscious about her appearance as she pulled open the door to the mill.

Altogether, the mill covered close to four acres, and stepping into its darkened halls was akin to entering a netherworld of fire and smoke. Molten steel rained down like droplets of lava as the slag was poured off a cauldron of steel fresh from the furnace. Further on, the furnace itself, its doors agape, glowed with unimaginable heat.

Elizabeth walked quickly, nodding to the men as she passed. Many of the faces were familiar to Charles, and he could tell from the expressions that many of the men recognized him in return.

Beyond the furnace, they turned to the left, passing a long series of molds in which the steel was cast into ingots. The cauldron they'd seen when entering was now overhead, its contents spilling down a series of corrugated ramps into the molds. They were near the center of the building, and across from them was a makeshift office consisting of a desk surrounded by wooden partitions. The floor master used it to do his calculations when determining the contents for a particular pour. At least that's how Charles had used it and, seeing a man emerge from behind the partitions, he assumed it was still the case.

"Miss Elizabeth, may I be of assistance?" the man asked, speaking with a distinct German accent.

"Johann, this is Mr. Jenkins."

The man looked at Charles. "Johann Stiller," he said, nodding his head sharply.

"I'm taking Mr. Jenkins to see the new rolling equipment," Elizabeth said.

"The new rolling equipment," Stiller repeated. "Yes, I would be happy to accompany you and demonstrate the machinery for Mr. Jenkins." Again he looked at Charles. "There are several mills in Germany using similar machines, but I believe it is unique in your country."

As he spoke, a deep rumble reverberated through the building, followed by a resounding crack boom as the furnace doors slammed shut. It was a sound instantly familiar to Charles, who braced himself for the ear-piercing blast he knew would follow. It was similar to a locomotive discharging a head of steam, only far more shrill, though, as Charles knew, it was not steam, but a stream of air injected into the furnace to burn off any impurities left from the previous pour. Charles knew this, just as he knew Elizabeth was leading him to the far end of the building, where the steel was put through the finishing process. He'd spent close to six years of his life inside that mill, and although he may not have been familiar with the new rolling equipment, he had no desire to be lectured to, especially by a foreigner some eight to ten years his junior.

Fortunately, he was spared the indignity, as the air blast was a signal the men were getting set to load the furnace with another charge, something for which Stiller had to be present. He apologized and took his leave, after which Elizabeth continued on toward the rear of the building.

The rolling equipment consisted of a moving conveyor some twenty-five feet long, on which the heated ingots were passed between pairs of moving rollers. Each pair of rollers was slightly closer together than the preceding one, so that the steel was squeezed along the way, a process that refined and toughened the metal.

At that particular moment, however, the conveyor was silent, as was the rest of the machinery in the immediate vicinity. Elizabeth and Charles were once again alone, only now it was worse. Her mind had already set to work. She could see herself at the train station, tears streaming from her eyes. It was the day Charles had first returned to London all those years before. She was crying, as if she'd known even then it was over. She could feel her body convulsing and the slight cant of her shoulders, as she leaned forward to keep the tears from falling on her dress. Charles had smiled at those tears—chuckled, even. He wasn't being mean. He'd simply seen no reason for it, since he would be seeing her again in only a few weeks. But it was the end, and she must have known.

Elizabeth shook her head to rid herself of the image. She didn't want to think of it. Still, she couldn't just stand there acting as if they'd never met before. That, too, would have been too much for her. She took a deep breath.

"So, how have you been?" She asked, not looking at him. She wasn't even facing him, but she could feel his presence. They were standing a few feet apart, both of them resting their hands on the edge of the conveyor.

"I suppose I've been well," Charles replied, glancing down as he answered. "And you?"

Elizabeth listened to his voice, suddenly realizing he hadn't said a word since her father had left them alone, which, if nothing else, meant Charles was probably nervous as well.

"Father has been kind enough to entrust me with a good deal of responsibility, so I keep quite busy," she said, turning to look at him.

Charles, who turned to meet her glance, nodded in acknowledgment before once more looking away.

"I imagine you must have children by now," she said after a moment.

Charles felt the muscles in his neck tighten. It was a reasonable question. He'd been married six years, during which they hadn't seen each other or spoken. Still, the mere fact that he had to answer yes was excruciating. Nothing could have been more obvious or undeniable evidence of everything that stood between them, a matter of no small importance in that, from the moment he saw her, whatever thoughts he might have had minimizing the significance of what they'd shared ceased to mean anything. As he'd watched her pause to pin up her hair, all he'd wanted was to reach out and take her in his arms.

In reality, though, he had no claim on her, no hold of any kind. And now this! Charles couldn't even look at her.

"One, a daughter," he finally said, as if the fact that there was only one might somehow make a difference.

"A daughter," Elizabeth said rather wistfully.

"Her name is Anne."

"Anne," Elizabeth repeated, and Charles thought about the fact that his daughter had been named after one of Victoria's grandmothers, something he certainly wasn't going to say right then.

"This is terrible. I send you out here to see the new rolling equipment, and the soaking pit isn't even fired up," Barrol said, coming up behind them.

Instinctively, Charles glanced toward the large brick kiln used to soften the metal for finishing.

"Really, sir, there's no need to go to all the trouble just for a demonstration."

"Nonsense, Charles. You have to see what these rollers can do. We can have the pit going in no time, a half hour at most. I'll get a couple of the men to stoke her up."

Charles turned slowly to Elizabeth, whose eyes were there to meet his, as he sensed they might be. The awkwardness could not have been greater, but like two animals caught in the same trap, there was nothing either of them could do to get away.

Chapter 19

The supper to which Barrol invited Charles was simply the family's evening meal. Besides Barrol and Elizabeth, there was Barrol's wife, as well as Kate, the younger of Elizabeth's two sisters. Sara, Elizabeth's middle sister, was married and no longer lived at home, as Charles had imagined would be the case with Elizabeth.

The fact that it was only the family was a relief, as it occurred to Charles that Stiller might also be included, a privilege Charles himself had enjoyed his last few years at the mill. Nevertheless, while Barrol surprised Charles with the enthusiasm of his welcome, there was no surprise where Mrs. Barrol was concerned. Her coolness toward Charles was obvious, and he was quite relieved when the meal ended and he and Barrol were able to retire to Barrol's study.

Barrol, too, was relieved to get away. Regardless of how it might have appeared, he was not the blundering idiot his wife and daughter imagined him to be at that moment. He was not entirely oblivious when it came to matters of the heart. The only reason he'd left Elizabeth and Charles alone to begin with was that he'd seen the way they'd looked at each when Elizabeth first came into the office. In comparison, anything he and Charles had to discuss could surely wait, and though he now realized that inviting Charles to supper probably hadn't been the best idea, Barrol thought he ought to be forgiven.

Besides, whatever happened in the past, Barrol didn't harbor the animosity his wife did. Over the years, his feelings toward Charles remained largely sympathetic. As far as Barrol was concerned, Charles could not have shown greater integrity in leaving the mill when he had. It was obvious to all he would have ended up running things had he stayed in Birmingham. But Charles hadn't come to Birmingham to run a mill. He'd come there to learn about steel so that he could apply that knowledge to bridges and railroads.

At the same time, had Charles stayed on at the mill, there would always have been questions as to whether or not he'd earned the position rightfully or if it had simply been the result of his relationship with Elizabeth. Barrol could understand Charles's need to do something on his own, just as he himself had done, and as he knew Charles's father had done as well. Though it certainly saddened him when things didn't work out between Charles and Elizabeth, it was almost to be expected. As he knew from his own experience, the course of love had as much to do with circumstance as anything else.

Right at that moment, however, any enthusiasm he'd felt upon Charles's arrival had long since been replaced by weariness. Charles, too, was weary, exhausted by the emotions of the day, and there was a heaviness to his steps as he followed Barrol from the dining room. They headed toward the back of the house to Barrol's study, which was positioned to look out on the mill, though at that hour there was little to see, other than its darkened outline looming in the windows. Barrol took a seat at his desk and gestured for Charles to sit down as well. Neither of them had spoken since getting up from the table, and for a moment they simply looked at each other, just as Charles and Elizabeth had done when first left alone. This time, though, there was no awkwardness, just a sympathy, as if they sensed each other's weariness.

"I shouldn't have come," Charles said.

Barrol, who, like Charles, was slumped slightly in his chair, smiled and shrugged as if to say don't blame yourself. Still, it was a sad smile and didn't hide the fact that he agreed, at least partly.

"The truth is, I never would have written if I hadn't found myself with my back so to the wall," Charles said.

Barrol looked at Charles quizzically, not knowing what he meant.

"Benjamin Farlow, the firm's senior partner, has been after me to contact you. He's been hoping I could use our relationship to secure a good price on the steel to give the firm an edge in the upcoming Forth competition." Given the events of the day, Charles saw no reason not to be frank. Barrol raised his eyebrows, clearly surprised by the information. "He's been asking me ever since he got word of the London & North Eastern's plans in Scotland."

"But you only wrote to me last week," Barrol said.

"I didn't want to impose. I didn't think it my place."

"Charles, I would never look on hearing from you as an imposition."

"But it had been such a long time."

"That's true, and I admit inviting you here probably wasn't the best idea. Still, I would never hesitate to lend a hand if I could be of help."

"I appreciate your saying so, but the fact is, I never would have written if it had only been Mr. Farlow pressuring me. I would have made up something—told him that I asked but you refused."

Again Barrol made a face, this time like a disapproving father, upset by the idea of his son lying.

"I told you, I didn't want to impose," Charles said. "And I never would have, only now something else has come up. I'm not the only one at the firm who's been asked to draw up plans for the Forth, and the way it stands, I'm not even sure I'll have something to show."

"Because of the cost of the metal?" Barrol asked.

"This has nothing to do with cost."

"What then?"

Barrol watched as Charles retrieved his portfolio case from near the door, where he'd left it when they'd come into the house before supper.

"I'm not sure what you know about the project. Are you aware of the site being considered?" Charles asked.

Barrol shook his head.

"Queensferry, a town just west of Edinburgh. Nothing is definite, but it's the most likely spot because there is a small island dividing the channel."

"I take it you're looking at two spans."

"Two spans of at least 1,700 feet each."

"Seventeen-hundred feet!" Barrol exclaimed.

Charles nodded.

Barrol shook his head in amazement. Seventeen-hundred feet was more than twice the length of any span then in Britain, and while no expert on bridges, he grasped the magnitude of what was being proposed.

Charles unbuckled his portfolio and removed a long sheet of drafting paper folded in thirds. "This is the reason I'm here," he said, placing it on the desk in front of Barrol.

Barrol unfolded the paper, which, when opened, extended the full length of the desk. It had been years since he'd last seen any of Charles's drawings but he immediately recognized his hand. As for the bridge, it was unlike anything Barrol had ever seen. At first glance, it looked like an enormous sea serpent with three enormous humps rising from the sea.

Barrol was fairly well acquainted with the cantilever principle from his work with Charles. He remembered the complex web of beams Charles had devised for the Devern project, but as Barrol looked at these plans, he realized that in spite of the bridge's colossal size, the arrangement of the beams could not have been more straightforward. It was simply a series of X's, larger toward the towers and gradually tapering as one moved out along the arms of the cantilever.

"I want a better look at this," Barrol said, reaching into his desk for a pair of eyeglasses.

"The overall scheme is really quite simple," Charles said, approaching the desk.

"I can see that—though for a moment I thought I was looking at a sea serpent."

"A sea serpent," Charles said, suddenly defensive. "You think it's ridiculous."

"Why would I think that?"

"You said it looks like a sea serpent."

"Well, it does, sort of," Barrol said, wrapping the stems of his spectacles around his ears. "That, or the bones of one of those dinosaurs they've been assembling at the museum in London."

Barrol could see that Charles was upset.

"Charles, I didn't mean anything bad."

"I don't see how you could have meant anything good."

"I didn't mean anything."

Charles made no reply, eyeing the plans as he had hundreds of times over the past few weeks. He was well aware of its unusual appearance, even for a cantilever. At the same time, he knew that, if built, the bridge would not only be the longest but also the strongest ever constructed—ten times stronger than any suspension bridge could ever be. No train traveling at any speed would have the least effect on it. But what did that matter? As he had feared, and as Barrol's response seemed to confirm, he'd be lucky not to be laughed at, let alone taken seriously.

"I should never have written to you," he said with resignation. "Clearly it was a mistake. I've come here, upsetting everyone, for nothing."

Charles reached for the plans, but Barrol pressed his hand down on top of them. "Why do you say for nothing? I'm still not even sure why you've come."

"What does it matter? No one is ever going to build it."

"Because I said it looks like a sea serpent? Charles, you surprise me."

"You see what's printed in the newspapers and magazines. Suspension bridges are all anyone can talk about. And the kind of words they use to describe them—graceful, noble, majestic. That's what I'm up against, because unless someone thinks he can build a pair of 1,700-foot arches, suspension bridges are all anyone is going to be submitting. After seven years, Roebling's bridge in New York isn't even half done, but it's all anyone can talk about. And to make matters worse, I'm not even sure my bridge can be built."

"That's the second time you've said that. What is it that makes you think it can't be built?" Barrol asked.

Charles pointed to the drawing. "Do you see these beams here— the ones that look solid? They're not standard beams. I tried to design a bridge entirely of the standard type, but beyond 1,500 feet, the forces involved were too much. I needed something stronger. You can't tell from the sketch, but these beams are hollow. They're really tubes, the largest of which is fourteen feet in diameter."

Charles was pointing to the main beams on which the entire structure was carried. They were not, however, the only beams in the drawing that were solid. As Barrol now realized, a full half of the bridge's beams were the tubular form, while the beams for the other half were the standard variety. The two types were used in juxtaposition, one to prevent bending, the other to prevent pulling apart. One could actually see the forces bearing on the structure and the manner in which it counteracted them to hold itself up.

"It's brilliant," Barrol said.

Charles looked at him. "What do you mean?"

"Don't give me that. You know exactly what I mean," Barrol replied. "Here I overlook your churlishness to give you a compliment. The last thing I need from you is false modesty."

Barrol was correct in assuming he'd been understood. Charles knew what Barrol had meant, but it wasn't so much false modesty as surprise. Charles had come to doubt whether anyone would see in the bridge what he did, and he was now embarrassed, realizing he'd been behaving like a child.

"Forgive me," he said. "It's just I've put so much into it."

Barrol looked back at the sketch. "How large did you say the beams are?"

"The largest are fourteen feet in diameter."

"Fourteen feet," Barrol repeated. "That does pose a challenge, doesn't it?"

Chapter 20

Both the sky and the water were gray, and except for the gap near the middle, the completed portion of the bridge formed a dark band between the two. Darrs gazed at it from the stern of a launch, having just set off from the Feeport harbor.

"No chance of not finishing her now."

Darrs turned to the boat's driver.

"Just a matter of time," the man added.

"I appreciate your certainty," Darrs replied, eliciting a bit of a smile from the man.

The seventy-first span had been bolted into position the previous day, and the seventy-second and seventy-third spans were in the process of being raised. Even unfinished, the bridge was an impressive sight. Darrs glanced back toward shore. The first fourteen supports were completed prior to the crews' breaking through the layer of hardened sediment in the riverbed. The supports were built entirely of brick, and knowing the complaints the bridge faced regarding its appearance, Darrs agreed it would have looked better if built as originally designed. With its masonry columns lined up one after the other, it would be, in its way, not unlike the great aqueducts with which the Romans had crisscrossed Europe in centuries past—which, in fact, was how Darrs initially imagined it.

Still, while it may not have been the most beautiful bridge, and knowing all that had gone into it, he remained proud, especially of the spans. For him they were the culmination of five decades of work, not just his own, but engineers around the world. In the fifty years since the railroads first came into being, thousands of bridges had been erected in Britain, more than half of which either collapsed or needed replacement within only a few years. The rails for the new trains were iron, and the men building them assumed the bridges should be of iron as well.

Trains, however, were unlike anything engineers had ever encountered. Although cast iron was strong when used for support, as Darrs was using it in the redesigned columns, it possessed no flexibility. It shattered under the strain of the new locomotives, leading many engineers and railroads to revert to massive structures of stone and brick. Others used timber, which, though not as strong as iron, was fairly flexible. Wood, though, was not a permanent solution, and masonry bridges took years to build. What was needed was a dependable structure that could be erected in minimal time. It's what Brunel and Stephenson had been searching for, but it wasn't really possible before the wide-scale production of wrought iron some fifteen years before. In addition to strength, wrought iron possessed a degree of flexibility. It could be used like wood to build trusses—great cages of metal that were quickly becoming the de facto standard of railroads around the world. The new wrought-iron trusses were more permanent than wood, and they could be longer. Indeed, the reason the bridge's central spans were to be 200 feet long was entirely arbitrary. Like the bridge's height, the length was dictated by the navy's requirements for clearance, but Darrs had no doubt that wrought iron could be used to build trusses up to 250 feet, even 300. It was with this in mind that he'd drawn up plans to replace the bridge's sixteen remaining spans with thirteen spans ranging in length from 220 to 245 feet.

Even with the new vacuum device, the excavation of the caissons remained the most time-consuming part of the work, and lengthening the spans would substantially reduce the number of foundations that had to be dug. At the same time, since beginning work on his plans for the Forth, Darrs had opened a correspondence with Sir George Larsen, the Royal Astronomer at the Observatory in Greenwich. Darrs had been looking extensively into the subject of wind, given that his Forth design was going to be a suspension bridge. In Larsen's opinion, while localized gusts could reach a force of forty or fifty pounds per square foot, the greatest pressure to which a bridge was likely to be subjected along its whole was just ten pounds per square foot.

It was a meaningful distinction, in that, while local gusts were clearly significant with regard to suspension bridges, which were constantly in motion, the gusts posed no threat to the spans on the Fee, which were fixed in position. As calculated by both Larsen and Stevens, the spans on the Fee, by their very nature, were capable of withstanding at least thirty pounds of pressure per square foot, if not more. It was one of the main reasons Darrs had chosen his design. Given the location, he didn't want to contend with the wind if he didn't have to, and given the rigidity of truss spans, as a rule of thumb, it was assumed if the span could support itself and the weight of a train, it was more than capable of withstanding anything it might be subjected to by the wind. The spans on the Fee were capable of supporting five times the weight of even the heaviest locomotives then in existence.

The launch approached the staging pier, where Darrs's assistant waited. Stevens reached out a hand, which Darrs took hold of as he climbed from the stern of the boat.

"I take it you received my wire."

"Yes, sir," Stevens replied.

"You'll have to check all my figures, but I believe there is still a chance of completing the bridge on time."

Chapter 21

Four weeks had passed, and Charles once again sat on a train bound for Birmingham. Barrol was excited by the idea of the tubular beams; he'd already put together a pair of small-scale prototypes. That was the reason Charles was on his way back to the mill. Of course, he very much doubted there would be an invitation to supper this time. The previous dinner had been awkward enough. Still, as the train neared Birmingham, it was Elizabeth he was thinking of. As his last visit had so clearly demonstrated, he was still in love with her. And not simply in love, but more so than at any moment in the past. For nearly a month now, she was all he could think about. He couldn't walk down the street or open a newspaper without finding some reminder of her. And while it was true that for years he'd been haunted by memories of her, they paled in comparison to the fresh sensations of longing and desire that now gripped him.

The two of them had stood only a few feet apart. With the smallest effort he could have reached out and taken Elizabeth in his arms, just as he'd reached out to her in his half sleep that very morning, not immediately realizing the woman in his arms was Victoria, not Elizabeth. That was hardly five hours before. He'd been in something of a daze ever since, and even now he moved slowly as the train entered the Birmingham station and he took his portfolio down from the overhead rack.

Though he'd been traveling in the third of a five-car train, he was one of the last to reach the archway leading to the station's main hall. The opening was like the mouth of a cavern. It was there that one emerged from the subterranean atmosphere of the train shed into the station proper, and had he not been looking at the ground, he would have seen Elizabeth, who stood off to the side, watching the passengers as they filed past.

"Charles," she called, catching sight of him.

He was still some distance away, and when he failed to respond, she called to him again. He looked up, but still not seeing her, or anyone else he recognized, he continued on until she said his name for a third time, which instantly brought him to a stop, as she was standing right in front of him.

"Elizabeth!"

"Charles, I know I shouldn't have come, but I simply had to see you."

"Has something happened? Are you all right?" Although he had no idea why she was there, he was overjoyed to see her.

"No, nothing has happened. Although I have no doubt my mother and sister must think I've lost my mind."

"They're here with you?" Charles asked, glancing about nervously.

"No. They're around the corner trying on dresses. As you can see, we came into town to do some shopping." Elizabeth gestured to her own attire, which was not at all typical for her. She wore a dark green dress, long green gloves, a black hat, and carried a black umbrella to match, something he would much more have expected of Victoria.

"Naturally, Father told me you'd be coming, and I think Mother made him feel so bad about last time you were here, he wanted to do something nice—that, or he thought it would simply be less awkward if I made myself scarce for the day. We never actually discussed it, but he suggested that Mother take Kate and me out on the town for the day. He even offered to buy us new outfits, so that's what we were doing, looking at dresses. At least Kate was. Father told me what train you were taking, so I knew when you'd be arriving, and the closer it got to the time, the more I thought I had to talk to you—I just couldn't leave things as they were."

Elizabeth paused, suddenly embarrassed, realizing she'd been chattering on as she sometimes did when she was nervous. And she was nervous; she could feel it in her stomach and her hands, which she thought might begin to tremble at any moment. It was terrible. In fact nothing could have been worse, as it so completely defeated her reason for being there.

For some time, Elizabeth had been of the mind that she had gotten beyond Charles. Not that she'd forgotten him, but simply that it was, at this point, far in the past. It had been six years, and while she was aware that her feelings were not nearly so indifferent as she'd feigned when her father first told her of the letter he'd received from Charles, it never occurred to her that she would react the way she had upon seeing him the previous month.

As she'd since realized, however, much of that may simply have been the shock at seeing him after so many years. Moreover, if the impression she'd gotten from her father was correct, this would not be Charles's last visit to the mill. Charles would be making a good many trips, in which case, she wasn't going to go off shopping every time he came. There was no reason the two of them couldn't behave in a civilized manner.

In the few moments since Charles's arrival, however, it had begun to dawn on Elizabeth how her actions must have appeared to him.

Whatever her intentions or whatever she might now say, from his point of view, her coming to the station could mean only one thing: She was still desperately in love with him, which is precisely what her mother and sister would have thought, had they known where she was.

Right then, however, there was little she could do, other than compose herself and try to go on as planned. With that in mind, she took a deep breath and glanced up at Charles, whose gaze she'd been avoiding.

"Forgive me, but clearly this is far more difficult than I imagined."

For his part, Charles had yet to look away, and, given the chance, he now fixed his eyes directly upon hers. "Elizabeth, what is it? What's happened?"

"Nothing has happened."

His expression turned skeptical.

"Truly, nothing has happened. It's just me. I didn't want to leave things as they were, so I came here to tell you I had given it a great deal of thought, and the awkwardness of my behavior the last time was simply the result of not seeing you in so long. But after all these years, there was no reason we couldn't behave toward each other in a civilized manner, especially if you and Father are going to be working together. That was before I came down here and began to chatter on in such a way that you must think me an absolute fool."

"You haven't been chattering on, and of course I don't think you a fool," Charles said with some force.

"There must be something I'm doing to make you ask 'what's the matter?'"

"It's nothing you've done. It's just my surprise at seeing you. It never occurred to me you'd be here."

"Well, that may be, but I have been chattering. The only reason you don't think so is because you know me and have heard it before." Elizabeth, who had been clutching her umbrella with both hands, let go with one of them. "Look at me! I'm trembling. Just being here with you—I'm so nervous, I can feel my stomach twisting itself into knots. There's no point in trying to hide it."

In keeping with her decision to go on as planned, she'd been speaking with a deliberate matter-of-factness. Now, as if suddenly realizing the significance of what she was saying, she again looked away, shaking her head. "I should never have come here. What was I thinking? How could I have made such a fool of myself?"

"You haven't made a fool of yourself," Charles replied. "Believe me, you're not the only one whose stomach is in knots. If you want to know, I haven't slept properly in a month." He wasn't entirely sure what she meant with her sudden show of emotion, but whatever her feelings, it was clear they were not the ones of abject hatred he'd so long imagined. In particular, the words "you know me" struck him as an acknowledgment that, in spite of everything, there were yet things between them that remained intact. With a single phrase, she'd brought their connection into the present.

"I know I shouldn't be telling you this," he said, "but ever since coming here, nothing has been the same. I can't walk down the street without thinking of you. I wake up thinking of you. It's all I can do just to get through the day, so don't you feel like a fool."

Elizabeth looked at him. What he said was not at all what she'd expected, or anything she'd even hoped for, but his gaze possessed an intensity she couldn't ignore.

Chapter 22

"What is that now?" Barrol asked.

"Forty-four tons," Charles answered. "We calculated the breaking point at just over forty-eight."

"Forty-eight and one-third," Stiller added.

It was a beautiful May afternoon, and the three men stood together near the coal bins behind the mill. This was the seventh time in a little over three months that Charles had traveled to Birmingham to test a new pair of beams, the latest of which was twenty-four feet in length. This was in comparison to the initial pair, which had measured just eight feet, and just as the beams had grown steadily larger, so had the apparatus needed to test them.

Tables in the office listed the load capacities of everything from cast and wrought iron to oak and pine, but there was very little information about steel, and none at all about tubular beams. The only examples of tubular beams on the scale that Charles was suggesting were Brunel's bridges at Saltashe and Chepstow, and those were of iron. Charles had also looked into the new arch bridge across the Mississippi River, in the United States, which did in fact use tubular steel beams, but they were only a quarter of the size needed on the Forth. To achieve any kind of certainty, there had been no choice but to stress the beams to the breaking point. Still, as the beams had grown larger, devising the means to break them had become as big a challenge as making them, and for this and the previous test, the men had used a steam jack, a rare and extremely expensive piece of equipment Barrol had paid for out of his own pocket.

The jack consisted of a steam-driven piston surrounded by a steel cradle that the three of them had fashioned at the mill. The center of the beam rested on the cradle, its overhanging ends curving downward to the ground under the weight of enormous barrels filled with scrap metal.

"I'm going up top for a look," Charles said.

Barrol nodded, as did Stiller. Although stronger and more flexible than wrought iron, steel was susceptible to something called shearing, internal fracturing of the layers within the metal. It was the greatest concern, because as the beams had grown longer, the metal plates from which they were fashioned had also grown thicker.

The second beam of the pair lay on the ground in front of the jack. It was so large that Charles sat down and swung his legs over the top to get past it. Beyond that, there was a ladder leading to the cradle atop the steam jack, and Charles climbed up.

"How are the seams?" Barrol called to him.

"It's not the seams I'm worried about," Charles replied.

"Yes, but I am," Barrol said, sharply.

Charles looked at him, surprised by his tone. Before he could say anything, however, there was a shrill blast. Inside the mill, workmen were getting set to load the furnace, and Stiller turned to Barrol.

"Excuse me, sir, but I must attend to my other duties."

Barrol nodded, after which Stiller turned to Charles, offering a quick bow of his head.

"Don't be too long," Charles called down to him. "I need you out here."

Again Stiller bowed his head, then turned and disappeared behind a line of freight cars by the loading dock.

Charles watched after him. "That was a very good idea of his to paint the beams. It is sure to crack before you'd see anything looking at the bare metal."

"I understand the purpose," Barrol said, again speaking with some irritation. "Now, will you please look at the seams and tell me if you see anything unusual." The beam was composed of overlapping steel plates held together by double rows of rivets. These were the seams he referred to.

"In all the tests we've done, not one seam has given way," Charles replied. "If you ask me . . ."

"I haven't asked you, have I?"

"I was only going to say . . ."

"Damn it, Charles, just do it. And then come down from there. We're coming very near the limit, and when it goes . . ."

"I know, rivets will be flying around here like bullets," Charles said somewhat dismissively, using one of Barrol's own phrases.

"Charles, whatever it is you think, let me tell you what I see. I see twenty-four feet of steel bent like a bow, and the only thing keeping it together are rivets I've rammed through it with a hydraulic press. You say you're worried about shearing. Who says the metal at the seams isn't already fractured?" Barrol was looking directly at Charles, and, after pausing for a moment, added, in a slightly different tone, "Besides which, if anything were to happen to you, I wouldn't want to be the one to have to inform your wife and daughter."

Barrol was on the verge of real anger, and even before he'd reached the part about the holes, Charles had already set about examining the seams. At the mention of his wife and daughter, however, he instantly turned. It was an unusual thing for Barrol to say, and Charles was about to respond when he caught sight of Elizabeth, who was making her way from behind the parked freight cars.

Realizing that Charles had shifted his gaze, Barrol also turned. On seeing his daughter, a low grumbling sound issued from his lips.

"Hello, Father. I came to see the new beams. I know how anxious you've been to test them."

Although addressing her father, she watched as Charles scrambled down from the cradle.

Barrol looked at her. "I'm going inside. Johann could probably use my help. If you're interested in the beams, ask Charles. He can tell you anything you want to know."

He glanced at Charles, who had come up beside them, but without saying anything, started away. He walked slowly, and Charles watched after him. As soon as Barrol was out of sight, Charles immediately turned to Elizabeth.

"I've been wondering where you were."

"I had some correspondence to finish up for Father, and I knew you'd be busy getting things ready."

Charles glanced toward the jack. "We did have quite a time getting the beam onto the cradle. But then again, we probably could have used your help," he added.

"What could I have done?" Elizabeth laughed.

"I'm not sure, but it would have been nice having you here. It always is."

Elizabeth glanced down, her expression undecided between shyness and disapproval. Charles was a married man, though at the same time, she would have been disappointed if he hadn't said something of the sort.

"Shall we take a walk? It's going to be a while before Stiller and your father come back, and I can't do anything without them."

Elizabeth glanced back at the mill, feeling a certain hesitance. Turning back, she nodded, and they started toward the path by the stream. Though it was a fine day, the week had been rainy, and the path was marred by puddles both large and small, and several times Charles offered his hand, which Elizabeth took hold of somewhat timidly. They stopped when they reached the outcrop of rocks they had so often gone to in the past, but rather than sit down, Charles walked over to the stream, which was running quickly with the spring thaw.

"Do you see the stones on the bottom?" he asked.

Elizabeth came up beside him. "You once told me you thought they were so perfectly placed that someone must have set them down one at a time."

Charles glanced at her. It was just what he was going to say, having forgotten he'd told her. "Before coming here, I'd never seen anything like it," he said. "I'd seen the Thames of course, but in London, you don't see the bottom."

"I know it would never have happened, but there was a time when I imagined we would get married right here. Mother would have insisted on a church, but if there was any place that was ours, it was here. And then afterward . . ." Elizabeth's voice trailed off. "I never even wanted to walk here."

Charles lowered his eyes. "I can imagine. It must have been terrible. But even so, these past few months, there have been moments when I've felt as if I'd never left."

Again he looked at her, and for a time they gazed deeply into each other's eyes. A moment later, Elizabeth abruptly turned away, something she had done before. In fact, it was just such an occurrence that usually put an end to their most intimate exchanges, as if in the same instant they found themselves at their closest, the reality of the situation would once again reassert itself. What she said next, however, very much surprised him.

"I don't believe Father is very happy about our becoming friends again. I think he sees it as improper somehow."

"Improper. Why would he think that?"

"Well, you are a married man."

"We haven't done anything improper. I've behaved as a perfect gentleman," Charles said.

"Father doesn't know what happens on our walks. Nor, for that matter, does my mother."

"Well, at least that explains his mood," Charles said, thinking back on Barrol's earlier comments. "He's been short-tempered all day."

"He fairly well groaned when he saw me coming."

"Have you tried talking with him?"

"What would you have me say? It's not as if he's said anything directly."

"Still, it's absurd. Can't a man and a woman be friends?"

It was a reasonable question, and for the most part, Charles felt justified in asking it. Not once in all his visits had he attempted to so much as kiss Elizabeth. Until a few moments before, he hadn't so much as taken her arm.

At the same time, while all they did when alone together was talk, it was talk of a very special kind. Although he had no aim to act on his feelings, one would have been hard pressed to describe their relationship as anything but a love affair, and a love affair of the most passionate kind. Circumstances prevented them from actually making love, but speaking in the most suggestive terms, they conveyed their wish that it could have been otherwise. It was as if the very purpose of their words was to achieve that moment in which, without having to say it, it was clear beyond all doubt that what they really wanted was to fall into each other's arms with the full force of their desire.

"You'd think we were living in the Dark Ages," Charles said.

"Maybe you should say something to him."

"Maybe I will. I know I'm not going to come up here and not see you."

Chapter 23

In the breakfast room of her parents' house, Victoria gazed through the window at the roses, which clung to the garden walls on trellises.

"We had quite a bit of rain this past month. I imagine that's the reason everything is doing so well," her mother said. "Usually, the roses aren't this tall until July or August."

Mrs. Cooper reached for her cup, waiting for some sort of response, but Victoria continued to gaze through the window.

"Still, you didn't come here to talk about the garden," Mrs. Cooper said, before taking a sip. Over the past two to three years, her husband's health had declined dramatically. It was not so noticeable in the beginning but recently had become quite apparent, and the last time Victoria and Charles had visited, Victoria seemed quite startled by her father's appearance. He was having trouble with his balance and had taken to using a cane, which Mrs. Cooper imagined was the reason for her daughter's visit.

Victoria turned to her mother, who smiled. Mrs. Cooper was right: Victoria had not come to discuss the garden. Given her father's condition, Victoria might not have come at all. She was pregnant, and not knowing the nature of her father's illness, she worried there might be some risk. Still, her suspicions with regard to Charles had been growing for months now, and she was desperate to talk with someone.

Victoria knew the purpose of Charles's trips to Birmingham, and at first it hadn't concerned her. The last two times, however, he'd traveled over the weekend rather than during the week, as he'd done to that point. Charles explained that, initially, Mr. Farlow had allowed him to travel to Birmingham on the firm's time, but that as the trips became more frequent, Mr. Farlow didn't want them interfering with Charles's other responsibilities.

It was a reasonable response, but unknown to Charles, Victoria knew of Elizabeth. Nothing specific; not even her name. But she knew from when she and Celia were roommates that Charles had had a girl in Birmingham—a girl who was none other than the daughter of the owner of the steel mill at which he'd apprenticed. At the time, Victoria had not yet met Charles, so the information meant little to her. Later on, however, when Charles continued to travel to Birmingham even after he was courting her, it had caused Victoria to wonder. Eventually, the trips ended, and even now she realized her suspicions might be nothing more than her imagination running away with itself. She didn't want to speak ill of Charles if her suspicions weren't true.

Still, if true . . . Just thinking about it made her sick, and she swallowed hard. Feeling flushed, she used her napkin to pat the moisture from her brow.

"My dear, is something wrong? Aren't you feeling well?" her mother asked.

Victoria turned abruptly to look at her mother. The question had startled her, and instinctively she thought to say something such as, "Yes, fine," or "Of course, why do you ask?" Instead, almost as if it were someone else speaking, she heard herself say, "No, Mother, I'm not. I'm not feeling well at all."

Chapter 24

Standing at his drafting table prior to the start of the firm's internal competition, Charles no longer had any doubts as to the feasibility of his design. His work with Barrol and Stiller had gone better than any of them had expected. He was certain that, given the chance, he could build his bridge. At the same time, like the Fee, the Forth was going to be a rail bridge, not a road bridge, and there was a strong case to be made for a cantilever design.

In spite of the bridge going up in New York, many doubts remained as to the ability of suspension spans to endure the stresses produced by racing locomotives. Of even greater interest to Charles was another of Roebling's suspension bridges, this one across the Niagara Gorge, a few hundred yards from the famous waterfall of the same name. The Niagara bridge had the distinction of being the only suspension bridge ever built specifically for use by a railroad. At 850 feet, it was also the longest rail span then in existence. The bridge, however, had been plagued by problems from the start, and at that very moment, serious discussions were under way for a second bridge across the gorge, this one a cantilever.

"Good luck, Charles," a colleague said as he passed by on his way to his own drafting table. "Don't let Fielding off too easily."

"No, I won't," Charles smiled.

The plans for both his and Fielding's bridges had been circulating around the office for the past week, and the response was far more encouraging than Charles had imagined.

"They're already starting to gather in the conference room," someone else said.

Charles nodded and began to gather up his materials. When Charles got to the conference room, Fielding was already there, speaking with Ashford Smith, another of the partners. Charles went to the front of the room and tacked his plans to the wall, as Fielding had done before him.

Fielding's proposal was very much based on Roebling's bridge in New York. Though two spans instead of one, the deck was suspended from four steel cables supported on stone towers. The main difference Charles could see was that, rather than the Gothic motif used by Roebling in New York, Fielding had based his towers on an Egyptian motif, just as Brunel had at Clifton, the one suspension bridge he'd ever built.

"Good morning, gentlemen," Farlow said as he entered the room.

He moved straight to the head of the conference table, where he stood, waiting for the others to take their places. Once seated, he took a moment to light his pipe, motioning for one of the ashtrays spaced along the table.

"Now then, I take it everyone has had a chance to familiarize himself with the plans."

"We have," and "Yes," came the replies from around the table.

"In that case, I see no reason for any great formality. Let us begin simply by having Mr. Fielding and Mr. Jenkins tell us about their designs, how they arrived at them, and why they believe they are best suited to the task at hand." Farlow glanced at Fielding and Charles. "You gentlemen are prepared to speak to those issues?"

"I am," said Fielding.

"Yes, sir," Charles replied.

"Very well. Mr. Fielding, please begin."

Fielding nodded and cleared his throat. "I suppose the best place to start is with the Forth itself, and the fact that to bridge it at the proposed site is going to require two spans of at least 1,700 feet each. They will be the two longest spans ever built. The only other span that even approaches that length is the suspension bridge now under construction in New York. In fact, the only bridges now in existence with spans that come within even 1,000 feet of those required at Queensferry are all suspension bridges—the longest nonsuspended span currently in existence being an arch of 500 feet.

"Based on that knowledge alone, one would have to believe a suspension bridge the obvious choice," Fielding continued. "But there is even more to suggest the selection of a suspension design. The origins of the modern suspension bridge can be traced back more than half a century to Telford's well-known Menai Bridge, in Wales. During that time, engineers here and abroad have had the opportunity to refine and improve upon the design in every possible way, from the choice of materials to the design of the road deck. It is not unreasonable to say that, as a form, the suspension bridge has reached a point of perfection heretofore unknown in the history of bridge building, an achievement all the more remarkable, given that, even to this day, measured against contemporary standards, the Menai Bridge remains one of the longest and most beautiful structures ever created. One can only imagine the effect of two such spans, one flowing into the next across the Forth."

Fielding spoke well, and as his remarks made clear, they would be getting right to the heart of the matter. Charles had no desire to sit through hours of preliminary discussion. He quickly stood after Fielding had finished.

"Sirs, I have no desire to appear disrespectful," Charles began, "especially because Mr. Fielding is a partner."

"You may speak freely," Farlow said, responding as Charles had hoped.

"Thank you, sir," he replied, before going on. "First of all, I must point out that while Mr. Fielding is correct in saying the only span now in existence that even approaches the length of those needed on the Forth is a suspension bridge, it is in fact only one bridge to which he refers, and that one is not even finished. At present, there are only four bridges in the entire world with spans longer than 1,000 feet, so to suggest the form has somehow reached a point of perfection seems highly presumptuous, to say the least. If anything, that number tells us just how meager our knowledge really is. In addition, another item Mr. Fielding has neglected to mention is that not one of those 1,000-foot spans he speaks of is used to carry anything heavier than a tram car. Two are restricted entirely to pedestrian and cart traffic. That being the case, the very notion of looking to them for precedent is mistaken. When it comes to the Forth, there simply is no precedent."

Like Fielding before him, Charles spoke with force and conviction, and if nothing else, he got the attention of several of the partners. But before Charles could go on, Fielding broke in.

"Gentlemen, I must apologize if I in any way created the impression that I look on the bridging of the Forth as a commonplace event. Nothing could be further from the truth. Given that, it will be the very last desire of the London & North Eastern to have its actions looked upon as rash or characterized by risk. The railroad will want to be seen as straying to the side of caution, and that being the case, the chances of it selecting a design so completely untried as the one Jenkins here puts forth are remote at best. If this firm is serious in its desire to pursue this project, it has no choice but to put forth a suspension plan."

"Like every other firm in town," Charles said loudly enough to be heard.

"And I will further point out," Fielding went on, "quite contrary to what Jenkins would have you believe, Roebling's bridge in New York is in fact designed with the railroad in mind. It is only the local authorities who have decided to restrict its use."

"And with good reason," Charles interjected. "They don't want to take any chances with it, once it's finished. "It's been eight years and it's barely half done."

"And the fact remains," Fielding went on, ignoring the interruption, "even now, Roebling continues to lobby to have the bridge opened to rail traffic."

"Then he is a fool. Unless he wants another Niagara on his hands—which is what we should be discussing. Niagara is the rail bridge. If it is the ability of suspension spans to carry rail traffic that we want to know about, that's the bridge we should be discussing, and that bridge has already had both its deck and cables replaced. It's hardly twenty years old, and now they're looking into replacing the towers as well."

"There's nothing wrong with the Niagara bridge," Fielding said. "The only reason for the work is that, when it was built, it wasn't designed to handle the weight of our new locomotives."

"That's nonsense. They've been having problems with it since the day it opened. You've all seen pictures of it," Charles said to the room.

"The thing is so flimsy, they've had to tie down the deck with cables running to the bottom of the gorge."

"That's merely a precaution. Added stays are not necessary on the New York bridge, and they won't be necessary on mine. I have made a detailed study of all the major suspension bridges now in existence, and I am convinced that, with the proper degree of stiffening, a suspension bridge of even 2,000 feet can be built to withstand not only the effects of the wind but also the weight and force of our heaviest trains."

"If that is so, why is a cantilever design the leading contender for the new bridge being planned at Niagara?"

"What of it?" Fielding scoffed. "At most, it will have a span of 900 feet. If you don't want to look to the New York bridge as a precedent for the Forth, how can you possibly look to a bridge that hasn't even been started. And besides, I've seen the plans for the Niagara cantilever. It in no way resembles the plans you've submitted here. It at least looks like a bridge, not some grotesque serpent rising from the sea."

Farlow, who, in the interest of candor, had been allowing the two men to speak without interference, cut in. "Gentlemen, we are all aware of the tremendous effort you have put into your proposals. Still, let me remind you that our purpose here is to secure this project for the firm. In that, we are all on the same side. There is no need to make matters personal." He glanced at Fielding and then at Charles, securing a nod of understanding from each. "Having said that, both of you raise important issues. Let us see if we cannot look at them in a more dispassionate light."

Chapter 25

It had rained hard the previous week, and there were still puddles in places as Charles and Elizabeth walked along the bank of the stream.

"Of course, by no stretch does this mean we'll be the ones to land the contract."

"It's an accomplishment in itself to have earned the right to represent Denney & Farlow," Elizabeth replied. "And from what you've told me, Mr. Farlow has as much interest in this project as you do. He wouldn't have chosen your design if he didn't think it gave the firm the best chance."

"I only hope he's right."

They came to a section of the path that was still quite muddy, and Charles stretched to pass it.

"You should have borrowed a pair of Father's boots."

Charles looked at Elizabeth. "I'm not sure that would have been the best idea."

"I know he was pleased to learn of Mr. Farlow's decision."

Charles had wired Barrol with the news, so what Elizabeth said might have been true. Charles, however, had not received a reply, and he had a fairly good idea of the reason. Over the past few months, it had become obvious to everyone at the mill that Charles's trips to Birmingham had as much to do with Elizabeth as with the beams for the bridge. This included Barrol, who as Charles had learned upon his arrival, was not even on the grounds. As Elizabeth herself had told him, her father had made a point of going into town before he'd ever gotten there, and Charles was surprised she'd brought it up, unless she'd actually wanted to call attention to her father's absence.

For appearance's sake, Charles stopped in to discuss a few matters with Stiller but was there to see Elizabeth. It was no longer possible to pretend otherwise, and while his relationship with Elizabeth was not exactly adulterous, it was plainly inappropriate, especially as Victoria was now some seven months pregnant with their second child. Though not planned, Charles had a fairly good notion of when it had happened, during the week or two before he'd first gone to Birmingham. There was some irony in this, he knew, but as he and Elizabeth neared their spot by the stream, it was of little concern to him. Even before the comment about the boots, he'd sensed a coolness to her manner.

"When I learned it was my design the firm was going to submit, you were the first person I thought of," he said. He was leaning against one of the rocks, looking at Elizabeth, who stood with her back to him, gazing at the stream. "You know that, don't you? I wired your father, but it was you I really wanted to tell. I even thought of getting on a train and coming that day."

Elizabeth said nothing; after a moment, he stood up and walked over beside her.

"Elizabeth, didn't you hear me? It meant nothing if I couldn't share it with you." He was looking at her, gazing directly into her eyes, and she glanced away.

"I do understand. Of course I understand."

"Then what is it? Why are you acting this way?"

"What would you have me do?"

Her voice quavered, and this time it was Charles who turned away.

"I don't know. I don't know," he said, shaking his head. "What I've done, there's no reason you should even speak to me. But my feelings for you, my love for you, it is real, you must believe that."

"I do," Elizabeth said.

"It's true. I swear it. Whatever I've done in the past, it doesn't change what's in my heart. It doesn't change the fact we are the ones who were meant to be together."

"That's what makes it so terrible."

Charles furrowed his brow, not understanding.

"Do you have any idea what it's been like for me these past six years?" Elizabeth asked. "For the most part, I've been trying to forget you, something I thought I had done. And do you know how I did it? I convinced myself that it was all my own doing. That, all by myself, I had built our love into something it wasn't, something more than it could have been."

"How can you say that . . .?" Charles began to speak, but she cut him off.

"I'm not saying you never cared for me, or that in your own way you might not have loved me. But it was just that: a love that lasted as long as circumstances permitted. It wasn't anything more than that. How could it have been, given what you did?"

"Elizabeth, please, you mustn't . . ."

"At least that's what I told myself. And as painful as it was, all I had to do was look at myself as a fool, a little girl who didn't know any better—which was far preferable to the alternative. Because the alternative was to think we really did have something special, something that could never be replaced. I realize now that I thought what I did simply because, otherwise, I could never have endured it. The pain would have been too much. But what am I supposed to do now? How am I to go on from here?"

"But Elizabeth, don't you see? It hasn't been lost."

"Oh, Charles, how could you? With all that we had, how could you?"

She was crying now, sobbing, enormous tears that seemed to pour from her eyes. Charles looked on, helpless. All he could do was watch. She'd turned away from him, but he could see her shaking and could hear the gasps that marked her breaths. It was as if, for the first time, he were confronting the full force of the sorrow he had wrought. He gestured, about to speak, but then stopped. He could feel his heart pounding and didn't know what to say. He'd had his own misgivings on the train ride north but had not anticipated anything like this.

Chapter 26

Unlike the British Northern, which received only seven proposals when it had announced its plan to bridge the Fee, the Forth Bridge Company received forty-six—the Forth Bridge Company being the nominal name of the entity under which the Forth project was being carried out. This was merely a formality, since, except for Taylor, the bridge company's board was identical to that of the London & North Eastern. Walter Blackman, the railroad's chairman, sat at the board's head, and he had no desire to waste time wading through forty-six proposals. With little consideration for anything other than the pedigree of those who'd submitted the proposals, Blackman quickly trimmed the list to twenty-five. Each of these was assigned a date and a time at which the engineer or firm responsible would be given the opportunity to speak.

Darrs was the third to present to the board, something his wife took as a good sign. She thought it better to go early rather than late, and as he stepped into the lavishly appointed elevator of the London & North Eastern's London terminal, he was not without optimism. In terms of the Fee, he'd received wires that morning from both Stevens and Pike, informing him that the fifth of the inverted spans had been secured into position.

Pike's attitude had improved considerably with the most recent modifications, which was just what Darrs had hoped. He knew there would be no way to complete the project successfully without Pike's full commitment. It also gave Darrs the opportunity when speaking with Pike to insist he use no beams with burned-on lugs in the supports for the inverted spans. Darrs considered it critical, given the additional height, and Pike agreed. Because he now had a chance at the bonus, Pike borrowed the money to build a second pier. To this point, they had managed one span a month, which is precisely what they had to do. Eight more spans at that rate and they would meet the September 1 deadline.

The elevator slowed, and Darrs watched as the uniformed operator brought it to a stop and slid back the brass gate.

"Here we are, sir. Top floor."

Darrs nodded his thanks and stepped from the car into a large reception hall. Like the elevator, it was richly paneled and trimmed with the finest brass and crystal fixtures. The floor was also wood, an intricate parquet, though much of it was covered by a thick maroon carpet, inscribed in gold with the London & North Eastern monogram.

Darrs had visited many offices in the course of his work and had also stayed in what were considered fine hotels. In terms of grandeur, however, he'd never seen anything like it, except for the concourse and waiting room downstairs. Those, however, were public spaces. This was another matter entirely, and Darrs was somewhat ill at ease as he announced himself to the receptionist.

The receptionist checked his log for Darrs's name and then led him to the conference room in which the competition was being held. The board members were already present, including Taylor, who was seated by himself toward one end of the conference table. Darrs nodded in acknowledgment. Beyond that, Darrs knew no one and realized he had never before faced competition so stiff. All the top London firms were represented, as were the prestigious firms from Birmingham, New Castle, Glasgow, and Edinburgh. In fact, it was only because of Taylor's presence on the board that Darrs believed he'd been included at all.

Darrs moved to the front of the room, where a set of his plans was tacked to the wall, in preparation for his coming. In addition to his plans, the plans for the other entries also hung about the room. As he'd assumed, most, like his own, were two-spanned suspension bridges. Still, glancing at the other drawings, he believed his plan did have certain features to distinguish it. Like Roebling's bridge in New York, the towers of most of the other proposals were massive structures of stone or brick. A number of the submissions even employed similar Gothic motifs. There were also several based on Greek and Roman styles, and one that employed an Egyptian motif.

In stark contrast, the towers of Darrs's bridge were entirely of metal. At the same time, though most of the other designs employed wire cables to support the road deck, as they were doing in New York, Darrs's plan was one of the few that used chains. Knowing what he did from the Fee, Darrs believed that using chains, although an older technique, would offer great advantage when it came to the actual construction.

The door opened, and the room suddenly quieted as one last board member stepped inside. From the response of the others, Darrs knew it to be Walter Blackman, who took a seat at the center of the conference table. He waited for the others to get settled, then looked directly at Darrs.

"Now then—Mr. Darrs," he said, like the receptionist, reading Darrs's name from the sheet of paper in front of him. "As I'm sure you know, the announcement of this project has generated a great deal of interest. The board initially received more than forty proposals. We have narrowed that to twenty-five, which is still too large a number to go through in any kind of detail. For the moment, therefore, we ask that you be as brief as possible, confining your presentation to only the most salient points."

Darrs, who was standing with his hands clasped, bowed his head in response.

"Very well then," Blackman said. "And please dispense with any rhetoric regarding the historic nature of what we are doing. We have heard it before."

Again Darrs nodded. He waited to make sure Blackman had nothing more to say and then began.

"In light of the chairman's remarks, not only will I forgo any discussion with regard to the historic nature of the undertaking, but I will also forgo any discussion of why I have chosen a suspension bridge, as it is clear from the other plans displayed around the room that the vast majority of the entries are also suspension plans. I will simply attempt to contrast my design against the others, beginning with the most obvious difference: the towers. While most of my competitors have chosen stone or brick for their towers, the towers in my proposal are to be constructed entirely of steel. The reason for this is twofold. First is time. Without any sacrifice in strength, steel towers can be erected in half the time. In this regard, I point out that the stone towers of the New York bridge have been a full nine years in construction. Second, being a suspension bridge, the Forth Bridge will always be in motion, however slight. The stresses where the supporting chains pass over the towers are likely to be enormous, and to have two different materials with two different sets of properties acting against each other at that point seems undesirable."

"But why steel and not iron?" one of the board members asked.

"Initially, I did consider iron for the towers, but the chains used to support the deck must certainly be made of steel, which again brought up the issue of having two different materials moving against one another. I realize in this country that steel remains somewhat suspect as a material, but when properly forged, there can be no doubt as to its greater strength, which brings me to the supporting chains themselves.

"Having glanced at the other proposals," Darrs continued, "I can see they divide into two groups; those that employ cables and those that employ chains. I imagine you will be hearing a great deal of discussion as to the relative merits of each—cables, of course, being the method being used in New York and chains being the more established method here in Britain.

"In this regard, let me say, having made a careful study of the matter, I have no doubt, properly constructed, either method would prove sufficient. The debate over which is superior is sure to continue for some years to come, but there can be no doubt that chains are simpler to construct and position. They can be manufactured off-site, brought to Queensferry, and hoisted into place. Cables, on the other hand, would have to be spun on-site using specialized machinery, a process which, given the uncertainty of the Scottish climate, could easily impede the pace of construction. As with the towers, the decision to use chains is therefore related not only to strength but also to ease of construction, a factor of nearly equal importance in a project of this size."

With that, Darrs was through, but because his presentation was even briefer than expected, the board members continued to look at him for several moments, imagining he'd say more.

"I take it you are finished," Blackman finally said.

"Unless there are any questions," Darrs replied.

Blackman glanced up and down the conference table, but no one made a move to speak.

"Very well then . . . Mr. Darrs," he said, once more glancing at his notes. "Thank you for your presence here. The board will inform you of its decision."

Chapter 27

Denney & Farlow was slated to be the twenty-first entrant to present its plans, something Farlow initially considered a stroke of luck. He'd wanted to be one of the last to present, but he now paced behind his desk, his pipe clenched firmly between his teeth. "Tenth or eleventh. Even fifteenth or sixteenth. But twenty-first of twenty-five!"

Charles sat in a chair across the desk from Farlow, watching as he paced. "You seemed pleased about it before."

"And I was a damned fool," Farlow said, coming to a halt behind his chair. "I might have been able to do something about it. As it is, how could Blackman and the others be thinking about anything but a suspension bridge? Of the sixteen proposals they've heard so far, all have been suspension designs. The only thing they can possibly be wondering is whether to use cables or chains."

"Have you heard something in particular?" Charles asked.

Farlow took the pipe from his mouth. "Yesterday, the board heard from Finch & Stanton," he said, sternly. "It was Stanton himself who gave the presentation, and apparently the board was very impressed. What he showed them was a suspension bridge, with towers patterned with an Egyptian motif."

"I see," Charles said, glancing down. Finch & Stanton was one of Denney & Farlow's main competitors and, like Denney & Farlow, had a long pedigree dating back to the early part of the century.

"Yes," Farlow said, returning his pipe to his mouth with a sharp jerk of his arm.

"Still, as you've said yourself, these presentations are merely preliminary," Charles said.

"They're preliminary only if one gets through to the next round."

"I'm sure we'll get through," Charles said.

"Even so, I've been reconsidering. I think I'll do the presentation myself."

Charles looked at Farlow, hesitating before responding. And when he did, he included the deferential "sir," which he had sometimes omitted of late. "Sir, if you don't mind my saying so, I believe that would be a mistake."

"You don't think I'm capable?" Farlow asked.

"No, of course you are."

"Well then?"

Again Charles hesitated, considering how best to proceed, given that he wasn't at all convinced Farlow fully grasped the principles involved when it came to the bridge. In terms of expertise, Farlow was a masonry specialist. Farlow had in fact overseen construction of the abutments and supporting columns for Brunel's bridge at Saltashe, and Charles had no doubt Farlow understood the basics of the cantilever principle. The specifics, however—the reason for alternating the tubular and standard beams—there, his understanding seemed superficial at best. Indeed, Charles had come to realize that his proposal had been chosen by Farlow based on salesmanship as much as on engineering. With all the suspension proposals in the competition, Farlow had concluded that it would be easier to convince the selection committee to reject the idea of a suspension bridge altogether than it would be to distinguish one suspension design from twenty-four others just like it.

"Sir, although there is no denying your presence would add an air of authority, as you've pointed out, whether or not the board is leaning toward a suspension design, or seemingly even set on one as the only serious alternative, we are almost certain to get through to the next round. That's why I say we keep to our original plan."

"Attack the whole idea of a suspension bridge."

"Yes. As I've shown you, I've got some excellent photographs of the Niagara bridge. The thing looks as if it's ready to fall into the gorge right now."

"But I'm just as capable of that as you."

"No doubt. But for you to give the presentation now makes no sense. What happens if we really need something more later on? Who can step in with your authority? Certainly not I, nor Fielding."

Farlow, who had been listening intently, suddenly sneered. "All right, Jenkins, that's enough. I realize now you're just trying to flatter me. I know what you're thinking. You think I don't know enough to explain the bridge. I also know you resent me for redesigning the approaches and think I did it strictly for reasons of my own vanity. Again, you're wrong."

The approaches to which Farlow referred were the long viaducts on either shore that would be needed to reach the bridge, which had to provide clearance of 150 feet in the main channels to meet the navy's height requirement for the Forth. In keeping with the rest of the bridge, Charles had designed the approaches as a series of small cantilevers. Farlow, however, scrapped Charles's plan and replaced it with a series of wrought-iron trusses supported on brick columns. In fact, to reach the height of 150 feet, the length of the approach viaducts was actually longer than the portion of the bridge over water, a fact that had at times led Farlow to speak of them as the major part of the project.

"I want to give the board members something they know," Farlow said. "I don't want them to think we're offering something different strictly for the sake of difference. It's true, I'm no mathematician, but that doesn't mean I don't understand the concept of tubular beams. You forget, I was with Brunel at Chepstow and Saltashe when tubular beams were first used. Granted, they were iron and not steel, but the principle remains the same, and if we are to secure this contract, my experience will be one of the primary reasons."

"Sir, I only meant to say . . ."

"I know what you meant to say," Farlow said sternly.

Charles looked at Farlow but said nothing in reply.

Farlow puffed on his pipe, then once more removed it from his mouth. "Now then, I want to again go over what we can expect from Barrol. There are bound to be questions about cost, and if I'm going to be the one giving the presentation, I want to know what I can say."

Chapter 28

Charles arrived home still upset over his meeting with Farlow. Regardless of comments to the contrary, Charles continued to doubt Farlow's ability to explain the bridge in any but the most rudimentary terms. Still, it was Farlow who was angry with him, and not only because he'd objected to Farlow's giving the presentation, but also because Farlow believed Charles had misled him about the extent to which Barrol was prepared to offer his support.

Charles's cantilever design was likely to cost 50,000 to 75,000 pounds more than a comparable suspension design, and while Charles had never promised anything specific, at the time of the Devern project he'd mentioned that Barrol had offered to supply the steel at cost. Farlow assumed Barrol would do the same now, but this time Barrol wanted ten percent profit on top of his costs. It was still an excellent price, but Barrol wasn't going to do it for free. Given the quantity of steel involved, it would take two years to produce, and that was working full time on one project alone.

Farlow, though, remained unmoved, and when Barrol first agreed to offer his help, the truth was that Charles, too, assumed the terms would be the same as those for the Devern. Still, they never discussed anything specific until after Elizabeth and he had already rekindled their friendship, and Charles was not at all sure that didn't have something to do with the ten percent figure.

Charles put his key in the lock and opened the front door. Immediately, he heard the sound of crying from upstairs. It was the new baby, Frederick, named in honor of Victoria's father. Charles would have preferred Samuel but hadn't argued. His father-in-law's health continued to decline, which made the choice seem only proper, and with everything else then going on, Charles hadn't paid much attention anyway.

Charles went straight to his study. He was in no mood to coo with the baby or play with Anne, who was undoubtedly upstairs in the nursery with her mother. Even with the door closed, however, he could hear the baby crying. The cries would stop and start, gather intensity, then suddenly break off, only to start up again at the very moment they finally seemed to come to an end. Charles tried to ignore the sound, but the cries were too piercing, too poignant, each and every one serving to remind him of the tormented state of his life. He could feel his chest tightening, and after a few moments, he got up from his desk to pour himself a drink.

Out in the drawing room, Charles filled a glass with whiskey and took a sip, wincing slightly as it went down. Even before his meeting with Farlow, he'd been struggling to maintain some semblance of coherence in his life. Elizabeth no longer spoke to him. He'd written to her dozens of times over the past two months, but she refused to answer, and given the way Victoria had been acting, he imagined she suspected something. She certainly wouldn't be pleased to hear he would be going back to Birmingham, but Charles didn't see that he had a choice. If he hoped to get Barrol to improve his terms, the men would have to meet face to face.

Upstairs, it seemed Frederick had finally quieted down. Charles took another sip of whiskey and then went back to his desk. The door to the study was open, and he could hear Victoria speaking to the nurse. No doubt his wife had heard him come in and was probably on her way downstairs. Charles put down his drink and reached behind his chair for a set of plans, which he unrolled across the desk. Victoria was now downstairs, and he could hear her steps as she crossed the drawing room to his study.

"I heard you come in. Why didn't you come upstairs?" she asked from the doorway.

"I could hear Frederick crying and thought it best not to disturb you. Besides, I've a great deal of work."

"Well, he's nursing now, but I can tell you it was no easy matter. He's much fussier than Anne ever was, but they do say boys are fussier than girls."

Charles, who had been looking at her, glanced down at his plans. "I think you've forgotten. As I remember it, you thought Anne was quite fussy in the beginning as well."

"Never like this. Every time it's a battle just to get him started."

"He'll learn."

"Soon, I hope, because this struggling with him is just too exhausting."

Charles made no response, continuing to look at the plans. "By the way, I have to go up to Birmingham again," he said after a moment.

"Really?"

"Yes. There are still matters Mr. Farlow wants me to discuss with Robert Barrol."

"And what might they be?" Victoria asked, her tone taking on a slight edge.

"Primarily, it has to do with the cost of the steel for the bridge," Charles said, looking up at her. "Mr. Farlow is hoping I can use my influence to get Barrol to lower his price. To tell you the truth, it's rather embarrassing for me. Barrol has already offered an excellent price, so I'm a bit annoyed with Mr. Farlow for even asking."

"Have you told him so?"

"Not in so many words. I did intimate that, only he didn't take the hint."

"What are you going to do?"

"There's nothing I can do. I have to go."

"But if it were up to you, you would prefer not to?"

"Absolutely," Charles replied, ignoring the obvious skepticism in Victoria's tone.

"And when might this be?" she asked.

"Sometime next week. I'm not exactly sure."

"It wouldn't be over the weekend?"

"No, why do you ask?"

"I thought that had been your habit of late—going up there on the weekends."

"What do you mean of late? I haven't been to Birmingham in months," Charles replied sharply.

Victoria paused. It was true, he hadn't been to Birmingham in months, and, given the time that had passed since his last trip, she herself had come to question her suspicions. Still, something in his manner continued to bother her. They certainly hadn't shared a great deal of warmth in recent months, and Victoria imagined that if he did have a mistress, it was she who was now traveling to London. It was something that made perfect sense, if, as Victoria suspected, the woman was in fact Robert Barrol's daughter. Now that the plans for the bridge had been submitted, there was no reason for Charles to travel to Birmingham. He would have no choice but to meet her in London. And while Victoria didn't know why Charles would suddenly be the one doing the traveling, the mere fact that he was going seemed to confirm the idea he and the woman had been seeing each other all along.

"Months. Has it really been that long?" she finally asked.

"It has," Charles replied.

"I didn't realize. Of course, I've had a great deal on my mind since Fredrick's birth. Still, for a time, it seemed you were off to Birmingham every weekend."

"It was never every weekend. Besides, as you know, the only reason I started making my trips on the weekend is because Mr. Farlow wouldn't have it any other way. He thought my work with Mr. Barrol was taking too much time away from my work on the underground project. Even now, with all I have to do for the Forth, he still has me working on both projects."

"Then I don't understand. Why is he allowing you to take the time now?"

Charles looked at Victoria. "Because now it affects him! As far as he's concerned, prior to his choosing my design, the work I was doing with Barrol was something I was doing for myself."

There was anger in his voice, and he could see he'd upset her. "I apologize. I know it's not your fault, and I shouldn't raise my voice. It's just that I'm under a great deal of stress, and it has me on edge."

He was looking directly at her, and for a moment they held each other's gaze. She could see the strain in his expression, and he did seem sorry. In fact, looking into his eyes, she felt closer to him than she had in months. At the very same moment, however, she felt a sinking in her stomach. Never before had she been so completely convinced of his infidelity. She felt herself flush and, for an instant, she again thought she might throw up. But it was only an instant; just as quickly, her body stiffened, going cold with a sense of betrayal that had been gathering for months. There was a fury within her, a rage greater than she'd ever imagined, but she could not bring herself to confront him directly.

"Why must everything revolve around your work? It is always Mr. Farlow this and Mr. Farlow that. If he ordered you to the moon, I suppose you would go there as well. Have you forgotten, you have a family, a new son you've hardly taken any interest in, to say nothing of Anne and me?"

Charles looked at her. He'd never heard her speak with such force, though at the same time he was relieved it focused on his work and not on something else.

"I have been neglectful," he said. "There's no excuse, and I assure you it won't continue this way forever. It's just the whole situation with the Forth. I've been hoping for an opportunity like this my entire life. This is going to be one of the greatest bridges ever built. People will be looking at it with amazement hundreds of years from now."

He spoke earnestly, in a manner he thought conciliatory, but not knowing the true nature of her anger, he only provoked her further.

"What people?" she asked. "The people who ride across it every day on their way to work? They'll be too busy reading their newspapers to notice. Who, then? Engineers like you? If they're anything like you, they'll probably sneer at its ancientness, assuming the bridge is still standing at all."

"Of course it will be standing," Charles said.

"Or that they'll even be using steel."

"What else would they use?"

"I have no idea."

"Are you quite finished?" Charles asked sharply.

Victoria looked at him. Her intention had been to hurt him, but it appeared she'd only angered him, something that seemed entirely unjust under the circumstances. Still, unless she actually confronted him about his infidelity, there was nothing she could do.

"I'm going to look in on Frederick," she finally said. "It might be nice if, at some point, you did the same." And with that she left the room.

Chapter 29

Charles stood at the end of the platform within the train shed of the Great Western's main London terminal. To his right and his left, the Great Western's famous green engines lined the tracks. Small streams of steam from the piston chambers wafted over the engines' great red and black wheels as they sat at rest. The track directly in front of him, however, was vacant. The morning train from Birmingham was due at any moment, and every few seconds he peered into the distance, looking for the train's approach.

Although Barrol had agreed to meet Charles, he'd done so on condition they meet in London, and only if Farlow was also present. It was better than his not agreeing at all, but it left Charles in an extremely awkward position. He and Barrol had not actually spoken directly in nearly five months, which was the reason Charles had come to the station to meet him in person. It would give them a few minutes alone on the ride to the office, where they'd be meeting Farlow.

Charles looked at his watch. On his way in, he'd glanced at the arrival board, according to which the Birmingham train was fifteen minutes behind schedule. Still, the fifteen minutes had come and gone, and he was beginning to worry they might be late for the meeting.

He heard a whistle blow, and then a loud blast of steam. Several tracks away, a train was pulling out, and he listened for the first few lurching sounds as the locomotive set in motion. He couldn't see the engine itself, but in time with the spasmodic churning of its wheels, puffs of smoke could be seen rising above the other trains. He was still watching the puffs when a second whistle blew, this one followed by the rhythmic tolling of a bell. It was the train from Birmingham, and though moving no faster than the outbound train a few tracks away, it was still running a full head of steam, and smoke poured from the stack, filling the upper reaches of the train shed with a great cloud.

Charles waited for the train to come to a stop and then stepped back a few paces to give himself a clear view of the passengers disembarking. As he descended from the train, Barrol saw Charles and walked directly up to him.

"I didn't expect to be met at the train," he said, glancing around. "Is Mr. Farlow with you?"

"No, we'll be meeting him at the office. I thought it would be best if I came to the station myself. Can I help you with anything?"

Barrol held a small leather valise, and it was this that Charles was offering to take. Barrol shrugged as if to say, "Help with what? This is all I have." Charles sensed antagonism in the gesture, as he did in Barrol's dour expression.

Charles motioned toward the archway leading to the main concourse. "This way; the cabs are through here."

"How far is the office? If it's not too far, I'd like to walk," Barrol said.

Charles took a moment before answering. Though they could walk, the office was some distance, and he didn't want to keep Farlow waiting.

"I think we're better off in a cab."

"Why? It's a fine day, and I've been sitting on a train all morning."

"It's not that we couldn't walk. But it is a bit far, and it's certainly faster in a cab."

"Very well then. It's just that I get so stiff sitting on the train."

"If you really would prefer to walk . . ."

"No, no, we'll take a cab. I wouldn't want to keep Mr. Farlow waiting."

Charles and Barrol crossed the concourse, Charles eyeing the marble floor as they walked. There was a derisiveness to Barrol's last remark, not only in tone, but the manner in which it presupposed the transparency of Charles's motives. Barrol was right, of course, and Charles assumed he also had a fairly good idea as to why Charles had come to meet him.

Outside the station, they walked to the first in a line of hansom cabs at the curb. Barrol pulled open the door, which Charles held. Charles gave the driver the address and then climbed in himself. The cab jerked starting from the curb, and Charles rocked in his seat. He was looking at Barrol, who was turned the other way, looking out the window.

"Sir, I have no doubt you know why I came to meet you. I thought it would give us a few minutes to talk—to clear the air, so to speak."

Barrol said nothing in response, but he turned to Charles, his expression stern, as it had been before.

"To begin with," Charles said, "I want to assure you I have done nothing to in any way bring shame on Elizabeth."

"I wouldn't be here if I thought otherwise," Barrol replied bluntly.

"At least I'm glad of that."

"But don't think for a minute that somehow excuses you. Charles, I never blamed you for the past. I'm no man of the world, but I know what can happen, and I don't believe you ever wanted to hurt

Elizabeth. But that was then. You have a wife and a child to consider. Where do they stand in all of this?"

Charles sighed. "I can't argue with you. All I can say is Elizabeth and I haven't seen each other in months."

"Yes, you came to your senses and realized just how inappropriate it was. That, or your wife began to have doubts about your running off to Birmingham every weekend."

"Sir, whatever you may think, the reason I haven't been to the mill in the last four months has nothing to do with my wife. It's because of Elizabeth."

"Oh, so now you're being protective of her. Isn't it a bit late for that?"

"It's not me, it's her. She won't see me."

"Oh, come now. You expect me to believe that?"

"It's true," Charles said, meeting Barrol's glance head on. "The last time I saw her—the day you made a point of not being there—she said she wouldn't see me anymore."

"And what of it?" Barrol went on. "For months now, Elizabeth has been moping, at times barely able to contain her tears, so whether it was you or she who put an end to it, what difference does it make? You should never have started up in the first place. Damn it, Charles, you're not some schoolboy. You're a man. You should have known better."

Charles looked away. For a moment he was silent, eyeing the traffic as it passed. "And that's the reason for the ten percent profit on top of cost," he finally said, though he continued to look away.

Barrol shifted in his seat, unprepared for Charles's directness. "Since you ask, I suppose that was part of it. But it wasn't the only reason."

Charles turned, but said nothing, waiting for Barrol to go on.

"You were no doubt thinking I would offer the steel at cost," Barrol said.

"You were prepared to do it for the Devern."

"The situation is different now. Back then I would have done anything just to find a place in the market."

"Just because a few shipyards have started to use steel doesn't mean anything," Charles said.

"It's not just shipyards. It's toolmakers and the weapons people, too."

"Still, not one locomotive or set of rails in the entire country is made of steel, and until that changes, you'll never be able to challenge the ironmakers."

"And the Forth is going to change all of that?"

"This bridge is going to be the first project by any railroad in this country to use steel."

"If that's the case, I don't have to worry, do I? Because this bridge is going to be built of steel, whether it's your design or not. I've already been contacted about chains for a suspension design."

Charles looked at Barrol. He knew his design was not the only one in the competition to use steel, and, in a way, it didn't really surprise him to hear that Barrol had been approached by someone else. Nevertheless, Barrol of all people should have known what this project meant to Charles, the years he'd been working for this chance.

Barrol took a deep breath, nearly sighing as he let it out. While still angry, he knew he'd been harsh and couldn't help feeling bad. Having learned the truth, he was no longer even entirely unsympathetic. He'd assumed that it was Charles who had once again abandoned Elizabeth; he'd never dreamed it was the other way around. And while he didn't believe that was in any way an excuse, it didn't give him any pleasure to see Charles hurting either.

"It's not as if I've offered nothing," he said. "It's still an excellent price."

"I'm aware of that, and I wouldn't be here if Mr. Farlow had not insisted."

Barrol shook his head. "Charles, I would love to have a hand in this project, but you also have to understand, it's not just me anymore. I'm not the only steelmaker in the country, and when it comes to breaking the iron market, we're all in this together. I can't be working for free, taking business from others. That said, if it really makes a difference, I am willing to work for five percent. Given the quantity of steel involved, it would mean two years running the mill full time."

Charles did not immediately respond. It was a generous offer, one that might even improve Farlow's mood, but it wasn't so much Farlow or Barrol that Charles was thinking of. He was thinking of Elizabeth, picturing her moping about the mill, fighting back her tears as Barrol described. And she wasn't alone in his thoughts. There was Victoria, who'd barely said a word to him since their quarrel the previous week. In some very basic way, she seemed to have withdrawn from him. Even when he told her he wasn't going to Birmingham she barely reacted. And just as with Elizabeth, he didn't know whether there was anything he could do at this point to undo the damage or put things right.

Chapter 30

"It's turned out to be quite a nasty morning," Mrs. Cooper said, handing her coat and umbrella to the maid. "It wasn't nearly so bad when we left, but now the rain seems to be coming down in buckets."

"Yes, I know," Charles replied. "It was quiet, and then, all of a sudden, I could hear the water racing down the gutter outside my study. Here, sir, let me help you," Charles said, moving toward his father-in-law, who was struggling with his coat.

Mrs. Cooper also moved toward her husband. "I'm afraid the combination of the cane and the umbrella was too much for him coming up the steps. Oh, dear, and the rain has soaked right through to his jacket. Charles, do you have something into which he can change?"

"Of course."

"I don't need anything," Dr. Cooper said.

"A sweater, or another jacket?" Mrs. Cooper continued, still looking at Charles.

Charles glanced at Dr. Cooper. "Sir, what is it you'd prefer? A jacket, and maybe another shirt as well?"

"Nothing. I don't need anything," the doctor responded with irritation. Supporting himself on his cane, he brushed at his shoulders with his free hand, as if to make the point clear. It was only then that he realized just how wet he was. But having spoken as he had, he was not now going to admit it.

"Dear, there is no shame in it. You got a little wet," his wife said.

Eyes to the floor, the doctor made no immediate response. Seeing that his father-in-law was embarrassed, and not wanting to make him feel any worse, Charles didn't push the point.

"Why don't we go into the sitting room? I'll light a fire."

"That's a wonderful idea," Mrs. Cooper said. "I don't care if it is July. With this rain, I've a bit of a chill."

Dr. Cooper said nothing, but glancing up at Charles, he nodded, and they were just about to start forward when Victoria appeared at the top of the stairs with Anne, who, seeing her grandmother, immediately raced down to her.

"Grandmother," she cried, arriving in Mrs. Cooper's outstretched arms.

Behind her, Victoria proceeded down the stairs at a much more deliberate pace.

"Anne, you should be more careful. You could have knocked your grandmother over," she said, reaching the bottom.

"Victoria, there's no need to worry. I'm quite sturdy," Mrs. Cooper smiled, swaying back and forth with Anne in her arms.

"You certainly have become a big girl. And a very pretty one, too," Dr. Cooper said.

Anne glanced at her grandfather. She hadn't seen him in some time, but without saying anything, turned back to her grandmother.

"Anne, your grandfather is speaking to you," Charles said.

Anne, who'd turned her head so she could see her father, looked back at Dr. Cooper.

"Hello, Grandfather."

"Hello, my dear."

Charles was about to suggest that Anne go over to him when Victoria placed her hands on the child's shoulders. It was almost as if she'd sensed what he was going to say and didn't want him to suggest anything of the sort. It was her parents' first visit since Fredrick's birth, and she still didn't know what it was her father was suffering from. He was thin, with hollow cheeks and sunken eyes, features all the more pronounced as he stood there in his wet clothes. Though not yet sixty, he looked at least ten years older.

"There's no reason to stand here," Victoria said, still holding onto Anne. "Let's go into the sitting room."

"Yes, let's," Charles concurred.

Victoria let go of Anne, who took hold of her grandmother's hand and led the way.

"My dear, where is the baby?" Mrs. Cooper asked. "I hope he's not napping just now."

"As a matter of fact, he fell asleep right before you arrived. He should wake up before you go, although he was quite tired, so I can't be sure."

Once in the drawing room, Charles helped Dr. Cooper get settled and then went to the fireplace and opened the flue.

"A fire? Do you think that's really necessary?" Victoria questioned.

"It's just until your father dries off," her mother replied.

Victoria said nothing but made a face, as if she thought it unnecessary, something that annoyed Charles. He thought it rude, and it was far from the only thing bothering him as he bent down to turn on the gas. He couldn't be sure, but he found the timing of Fredrick's nap a little coincidental and had been listening for his cries, wondering whether he was really asleep. Charles thought it more likely that Victoria was simply keeping the boy at a distance from her father.

Charles was also ignorant when it came to the nature of his father-in-law's illness, but he thought it highly unlikely either of Victoria's parents would do anything to endanger the children. Her father was, after all, a physician.

Charles also knew that, at this point, his opinion carried very little weight with Victoria. It had been months since he'd last been to Birmingham, but her coolness toward him continued. She rarely spoke to him unless it was absolutely unavoidable, and she'd even intimated that if the house were large enough, they would no longer be sharing the same bedroom.

Charles stood up from the fireplace. "That should help."

"Thank you, Charles. I can feel it already," Mrs. Cooper said.

"Can I get either of you anything? Sir, perhaps a brandy?"

"Please," Dr. Cooper replied.

"And you?" Charles asked, turning to Mrs. Cooper.

"No, thank you, Charles. Nothing for me."

Charles poured two brandies, which he carried back across the room, taking a seat next to his father-in-law.

Dr. Cooper nodded his thanks and reached for the glass, his hand trembling noticeably as he lifted it from the table. It was the first time Charles had seen the shaking, and he immediately connected it with the stray hairs on his father-in-law's neck and jaw, spots he'd obviously missed while shaving.

Despite their early differences, Charles and Dr. Cooper had grown close. His in-laws had been very generous over the years, and while Charles realized his inclusion in this generosity was primarily the result of his being married to their daughter, it was also, to some extent, an indication of their acceptance of him as well.

With that acceptance came responsibility. It implied a trust, something that pained Charles to think about as he watched his father-in-law work to take a sip. Though right at that moment Charles was the one annoyed with Victoria, he knew in a larger sense that he was the one at fault. It was he who'd betrayed the trust, and yet, even now, feeling as he did, it in no way changed the fact that not five minutes passed without his thinking of Elizabeth.

"Charles," Victoria said.

Charles did not immediately respond, and she called to him again, this time more emphatically. Charles jerked his head around, and Victoria, who was sitting on the sofa with her mother and Anne, motioned to her father, who had brandy dribbling from his chin.

Charles took out his handkerchief. "Sir, forgive me, but I think you might want this."

Seeing the handkerchief, Dr. Cooper reached for his chin and made a grumbling sound.

"Blasted shakes. I can't even take a drink without spilling." He took out his own handkerchief, which he used to wipe his chin and mouth. "It's even worse than the trouble with my legs; the only difference is, the brandy seems to help with my hands."

Charles glanced inquiringly at the doctor's empty glass.

"Please," the doctor said, showing his appreciation with a small smile.

Charles put away his own handkerchief and went to pour the doctor another drink.

"Yes, and it's only just started," Mrs. Cooper said.

"Ah, it's been coming on for months now," Dr. Cooper corrected her.

"Well, yes, I suppose so. But it was never like this."

"No, it never was. But that doesn't mean you have to treat me like a child. Nor you either, my dear," Dr. Cooper said, looking at Victoria.

"I? What did I do?"

"If you have something to say to me, say it. For the moment at least, I'm still capable of wiping my own chin."

Charles returned with a second glass of brandy and set it down next to his father-in-law.

"As you can see, the brandy not only helps with the trembling. It gives his spirits a lift as well," Mrs. Cooper said.

"I think I'm entitled," he said, sharply. He was looking directly at his wife, and as his annoyance was clear, she let the matter drop and turned to Charles, who was once again seated.

"Well, Charles, with the new baby here, I imagine you and Victoria will again be looking for a larger house."

Charles reached for his own glass of brandy. Under normal circumstances, what his mother-in-law said was true, but as things were, it was an awkward question.

"Well, as I'm sure you know, we were looking for a time last year."

"But then you put it off when Victoria became pregnant, which only made sense. But now, I'm sure you'll be wanting more room."

"It would be nice. But actually, Victoria's pregnancy was not the only reason for putting off the move."

"No?"

"It also had to do with my work. With both the Forth and the underground projects to contend with, the thought of also having to find a house was simply too much, and that hasn't changed."

"Really," Mrs. Cooper said, seemingly both surprised and disappointed. "At some point your projects will have to come to an end. One of them, anyway."

Charles finished off his drink and set down the glass. "Unfortunately, one of them might be coming to an end quite soon," he said somewhat lamentably.

"Which one is that?"

"The Forth."

"The bridge. Oh, Charles, I'm so sorry. I know how excited you were about it."

"Yes."

"And just a few months ago you seemed so optimistic about your chances."

Although Charles was the one to bring it up, as he now realized, it was not something he really wanted to discuss, but Mrs. Cooper persisted.

"Tell me, what's happened to change that?"

"Well, it's not over yet. In fact, ours is one of only five proposals still in the running."

"Then I don't understand. If you've made it this far, it seems to me your chances have only improved."

"Theoretically. In the end, though, I fear my design is simply too unusual to be chosen."

"Yours is the only one in steel, I suppose," Dr. Cooper interjected.

His tone was somewhat derisive, and Charles turned to him. "In this case, all five of the entries still in the running employ steel."

"Really! Is that so?"

"Yes, that's so," Charles replied sharply.

Dr. Cooper shifted in his chair, attempting to set down his drink without spilling it. He could see he'd really offended Charles, which had not been his intention.

"I only meant . . .," the doctor started to say, but Charles cut him off.

"That you would have thought I had given up by now on my foolish notion to build in steel."

"Charles, it's just my husband putting his foot in it again. As you no doubt know by now, he simply can't help himself," Mrs. Cooper said.

"Still, Charles, that's no excuse for you to react so," Victoria said.

Charles, who'd turned toward Mrs. Cooper, shifted his glance to Victoria. Her comment only added to his irritation. She could see it gathering in his eyes, but she didn't let it deter her.

"I'm sure Father didn't mean anything by it. And, even then, one can hardly blame him. Given the past, it's not an unreasonable assumption."

"Victoria, I think it would be best to let the matter drop," Mrs. Cooper said. She also sensed Charles's anger and hoped to avoid a scene.

Victoria turned abruptly to her mother, annoyed by her interference. Still, not wanting to say anything in front of Anne, Victoria kept silent and, for a time, so did everyone else.

Charles and Victoria barely spoke for the rest of the day. After the Coopers left, Charles retired to his study, and though still angry with Victoria, he was also feeling bad about his own behavior. Though his father-in-law had, to some extent, brought it on, Charles's reaction was uncalled for. What point was there in attacking an old man? And besides, even if it did prove that Charles had been right about steel, in and of itself that meant nothing, not if he wasn't the one to benefit from it.

Charles looked up at the ceiling. He could hear Victoria walking around, and he sighed wearily as he took a sip from the glass of whiskey he'd brought into the study. There was a certain irony to Charles's pessimism in that, contrary to his fears, Farlow had been impressive in his presentation before the board. In a move Charles had not anticipated, Farlow began his presentation by explaining how, in making its own decision, Denney & Farlow had gone through a process very similar to the one then being employed. That, in fact, Denney & Farlow had staged its own internal competition, pitting cantilever against suspension bridge, a competition in which the cantilever had clearly proved to be the superior design.

It was a brilliant maneuver, as was the way he handled the cost issue. He made no excuses. The cantilever bridge was more expensive, but it was also stronger, and as all the proposed bridges were going to cost in the neighborhood of half a million pounds, a difference of 50,000 or even 75,000 was hardly worth discussing. If theirs was truly the best design, cost alone would not end their chances, but it was here that Charles had come to have his most serious doubts. Sitting to the side while Farlow spoke, Charles, for the first time, had a chance to see some of the other proposals, including the Finch & Stanton entry Farlow had been so worried about. It was tacked to the wall close to where Charles was sitting, and having seen it for himself, he too believed there was reason to worry.

Superficially, the proposal was similar to the one Fielding had submitted during the internal competition at the firm, in that the towers were based on an Egyptian motif. The similarity, however, ended there. Like most of the entrants, Fielding had based the cable work for his bridge on Roebling's bridge in New York, a complex system of cables interwoven to resemble an enormous spider web. In stark contrast, the Finch & Stanton bridge omitted the diagonal cables. What was left were just the main suspension cables and the vertical stringers used to support the road deck. Nothing could have been simpler. Indeed, when viewed alongside the Finch & Stanton entry, the other bridges in the competition looked distinctly outmoded, which, in a sense, they were.

Despite the fact that the New York bridge was not yet complete, it had been under construction for almost a decade. Adding to that the years that had elapsed between the time Roebling first produced the plans and the time they were finally approved, one was looking at close to twenty years. It took the bridge back to a time when steel was in its infancy, so that one could understand Roebling's caution. Knowing what they did now, however, there was no reason for such caution. Any need for stability could be handled directly by a stiffening truss, which in the Finch & Stanton entry took the form of a simple steel cage running beneath the roadway. Here again, nothing could have been more straightforward. Even when it came to the towers, Charles could find little to fault. While he was not one for elaborate architectural treatments, in this case the Egyptian motif referred to nothing more than the fact that the towers were tapered and culminated in a flat top. Beyond that, they were virtually unadorned. Like the pyramids themselves, they relied on nothing but their size to make what Charles had no doubt would be an extremely powerful impression.

It was an excellent piece of work; so excellent that it was not only the other suspension proposals that suffered in comparison but also his own. All the things Charles had done to make it work—the enormous size of the beams, the mix of tubular and standard forms—rather than strokes of genius, they now seemed to be indications of the inherent weakness in the design itself. No doubt his bridge would be strong—500 times stronger than it would ever need to be. It was absurd. In fact, as he now saw it, he'd been wrong all along. Not about steel, but about how to use it, which, in addition to everything else then going on in his life, left him with a feeling of defeat beyond anything he'd ever imagined.

Chapter 31

The eighty-fifth and final span of the Fee Bridge was raised into position the second week of August 1878, more than six and half years after breaking ground. Darrs was on hand for the occasion, and Pike was literally bursting with delight, seemingly undaunted by the height, as he led Darrs and Stevens on an inaugural crossing. They started from the bluff on the south shore, where a number of the men stood with their hats in their hands as Darrs passed. Others were still at work on the bridge, laying the rails, but here, too, most paused as Darrs passed.

Darrs shared glances with many of them, acknowledging them and the role they had played. There was still work to be done. It was not just the rails on the bridge that had to be laid but also the permanent connections between the bridge and the Feeport and Brindee stations—not to mention the fact that the bridge still had to be inspected by the Board of Trade.

The official opening was at least two months away, but Taylor and the other board members had planned a ceremonial crossing for the following week, as soon as the rails were laid. Darrs was looking forward to that day with great satisfaction, as was his wife, who, he knew, was already planning what she would wear. Nevertheless, there was something extremely personal in this walk. Laying the rails was hard work, no doubt. It took steady aim and a heavy sledge to fix a six-inch spike with three to four blows. In kind with his own feelings, he imagined there was a fair amount of satisfaction in it is as well, and the rhythmic tolling was as pleasing a sound as Darrs could imagine. Stevens walked next to him, and Darrs grasped his arm, wanting to share what he was feeling.

They were about half a mile from shore, and before them the entrance to the inverted spans loomed, not unlike the start of a lengthy tunnel. Compared with the open deck on which they were walking, the interior was cast in shadow by the surrounding bridgework. There was also a low whirring sound, that of the wind, swirling among the beams. But that was not the only sound Darrs heard; there was something else—a clattering. Not from the span but from the support beneath it, and Darrs knew right away what it was. It was a loose bracing bar, chattering in the wind. And it wasn't just one. He could hear several of them at different points below him.

"No doubt, some final adjustments have to be made," Pike said, seeing the change in Darrs's expression. He could hear the clattering as well.

Darrs gave a slight nod but said nothing, instead turning to Stevens, assuming he heard the noise as well.

"As you expected, there was some shifting as the final spans were lifted into place. The bracing bars are still in the process of being re-tensioned."

"Even as we speak, the men are going through the supports, making sure all the connections are tight," Pike added.

Darrs knew the crews had been rushing to make the deadline and, to some degree, that was understandable, and final adjustments were to be expected. But he'd already spoken to Pike about the bracing bars twice in the last month, and just as Darrs had insisted that Pike use no beams with burned-on lugs in the supports for the inverted spans, he'd also insisted that all the bracing bars be secure. It was essential that they bear their share of the load, and for that, the connections had to be tight. As the men continued to walk, the chattering grew more pronounced. By the time they reached the fifth of the inverted spans, at which point Darrs stopped, it wasn't just four or five bracing bars per support, but seemingly dozens, clanging and rattling in the wind.

"Mr. Pike, I will not risk a train on this bridge until every one of the bracing bars has been properly secured."

"Sir, as I said, right as we speak there are men going through the supports."

"If any idea is entertained of running an engine across the bridge before this is done, I will immediately resign my position as chief engineer to escape responsibility."

Pike said nothing in response, but, having looked into the matter, he knew that fixing the problem was not nearly so easy as Darrs imagined. While in most cases it was simply a matter of tightening bolts, there were problems with some of the bracing bars themselves. Like the parts for the spans, the bracing bars were wrought iron. They'd been made in Clevelandham and shipped to Feeport, and not all of them fit properly. Some were nearly two inches too long, and no amount of tightening was going to secure them. They had to be cut down, which could take weeks, something he had yet to mention to either Darrs or Stevens.

Chapter 32

Farlow was unaware of Charles's pessimism and, for his part, was fairly optimistic about their chances, especially when they were included in the final round of three. Farlow knew Blackman personally. The firm had only recently completed a large undertaking for the London & North Eastern, during which the two had met numerous times. That undertaking was the renovation of the Chatham line, a project in which Charles had played a key role.

The Chatham line was one of London's busiest commuter routes, and also one of its oldest. The London & North Eastern had acquired the line seven years before, hoping to capitalize on the growth then transforming London's rural outskirts into a series of exclusive suburban villages. The Chatham line was so antiquated, however, that it was a struggle just to keep it operational. It needed a complete overhaul, not only new rails but also a second track, and it was because of this that Farlow and Blackman had met so many times.

It was no secret that the railroads had grown stupendously in their power and influence over the past twenty years. With that power, however, came increasing scrutiny. Lawsuits were a constant concern, on top of which there was growing pressure for the railroads to act in accordance with what was termed the "public good." For the most part, this involved an increasing mountain of regulations that were both costly and difficult to implement, and while Blackman had had to deal with them before, never had they been so overwhelming as on the Chatham line, a seventeen-mile run through some of the most exclusive estates and residences in the London area.

One of those regulations required pedestrian bridges at all regular stops, and it was here that Charles came in. Combining the decorative qualities of cast iron with the strength of wrought iron, and even elements of steel, Charles created a series of bridges that not only were durable and easy to construct but also satisfied the aesthetic demands of the community boards. So far as Blackman was concerned, that was all well and good.

At the same time, however, the London & North Eastern was being asked to bear responsibility for the manner in which its coal bins and telegraph wires marred the landscape, and it was here that Blackman's patience came to an end. Farlow remembered the conversation distinctly. "The London & North Eastern is not the government," Blackman had said. "It is a corporation. Its function is to make money. So far as that must coincide with public safety, so be it. Beyond that, however, the railroad is beholden to no one."

It was an attitude Blackman maintained to this day, and in terms of sheer strength, there was no question the Denney & Farlow cantilever proposal was by far the strongest of the three designs still in the competition. It was also the most expensive, and in choosing it, Blackman believed he would be beyond reproach. The railroad would be putting the well-being of its riders ahead of cost—even if the bridge was, as several members of the board put it, a monstrosity. Indeed, from what Farlow was able to find out, the notion of its seeming ugliness rather appealed to Blackman.

Chapter 33

It took close to four weeks to correct the problem with the bracing bars to Darrs's satisfaction, which meant it wasn't until the middle of September that the Director's Special left Feeport on the inaugural crossing of the Fee Bridge. It was a three-car train, carrying the British Northern board members and their wives. There also were people who'd been involved in constructing the bridge, including Darrs and Pike, as well as other dignitaries and notables from both north and south of the Fee.

The first car was an open coach with an aisle down the center, and Taylor, shaking hands and chatting, moved about with an ease unexpected in such a large man. He was just turning from the mayor of Feeport when the train rocked slightly and he took hold of a seat to steady himself. Looking out the window, he realized the train had entered the inverted spans. It was a mild day, but even so, within the spans one could hear the wind whirring past; for a time, he continued to watch the beams pass, one after another, in an endless stream. The train had been traveling for three or four minutes. He didn't know of another bridge that took even a minute to get across; the vast majority were crossed in only seconds. Sitting on a train, one might not notice at all, and the reason the bridge had taken so long was suddenly apparent to him in a way it never had been before. It was an extraordinary accomplishment. He felt himself swelling with emotion, and knew he was not alone in deserving credit. There were others who had played a major role as well, including Pike, who at that moment seemed to be clutching the seat in front of him as if for dear life.

Pike, by necessity, had walked the bridge dozens of times, and by the end had even come to tolerate it. Inside the train, however, was another experience entirely. While one was not forced to look through the bridge's slatted deck at the water below, the fact was he could not see the bridge at all. The bridge was so narrow that until they entered the inverted spans, he would have had to stick his head out the window and look straight down to see anything at all. It was as if they were flying, and, in fact, birds could be seen gliding alongside the train.

"Come now Mr. Pike, it can't be as bad as all that," Taylor said, making his approach. He was smiling and meant the comment in jest, but Pike grimaced in response.

"I've never been fond of heights."

"Don't tell me you're frightened?"

"Not frightened, I just don't like the view. It upsets my stomach."

"I hope that's not the case with our passengers," Taylor said with some amusement.

Pike looked up at the chairman. "Sir, I was wondering if you had given any more thought to our most recent discussion?"

"Regarding your bonus," Taylor replied. "I did, and I will be happy to discuss the matter at a more appropriate moment."

"Sir, I do not wish to interfere with the day's celebration, but it is of considerable importance to my firm and here we are, crossing the bridge less than two weeks beyond the specified date."

A gust of wind rushed through the open windows as the train exited the inverted spans, and for an instant, both Pike and Taylor glanced away. A moment later, however, they were again looking at each other.

Feeling as he did right then, Taylor had considerable sympathy for Pike, but even so, it wasn't as if the railroad had 50,000 pounds sitting in the bank waiting to be handed over. The railroad remained extremely short on cash, and that was to say nothing of the fact that to use the bridge to its full potential the railroad was going to have to purchase new coaches and at least two or three locomotives as well.

"Mr. Pike, I do appreciate your position and as I said, I will be happy to discuss the matter further. I am simply not prepared to discuss it right now."

With that Taylor started away, continuing down the aisle toward Darrs. Darrs sat toward the back of the coach with his wife, to whom the chairman offered a deep bow.

"This must be a very proud day for you as well," he said.

"It is," Mrs. Darrs replied. "More than anything I had imagined."

Taylor turned to Darrs. "And you, sir, how does it feel?"

"As much as anything, I am relieved," Darrs replied.

"I understand, though depending on how things go in London, there may not be much time for rest. Developments here bode extremely well for you when it comes to the Forth."

Darrs said nothing in response. He did not think it proper to be discussing, seeing as the chairman would be one of those deciding the matter.

"By the way, have you heard of our plans for the new tickets and schedules?" Taylor asked. "The bridge is to become the official symbol of the British Northern. From this point forward, it will appear on all stationery, schedules, and tickets."

"Still, to truly appreciate it, I believe one must ride across it as we are now," Mrs. Darrs said.

Darrs glanced at her and then at the chairman.

"I can't say I ever imagined what it would be like, but it is not the same as walking the bridge on foot.

Taylor motioned toward Pike. "I can't say Mr. Pike is especially enamored with the view."

"We're through the inverted spans. It won't be much longer now," Darrs said, looking in Pike's direction.

He did not feel good about how things stood and was hoping Taylor would see fit to pay the bonus, at least the main share of it. That being said, as Darrs saw it, he'd had no choice but to delay the crossing. The supports were designed to function as if they were solid brick or stone. Rigidity was key. Pike was an experienced engineer himself. He knew that as well as anyone.

Chapter 34

The completion of the Fee Bridge was front-page news across the country. At nearly two miles, it was by far the longest bridge in the world. Originally estimated to take three years, it had taken more than twice that, but when the stories started coming down from Scotland—hurricanes shutting down operations, men blown to bits the digging chambers used to excavate the bridge's foundations— the delay seemed secondary. Hundreds of men had worked on the project, risking life and limb. It was a remarkable achievement, and almost immediately there was talk of knighthood for Darrs, who was suddenly the most famous engineer in Britain.

For the past decade, the vast majority of "firsts" had been coming from the United States. If it wasn't Roebling's bridge in New York, it was the two transcontinental rail lines the Americans had completed in that same time. Still, it was in Britain that the railroads had been born and risen to their position of prominence. Regardless of what was happening across the ocean, in the minds of many, Britain remained the greatest industrial power on earth. Even when finished, the Brooklyn Bridge would be only a third as long as the Fee from end to end, a fact the newspapers could not have gone to greater lengths to emphasize.

"Mr. Chairman, I am in complete agreement with you. What the bridge looks like is not relevant and should not even be a consideration." Taylor said, looking across the desk at Blackman, in whose London office the two men sat. "At the same time, as you know, it is not the business of railroads to act as laboratories in which to test the latest ideas and inventions to come along—I know the British Northern isn't. Other industries may have that luxury, but we have other concerns, not least of which are issues of public confidence and safety."

"Exactly," Blackman replied firmly. "Of all the designs presented to the board, that of Denney & Farlow is by far the strongest. It is a fact attested to not simply by Benjamin Farlow, but independently confirmed by the board's own consultants. That being the case, propriety alone would dictate that it be our choice."

"If it is the strongest of the designs, it is so in theory only. Mr. Darrs's design is based on principles that have been employed with success both here and abroad."

"Yes, for pedestrian and wagon traffic. As Mr. Farlow has pointed out on numerous occasions, when a second bridge was needed at Niagara, the Americans chose a cantilever design. Suspension bridges are simply not suitable for either trains or wind, which, from what I've been told, is a major concern on the Forth."

"Sir, in that regard, when it comes to the Forth, the fact is that Mr. Darrs is the only person with any comparable experience as chief engineer on a project of this magnitude."

Blackman made no response. In spite of Darrs's sudden fame, he remained, in engineering terms, unknown outside of northern Britain and Scotland. While the British Northern, operating in the hinterlands of Scotland, might rely on his services, the London & North Eastern was in no such position. Blackman had learned from experience it was best to confine his dealings to only the most reputable firms, which meant Denney & Farlow or, if absolutely necessary to appease the other directors, Finch & Stanton. The only reason Darrs's design had been included among the final three was Taylor's presence on the board. Blackman thought it an easy enough gesture, given that he hadn't imagined it would actually come into play.

With the completion of the Fee, however, Taylor's sense of himself had swelled substantially. For months, he hadn't bothered to attend the proceedings, yet suddenly he'd begun to act almost as if he were chairing the bridge company's board of directors. At the same time, while technically a joint venture, the Forth Bridge, when completed, would lie entirely within the British Northern's right of way. Even at this late date Taylor could pull out and build the bridge on his own, and with the Fee complete, he could very well find the backing to do it.

The irony of the situation was not lost on Blackman, who, for years, had been waiting for the British Northern to go under. From what he knew, the company had been on the verge of bankruptcy for more than a decade. He'd stepped in only because of the agreement between the Great Western and the Scottish Central. Blackman wanted Scotland for the London & North Eastern, which meant that if Taylor insisted on Darrs, Blackman would go along. It wasn't what he wanted, but he took comfort in the fact that, if nothing else, the bridge would not have stone towers, something certain to stir controversy in itself.

Chapter 35

The Fee Bridge opened for business the last week of October 1878, following a three-day inspection by Major General R. M. Hudson, of the Board of Trade. Hudson walked the bridge from end to end five times. He also visited each of the bridge's eighty-six supports and tested the structure under the weight of a ten-car train loaded with gravel.

The benefits of the new bridge were immediate. Barring bad weather on the Forth, travel time between Edinburgh and Brindee was cut in half. In direct competition with the existing ferry lines, the British Northern also initiated a shuttle service between Feeport and Brindee; within a month of the bridge's completion, ridership doubled and then tripled.

Darrs's fame increased with the bridge's success, and as with the Fee, he was awarded the contract for the Forth, something that once again had immediate consequences for Charles. During the competition, Charles could be seen coming and going from Farlow's office four or five times a day. It was widely assumed he was in line for a partnership, and it wasn't lost on anyone when his frequent visits to Farlow's office came to an abrupt end once the competition was over. In fact, he and Farlow had barely spoken since, and then only in meetings or when passing one another in the hall. As far as Charles could tell, his standing at the firm was actually lower than it had been before the competition began.

"Jenkins, you are clear on what you must do? There can be no delay. The work must be completed Friday, no later, in order to give the draftsmen the weekend to do their inking."

"I understand," Charles said impatiently.

The person speaking was Otto Fein, the man in charge of the underground project. His accent grated on Charles, as did his butchered English. If Fein was making London his home, he could at least learn to speak the language properly. Just as frustrating, Charles knew Fein would never have dared spoken in such a manner only a few months before. During the Forth competition, he'd gone out of his way to show Charles great deference. He'd even let Charles set his own timetable, often arranging meetings around his and Farlow's schedule.

Back at his seat, Charles unrolled the plans across his drafting table. In spite of his feelings about Fein, the underground extension was a project Charles had been fairly excited about, in the beginning at least. The LMR was the first underground railway in the world, and when it opened fifteen years before, Farlow had been touted as the savior who would deliver London from the impassable traffic that clogged the city's streets on a daily basis.

Farlow was not the first person to think of putting a rail line under London, but he conceived of two innovations that made it possible. First, rather than tunnel under any buildings, something that would have required digging down hundreds of feet, he'd come up with the idea of having the tracks follow the path of existing streets. In that way, all one had to do was dig a trench, lay the tracks at the bottom, and then cover it over again. Referred to as cut-and-cover, the technique essentially turned a street into a gigantic bridge. In fact, Farlow's ultimate goal was to build a system of underground routes that would make for the longest and most complex series of bridges ever created. Being underground, it was unlikely to be recognized as such, but the idea was not lost on Charles.

Farlow's other innovation, however, did not turn out nearly so well. Besides tunneling, the other major obstacle to putting a rail line underground was the smoke from the locomotives, and it was here that Farlow introduced his most revolutionary creation. When it opened, the London Metropolitan Railway featured a locomotive of Farlow's own devising, specially fitted with cold-water condensing tanks that he believed would swallow up to seventy-five percent of the exhaust smoke. The one time the engine ran, however, boiling water blew out of the air pump, and the locomotive came hissing and frothing to a stop in front of the crowd gathered to see it.

Since then, the London Metropolitan Railway operated using standard steam locomotives, and there were many Londoners who refused to use it because of the smoke and filth. Early on, there also was a panic, in which a woman had been trampled to death. That was now more than ten years before, but Farlow was well aware of the line's shortcomings, and though he was head of one of the nation's most prestigious engineering firms, he knew his reputation was not one of universal acclaim. He was constantly looking to redeem his earlier effort, which was the reason he'd hired Fein, the pneumatics expert. If the underground system was ever to achieve its full potential, it was going to need an alternative power supply. It was also the reason Farlow had nearly a quarter of the firm working on the project, even though there was no guarantee it would even be approved.

As Charles saw it, what Farlow was really after was a knighthood, an honor that in one stroke would raise him to the ranks of men such as Denney, Stephenson, and Brunel. And whether that knighthood came as a result of his building a record-setting bridge or perfecting his underground rail system, he didn't care. Charles burned, thinking of how quickly Farlow moved on after the Forth. He simply turned his attention back to the underground. In addition, only the previous month Farlow had been elected president of the Royal Society of Engineers, an honor nearly as great as a knighthood itself.

Charles, however, felt as he did after losing the Devern contract, when it seemed all he had to look forward to were long hours in a steel mill. That was the reason he'd returned to London. Charles actually took some comfort in the fact that it was Darrs who had been awarded the Forth. He'd seen Darrs's plans and certainly gave him credit for his lack of ornamentation. Still, compared to the Finch & Stanton entry, Darrs's design harkened back to an earlier time. Instead of using cables to support the road deck, Darrs planned to use chains, a technique dating to the early part of the century and the first major suspension bridges. Darrs believed they would be easier to construct and position than spinning the cables in place, as was done with the Brooklyn Bridge, in New York. But in Charles's opinion, chains did not take advantage of steel's real superiority, which, with regard to suspension bridges, was its ability to be spun into wire infinitely greater in strength and resilience than individual chain links. It wasn't that he thought Darrs's plan wouldn't work, but it helped Charles view his own failure in terms of circumstance and politics rather than anything to do with engineering.

As consolation, this was very little. If possible, his relationship with Victoria had only gotten worse. He was beginning to think he was paying a very high price, given that there never was any actual infidelity. Still, this was nothing he could say to Victoria without having to explain what had actually transpired or, why even now, despite the fact that it had been nearly a year since he'd last received a reply, he continued to write to Elizabeth at least once a month.

Chapter 36

For Taylor and the British Northern, 1879 could not have started with higher hopes. In addition to the new shuttle service across the Fee, the railroad had added new trains to accommodate holiday travelers from across the country, visiting Feeport and Brindee just to see the new bridge—a huge, hand-colored engraving of which now graced the company boardroom. This was in place of the twenty-five-year-old print of the *Coast Flier*, the line's premier train, and it wasn't just the picture that had been replaced. Over the past three months, the British Northern had taken delivery of three new locomotives and three sets of coaches—one six-car train of deluxe carriages for the main run from Edinburgh to Aberdeen, and two ten-car trains with open seating for both the morning and the afternoon shuttle service.

Right at that moment, the company treasurer, Robert Kendall, stood before the other board members, totaling up the costs, along with those for the expanded rail facilities and new sidings in Feeport and Brindee. These were needed for the shuttle trains when not in service, and there was also the printing of all new tickets and schedules for the entire line. Since the bridge opened, it didn't seem that the railroad could make a move without spending money. In compliance with new regulations, the British Northern was installing crossing signals and building footbridges or under-track passages at all major stations. These expenditures were perhaps unavoidable, but Kendall finished his report enumerating items from a list of 10,000 pounds that had been spent on either the opening festivities for the bridge or the refurbishing of the company's offices, which, it was clear, from his tone were not at all unavoidable.

"Mr. Kendall, have you failed to notice the company's receipts for last month?" Taylor asked a bit impatiently. Like most everything else, the items had been purchased on credit, so that to Taylor they were merely numbers on paper—or so to some extent he had come to think of things over the past several years. And from his perspective, there were times that had been much worse.

"Receipts are nearly double what they were prior to the bridge's opening," the treasurer replied, his dour expression remaining as it was.

"And that's simply on the through run," Taylor said.

"It doesn't include the Fee shuttle," another of the board members added.

"The receipts of which are nearly equal to what we have been earning on the main line," Taylor finished the thought.

"That may be, but to this point, we haven't made a penny—not when you account for all the expenditures."

"And what might those be?" Taylor asked testily.

"The ones I just mentioned," Kendall responded with impatience of his own. "The new locomotives and coaches, the new sidings, the new tickets and schedules." He looked directly at Taylor. "This is no time to be spending money indiscriminately."

Taylor made a face. He and Kendall had already had this conversation in private, and he had hoped it would remain that way. As treasurer, Kendall had served the company well during difficult times, and Taylor supposed he was just looking for acknowledgment or recognition of some kind. But it was becoming more and more obvious to Taylor that their sense of accounting was no longer fully aligned.

Taylor had no doubt that, when tallied up, the cost of everything the company had purchased over the past threes months was far greater than any money seen in increased revenue. In reality, however, the railroad had not yet paid for any of it, other than a down payment—not the new locomotives and coaches, not the new sidings, not the new tickets and schedules. Not even the opening ceremony for the bridge or the new furnishing for the offices. The only items the railroad was currently paying cash for were wages and loan obligations, and their funding was gathered directly from daily ticket sales. If there was money left over after that, and there had been since the bridge opened, Taylor was not going to worry. After all, that had been the whole problem—not enough money coming in to pay the bills.

"And it doesn't end there. Coming this spring, the bridge must be painted," the treasurer went on. "I've only now begun the computations, but given its length, painting is a major project in itself, involving substantial materials."

"You are referring to the paint," the chairman snapped, surprised Kendall had continued at all.

With the railroad's sudden change in fortune, it was as if the treasurer suddenly wanted things done in a way neither he nor anyone else on the board had paid much attention to in recent times. Indeed, it seemed to Taylor that Kendall's primary concern was protecting himself, and there was no question that, should anyone come looking, it was the treasurer who would be most exposed

Still, while he understood Kendall's concerns, Taylor was not overly sympathetic. One of the expenses he and Kendall had argued about that morning was 375 pounds for a second commemorative plaque. The first one did not include de Forge's name, so the chairman had ordered a second one at Darrs's suggestion, wanting to avoid any sort of scene with de Forge's widow at the opening ceremony.

With all that had transpired in the past seven years, it seemed a remarkably small sum over which to be making a fuss, in addition to which, as he'd mentioned to Kendall, Taylor had also heard again from Pike the previous day. The railroad had yet to settle with Pike over the bonus, and to that extent the treasurer's remarks would be useful when Taylor was once again forced to tell Pike that the railroad did not have 50,000 pounds to hand over. Or even 25,000 pounds, which is the figure Taylor believed fair under the circumstances. As he'd also discussed with Kendall that morning, Taylor had no doubt Pike would accept the lower figure, but Kendall remained adamant in his refusal to pay any portion of the bonus because the contract was explicit in its stipulations.

Still, as Darrs had once again recently reminded Taylor, the bridge had already forced De Forge & Company into bankruptcy. Given the bridge's success, there was no reason for it to do the same to Hodges & Pike.

Chapter 37

Charles reached for his watch as he gazed through the window at the workmen lining the tracks. It was Sunday, and there was construction on the line, which was typical, because the Great Western, like most of the larger railways, tried to schedule maintenance and repair work for the weekend so as to interfere as little as possible with weekday operations. Still, the train had been moving at a crawl almost from the moment it left London more than two hours before. It was already past 1:00 p.m. At the present rate, it would be 2:00 or 2:30 before he reached Birmingham, and that was to say nothing of the fact that he would still have to get home again.

A few days before, at dinner, Charles had informed Victoria he would be working over the weekend, a remark that initially brought little in the way of a response. When he went on to say that this particular weekend he would have to go into the office, Victoria became suspicious, wondering why he couldn't simply do his work at home as he normally did on Saturday and Sunday. He'd had no good reply, and her suspicions were sure to increase if he didn't get home until nine or ten that night.

Of course, given the state of their marriage, it was not as if it really made much difference. Victoria was barely talking to him as it was, and the fact that he had nothing to lose was one of the main reasons he'd even dared the trip to begin with—that, and the fact that, if he ever hoped to see Elizabeth again, he had no choice. Although he continued to write to her, Elizabeth had refused to answer him until two weeks before, when he'd written to say that if she didn't at least respond, he would have no choice but to come to Birmingham in person. He'd reached the point where he was prepared to do anything just to hear from her, and in this, at least, his efforts were successful. Her reply, however, was simply to tell him that she had no desire to see him or hear from him, and would he please have the decency to leave her alone. It would have been an exaggeration even to call it a letter, as it consisted of a mere two lines. Charles, however, was not prepared to let it end there. He wrote back telling her he would do as she asked, but only if she would consent to see him one last time.

Charles thought back on the day he'd first been offered the job at Denney & Farlow. When he left the interview, the world itself had seemed different. Being in Westminster, Denney & Farlow was also located fairly close to where the Coopers lived, and the idea of telling Victoria he'd been offered a position at one of London's most prestigious engineering firms had seemed especially appealing right then. As a memory, however, it held no pleasure.

When the train reached Birmingham, Charles moved quickly. He still had to get to the mill, and there weren't always cabs on Sunday. Heading up the platform, he weaved around those ahead of him, though, as he neared the station proper, he slowed abruptly. He could see Elizabeth standing in the archway leading to the main hall, and it was clear she was not at all happy to be there.

"I didn't expect you to be here. I was just on my way to get a cab to the mill."

"I thought it would be better if I met you here at the station. I saw no reason to upset mother and father with your coming. I didn't even tell them why I was going into town."

"I see," Charles said, glancing down.

"Though I don't doubt they have their suspicions. They know you've continued to write to me."

Charles raised his eyes. "Still, it was good of you to come. I do appreciate your taking the time to see me."

"It's not as if you left me very much choice."

Again Charles looked down. "I suppose that's true," he said softly.

"You suppose!"

"Well, what would you have me do? You wouldn't answer my letters." Though still speaking quietly, Charles's tone was suddenly quite sharp.

"Where was I supposed to write to you? At your home? No, of course not. You wanted me to write you at your office. Do you have any idea how that would have made me feel? It was bad enough I had to do it this time."

"Elizabeth, please don't do this. I know I've put you in a terrible position. But don't you see? That's the reason I've come—to change all that."

"And how do you plan to do that?"

Charles glanced around. Because it was Sunday, the station was fairly quiet, but they were standing close to the entrance of the train shed, and the few people who were there had no choice but to walk around them to get to and from the trains.

"Can we please go someplace else to talk?" he asked.

"I really don't think we have anything to talk about."

"Please. We can't stand here. Let's just go over to the restaurant."

Elizabeth hesitated. As angry as she was, she did not want to concede anything. Still, she, too, was feeling self-conscious, and even as she considered her answer, she spotted a woman eyeing them as they walked past.

"Very well. But I will tell you now that I do not plan to stay long."

"Fine."

They crossed the main hall and went into the station restaurant, which, like the station itself, was practically empty. They sat down at the closest table, and a waiter came over with menus.

"That won't be necessary. I won't be ordering anything, thank you," Elizabeth said, declining the menu.

"Ma'am, you cannot use the restaurant as a waiting room. If you are not going to order anything, I'll have to ask you to leave."

"What if I order something?" Charles asked.

"I'm sorry sir, but both parties must put in an order."

"But we're not keeping anyone from the table."

"I'm sorry sir. Those are the rules."

"I could understand if you had people waiting. But what's the point of it now?"

"I'm sorry sir. Those are the rules."

Charles shook his head, clearly annoyed, but it wasn't something he was going to bother with then. "Elizabeth, just order something, you don't have to eat it."

"Very well, I'll have a cup of tea," she said.

"A cup of tea," the waiter repeated. "Is that all?"

"Of course that's all," Charles said. "The lady doesn't even want that. Or weren't you here a moment ago?"

"Well, sir, generally there is a minimum order, but since we aren't crowded, I suppose I can overlook it in this instance."

"Thank you," Elizabeth said.

The waiter nodded to her and then turned to Charles. "And for you, sir?"

Charles looked at the menu. Although he hadn't eaten anything since breakfast, his stomach was in knots, and the thought of putting food into it only made it worse. If anything, he would have liked to order a whiskey, only he worried over what Elizabeth might think, especially at that hour.

"I'll have a cup of tea as well."

"And to eat?" the waiter asked.

"Nothing for me either. Just the tea."

"Sir, I realize I made an exception for your wife, but I only did that assuming you would be ordering."

"Whatever the minimum is, I'll pay it," Charles said, sharply. "Please, just bring us the tea."

"Very well then, two cups of tea. But you do understand you will have to pay the minimum."

"Yes, yes, whatever it is, I'll pay it."

The waiter left, and for several moments Charles and Elizabeth remained silent.

"I apologize for that," he said.

"For what? You did nothing."

"Nevertheless, I know that must have been awkward for you."

"Hearing the waiter refer to me as your wife? It was bound to happen."

"Yes, but still . . ."

"It was not half so awkward as having to come here to meet you in the first place," Elizabeth said grimly.

Before Charles could say anything in reply, the waiter returned with a pot of tea and two cups, which he set down in front of them, along with a sugar bowl and a small pitcher of milk.

"If there is anything else I can get for you, please let me know."

"Thank you, that will be all," Charles said.

He watched after the man, waiting until he was out of sight before turning back to Elizabeth.

"My intention was never to cause you any awkwardness or to force you to see me. But you refused to answer my letters. I simply had no other choice."

"I thought we went through that. Where was I supposed to write you?"

"One letter. You could have written one letter. You have no idea what it's been like for me the last year. You're all I think about."

He was looking right at her, his eyes suddenly inflamed with emotion, and her first thought was "how dare he!" Still, it was not passion she saw, but pain, an overwhelming anguish, and while there were certainly times she'd wanted him to suffer as she had, it disturbed her to see him so.

"Charles, my intention was never to hurt you. I just thought if I didn't answer you, you would eventually stop writing. Certainly by now."

"Well, I didn't," he said, his eyes still fixed on her. "Besides, if your real desire was that I stop writing to you, why would you bother reading my letters in the first place? And I know you must have been reading them or you wouldn't have known to meet me here today."

Elizabeth looked down, having no immediate response. In a way, she'd actually looked forward to his letters, even to the point of worrying if more than four or five weeks passed without one. There was no question that her greatest wish was that they could go back to a time before any of this had happened, but that in no way prepared her for what he said next.

"I know how shamefully I've behaved, and how wrong it was for me even to write you, expecting you to carry on some sort of illicit correspondence. You deserve better. Far better. But I also know you must still have feelings for me, and that's the reason I've come today, to beg your forgiveness and to ask you to marry me, so you never have to be in that position again."

As he spoke, Charles took hold of her hand, which he now held firmly in his own. Still, it was not so much the force of his grasp that kept it there, as her astonishment. Although she was fairly certain Charles had come there to declare his love, it never occurred to her he would ask her to marry him.

"But you're already married," she replied.

"I'll get divorced."

"Charles, do you have any idea what you're saying?"

"I do. I don't love Victoria. I never loved her. As you know, I was simply too cowardly to back out of the marriage when I had the chance. But I'm no longer so timid."

"But you have your daughter to think about. What about Anne?"

Elizabeth looked directly at him, and Charles felt himself cringe. Even now he had yet to tell Elizabeth of Fredrick's birth.

"It's terrible, I know. But I also know I couldn't expect you to settle for anything less. And the truth is, I can't go on without you. I need you."

As Elizabeth listened to him, she saw that her hand was still within his, and she withdrew it. What he was saying was scandalous. That he was even considering it or thought he could somehow make up for everything by divorcing his wife—the very idea of it was horrifying. It seemed to expose something so deeply self-serving that it made her question why she'd ever loved him to begin with.

Chapter 38

It was a breezy June evening, and the elongated rays of the sun shimmered on the water as Henry Markum approached the bridge. Markum had been with the project from the very beginning and, at Darrs's suggestion, had been appointed permanent inspector when the bridge opened in the fall. With him was Martin Kinney, the seventeen-year-old lamplighter. Twice a day, Kinney climbed down each of the columns supporting the inverted spans, which everyone in anyway familiar with the bridge had come to refer to as the high spans. Each of these columns was marked by two navigation lamps, one on either side. There were twenty-eight in all, and Kinney would light them in the evening and then put them out again the following morning.

The two men were on foot, and before starting onto the bridge, they paused at the signal box located at the south end of the bridge.

"Good evening, Mr. Markum," the signalman said. He'd seen their approach and stepped outside to meet them.

"Mr. Berkeley," Markum said in response.

"And good evening to you too, lad," the signalman added, glancing at Kinney.

"Good evening, Mr. Berkeley, sir."

"The eight o'clock is on time, I expect," Markum said.

"Yes, sir. I just got done speaking with Mr. Shap on the north side. She should be through in about ten minutes."

Markum took out his watch to mark the time.

"Accompanying young Martin, here, on his rounds?" Berkeley asked.

"I have something to check on the high spans."

"Aye, you'll be wanting to check on the painters," Berkeley said. "Happy just to slop it on, or so it would seem, the way they've been getting on with the job."

Markum grunted thoughtfully but said nothing in response. He simply returned his watch to his pocket and continued up the tracks to the bridge, with Kinney at his side.

The painters to which the signalman had referred were a crew of some two dozen men who'd been at work on the bridge the past three weeks, one of whom reported a cracked beam in one of the columns for the high spans. Given the Fee's currents and the fact that the bridge was not founded on bedrock, both Markum and Darrs were especially concerned about the underwater parts of the bridge, and, when first appointed inspector back in the fall, Markum had hired four other men, two of whom were divers. The third was Kinney, and the fourth was a boatman, who, together with the divers, had carried out two series of soundings around the bridge's foundations, the first when it opened, and the second six months later, back in March.

Faced with the cost of having to paint the bridge, however, the railroad had abruptly dismissed the boatmen and divers the previous month. The directors had seen no reason to pay for twelve months of work when the duties required two or three at most, so they informed Markum that, henceforth, only one set of soundings would be required per year.

With the divers' departure, however, that left only two men permanently employed on the bridge: Kinney, and Markum himself. The track and spans were inspected twice monthly as part of the roadway; for anything important, Markum could consult Darrs. But on a day-to-day basis, Markum was on his own, and he'd seen the painting crew as a great opportunity. Realizing the bridge was going to be under the greatest scrutiny since its initial inspection, he'd asked the painters to keep an eye out for anything unusual, though he was beginning to question the wisdom of having done so.

It was about a half mile to the high spans, and Markum and Kinney walked in silence, one on either side of the track. Iron handrails made of cast-iron pipe had replaced the wooden two-by-fours used during the bridge's construction, and it was within the handrails themselves that the gas was delivered to the navigation lights. On Markum's side, there was also a five-inch water main running along the base handrail. It was a new addition, giving Brindee access to a freshwater source south of the Fee, in return for which the city was paying the railroad a sizable fee.

Across from him, Kinney walked close to the edge, running his hand along the pipe railing. The seventeen-year-old liked his job, especially the evening rounds. It was a beautiful time to be on the bridge, the sun sparkling on the water.

"There she is, sir."

Beyond the high spans, the bridge curved to the east, and glancing ahead, Markum spotted the train as it neared the northern approach.

"Sir, if you don't mind, I'm going to hurry. I want to get over the side before she reaches us."

Markum nodded. They were nearly to the high spans, and he watched Kinney trot ahead. He was just disappearing over the side as the train reached the bridge. It was more than a mile away, but

Markum could feel the vibrations in the deck under his feet the instant the train started on the bridge.

Right at that moment, the train not only was more than a mile away but also was headed south. Because there was no bluff on the Brindee side of the firth, the crossing from Brindee to Feeport was uphill, which slowed the trains. Traveling from Feeport to Brindee, however, the trip was downhill, and the trains could pick up considerable speed. This was especially true of the morning and evening shuttle trains, which were not only headed downhill but also consisted of ten packed coaches, making them much heavier than the through trains, which consisted of only five or six. As well, since the bridge had opened, a rivalry had developed between the shuttle drivers and the ferry captains. General Hudson, the inspector, had set a speed limit of twenty-five miles per hour, but heading north, the morning and evening shuttle trains regularly exceeded thirty-five and even forty miles per hour. The station and ferry terminals were across the street from each other, on the Brindee side, and from what Markum had heard, the drivers took considerable sport arriving ahead of ferries that had left ten and even fifteen minutes before the trains.

Markum had been on the bridge and knew that, at such times, the vibrations could become quite severe. Some of the painters even claimed to have seen the deck develop a waving motion, though he doubted that was the case. He'd never seen anything like that and thought it was more likely it was the painters' own sense of vertigo at the passing train. He also took it as something of a personal affront when he heard the foreman of painters had warned his men to trust their weight not to the bracing bars but only to the main beams in the columns. Markum knew of the problem. One could hear the chattering whenever there was a train on the bridge, but it was no more than one or two per column, not every other one as the painters had complained.

Markum was now inside the third of the high spans, and he glanced ahead at the approaching train. He could feel the rumble in the deck growing, although in this case he doubted even the painters would have found anything to complain about; the train was traveling at no more than fifteen miles per hour. Still, Markum stopped where he was and took hold of the handrail. Regardless of the train's speed, given the bridge's narrowness, it was wisest to stand still when a train was passing.

The sun had yet to set, but the train's headlamp was already lit for the evening run. Markum could see the flame burning behind the glass—that, and the blasts of white steam pumping from its cylinders with each stroke of the pistons. It was no more than a few hundred feet away, and the driver gave a short pull on his whistle. Markum held up a hand in response, though he tightened his grasp on the railing with the other. He could feel the weight of the locomotive on the span, the driving force of its wheels as it steamed toward him. The sheer magnitude of its presence was impossible to ignore, even for an experienced man, and Markum felt his body stiffen in a combination of fear and awe. It took no more than a few seconds to pass, but Markum remained transfixed, watching after it for some moments before continuing on to the second to last of the columns supporting the high spans. There, Markum ducked under the handrail and stood for a moment, looking down at the water some ninety feet below.

The beam in question was near the bottom of the support, and Markum started to descend a series of cast-iron rungs that ran down one side. The cast-iron portion of the supports for the high spans were made up of eight tiers, each ten feet in height, the crossed bracing bars forming a column of X's down each side.

From what the painter said, the crack was in the third tier from the bottom, and although the rungs were dry, about halfway down Markum could see the beams had already been painted and were still fairly wet. The same was true when he reached the third tier, but even with the paint, Markum could see the crack. It was on the other side of the support, and Markum made his way around the outside, careful not to slip. His hands were already dirty, and he wasn't worried about the paint, but he was still some thirty feet above the water and not looking to have a foot slip.

When he reached the spot, Markum took a measuring tape from his pocket. He'd been skeptical of the painter's description, but the crack, which ran lengthwise down the center of the beam, did in fact measure more than six feet in length. Markum put away the tape measure and took out his pocketknife, using it to probe the crack, which, at its widest point, was possibly an eighth of an inch. The crack did not penetrate into the beam's cement core, something he was glad of. Markum had never seen the crack before, and Kinney, who was up and down the supports twice a day, had never mentioned it, either. Markum could only assume it had just opened, something he immediately tied to the speed of the northbound trains. Indeed, he had no doubt racing the ferries was one of the main factors behind the loose bracing bars as well.

Markum looked at his watch and then at the sky. The sun was beginning to set, and as he was on the east side of the bridge, he was in shadow. In the thirty minutes or so that he'd been on the bridge, the temperature had dropped noticeably, but he wanted to see how the crack responded with a train passing overhead, and the next train through would be the evening shuttle from Feeport, an excellent test. Markum put away his knife and tore a sheet from a small notebook he carried. He pasted the sheet over the center of the crack, using the wet paint to hold it in place, then made his way around to the other side of the support, which was still in sunlight.

From his perch on the support, Markum gazed to the south. Within a few minutes, he could see the train approaching the bridge along the bluff. Coming from the south, it was traveling a good deal faster than the previous train, and the vibrations were immediately more pronounced. He could feel it in his hands as he made his way back to where he'd placed the sheet of paper. Markum could also hear a number of bracing bars chattering nearby. They became louder, the closer the train came, but at that moment, his focus was on the crack. He kept his eye on it the entire time the train was passing, then carefully peeled it off, pleased to find it had not torn. He took this as a good sign, though not wanting to take any chances, he wired Darrs with the information the very next morning.

Chapter 39

Upon completion of the Fee, Darrs immediately turned his attention to the Forth. He very much wanted to avoid the difficulties that had plagued the Fee, and he'd spent much of the time carrying out an exhaustive study of the riverbed and shoreline in preparation for the bridge's foundations. But it wasn't just the problems with the survey he wanted to avoid. Over the past few moths, Markum had sent several reports to Darrs, informing him of cracks in the supports for the inverted spans. Such cracks were not uncommon with cast iron, which was one of the reasons for the cement cores. As an added precaution, Darrs also had Markum strap the affected beams with iron collars, which was standard practice. Still, after eight years, Darrs was unaware of any cracks in the supports at Birkendale, which made him think of the molders grumbling about the quality of iron. Given the type of bridge, Darrs was not concerned, but he had no doubt that additional cracks would be found, and he imagined he'd be strapping the beams with collars for years to come, something that would never do on the Forth.

Darrs's only break from work came that fall, when the queen made a special point of crossing the bridge on her return from her annual holiday in Scotland. There had been talk of a knighthood from the moment the bridge was completed, and with the queen's visit, it became a virtual certainty. People lined the shores in Feeport and Brindee, and an immense crowd gathered at the Brindee Station, where flags and banners waved in the wind as councilmen made speeches in anticipation of the queen's arrival. Darrs himself received a thunderous ovation from the crowd when presented with the key to the city.

Despite all of the preparation, however, the visit lasted only a few minutes. The ladies of the city presented bouquets, after which the queen asked for Darrs, who bowed deeply in her presence.

"I was told there were great difficulties in laying the foundation and that some lives were lost," the queen said when he straightened up.

"Yes," Darrs nodded, surprised by the seriousness of her words and tone. "We employed several new techniques during excavation, and there was an explosion in one of the digging chambers. Four men were killed, for which I take complete responsibility."

"The bridge is more than a mile and a half long," the queen said in response, her expression unchanged.

"Closer to two miles from end to end," Darrs said, with no particular inflection of his own.

"And it took almost seven years to build?" the queen questioned.

Again Darrs nodded.

"I am quite looking forward to the view. I was told it takes nearly ten minutes to cross, and that at times one can imagine oneself flying?"

"I don't know about flying, but yes, the southbound trip often takes nine or ten minutes."

"I will tell the driver to take his time," the queen said, taking her leave.

Again Darrs bowed, and within moments the train was pulling out. The engineer took his time, as the queen had requested, and the royal train crossed the bridge to a salute of cannon fire from the three naval gunboats stationed on the Fee.

Chapter 40

The signalman, Thomas Berkeley, walked with his head down, but the rain, which one moment beat down upon his back, would just as quickly turn about, striking him in the face. He glanced to his left. With him was Martin Kinney, the lamplighter. It was December 28, and they were in the midst of a serious winter storm.

Berkeley had seen Kinney returning from the bridge a few hours before and, knowing the boy lived on the far side of town, had invited him home for supper. To return the favor, Kinney offered to accompany Berkeley back to the bridge for the seven o'clock train, though looking at him now, Berkeley imagined Kinney regretted it. He, too, was bent over against the storm, and they were both grateful to reach the shelter of the signal box, meager as it was. The signal box had one four-paned window that faced north to the bridge. Each pane rattled violently. Even worse was the cold air slicing through the slatted walls, and upon entering, Berkeley set down his lantern and moved quickly to add more coal to the stove. Almost immediately, however, the telegraph sounded. It was the wireman at the Feeport station, saying the seven o'clock train had just pulled out and would be at the bridge any minute.

"You know, I wouldn't stand so close to that window," Berkeley said, as he turned from the desk.

Kinney glanced back at him.

"You hear the panes rattling," Berkeley said. "A good rush of wind and one or two of them might decide to come popping out."

Kinney looked at the window, evaluating its strength for himself.

"I'm not saying they will, but I've seen it happen."

Just then a blast of wind shook the signal box, and Kinney jerked backward. Berkeley let out a small chuckle and picked up his lantern, along with the bridge baton, which sat on the desk next to the telegraph. The wind had yet to subside, and a spray of icy rain rushed in the instant he opened the door.

Outside, he made his way to the track. He could see the flame of the headlight as the train approached. It was no more than twenty yards away, and he held up the baton. From inside the cab, the fireman leaned out, snatching the baton away as the locomotive passed.

"My God, she's blowing. Great guns in every direction and getting stronger," Berkeley said, returning to the signal box.

He crossed to the stove and resumed adding coal to the fire. Kinney continued to look out the window, although from a distance of two or three feet. He could see the train on the bridge, its form illuminated by the interior lights of the passenger compartments, which produced a sort of halo around the coaches. It was a sight he'd witnessed many times, and he was not surprised when sparks began to fly from the wheels.

"She's sparking," he said, still looking out the window.

"I don't doubt it in this wind," Berkeley replied. "Which rail? The east or the west?"

"The east."

"Well, at least we know which direction the wind is coming from—for the moment anyway."

Kinney continued to watch the train. He could no longer see the glow from the coaches, only the intermittent sparking of the wheels and the two red lamps on the back of the last coach. The train was perhaps three-quarters of a mile from the signal box when he saw a sudden flash of light. It didn't last more than a second or two, but afterward he could no longer see the taillights.

"Something's happened."

Berkeley, who was just finishing up with the fire, gave the contents of the stove one last turn with a poker. "What's that?"

"Something's happened to the train!"

"What do you mean?" Berkeley asked, his voice taking on a more serious tone.

"I was watching when, all of a sudden, there was a flash. I can't say what it was, but it was out by the inverted spans, and afterward I couldn't see the taillights."

"Well, if it was out by the inverted spans, it was just the train starting down the other side of the bridge. You always lose sight of it there. You know that."

"But the flash, I never saw that before. Besides, I don't think the train was so far out to have started down the other side."

Berkeley walked to the window and looked out. There was little to be seen, but at that moment he was actually more concerned with the window, the panes of which continued to rattle violently.

"Keep watching," he said, returning to the stove to warm himself. "She'll come back into view any minute now, as she swings around on the north side."

Perched atop the bluff, the signal box offered an excellent view, and Kinney kept his eye on the far shore, waiting for the train to reappear. He could make out a faint glow from the signal box at the other end of the bridge, but the train did not reappear. Five minutes passed. Then six and seven. The bell on the telegraph should have rung, signaling the train's arrival on the other shore.

Berkeley joined Kinney by the window.

"Nothing yet?" he asked.

"No sign of her."

Berkeley reached into his pocket for his watch. It was now a full twelve minutes since he'd handed off the baton. He picked up the earpiece and cranked the handle on the newly installed telephone that connected the north and south signal boxes. The line remained silent, so he cranked again. By that point, both he and Kinney were visibly concerned, something evident in their expressions.

"Try the block," Kinney said, referring to the telegraph, but that line was dead as well.

Berkeley went to the window and peered hard into the night. With both the telephone and the telegraph lines out, he was beginning to fear the worst. Like all newer bridges, the Fee was equipped with safety rails, a second set of rails running inside the main ones to prevent a train from derailing on the bridge. Given the strength of the storm, however, it was possible the wind had simply blown the train over the side. At thirty tons, the locomotive was no doubt still somewhere on the bridge, but the coaches weighed practically nothing. They could easily have gone over, which would explain the lines being out, as the coaches would likely have cut the wires as they went over.

Berkeley went back to the desk to telegraph the Feeport station. It was on a separate circuit from the bridge, but it, too, was dead.

He turned to Kinney. "Lad, get into town. Tell the stationmaster there's been an accident."

"What about you?"

"I'm going onto the bridge."

"In this storm!"

"Someone has to see what happened."

"What happened? I'll tell you what happened: The train went over the side."

"We don't know that for sure. She could be sitting just on the other side of the inverted spans where we can't see her. At least part of her."

"Then I'm coming with you," the boy said.

Berkeley shook his head. "I can't let you do that. Besides, someone has got to get into town to tell them what's happened."

Kinney looked at him, still unconvinced.

"Don't argue with me, lad. You get into town and tell the stationmaster what's happened."

With that, Berkeley grabbed his lantern and headed out the door. He made his way to the start of the bridge, where he stopped and held up the lantern. Like many bridges at the time, the Fee was built to carry only a single set of tracks. That was the reason for the baton: To prevent collisions, only one train was allowed on the bridge at a time, and to cross, the driver needed the baton. What it also meant was that the bridge, though nearly two miles long, was a mere fifteen feet wide, and the only thing to keep one from going over the side were two slender handrails. Kinney was right, Berkeley thought, starting down the center of the track. It was madness.

He could feel the rain beating down on his hood and the back of his coat, but the wind, which was what he'd feared most, was not as bad as he'd expected. Beneath him, he could hear the wind whining among the beams—that, and the chattering of the bracing bars, which told him whenever he was passing over the top of one of the bridge's iron columns. Across the firth, the lights of Brindee glowed in the distance, but he didn't look at them. He kept his eyes focused on his feet, except for those moments when he glanced ahead, hoping to see something of the train.

He was doing just that when a tremendous gust of wind ripped at his coat, tangling the hood over his eyes. Blinded, he dropped to the deck, smashing the lantern against one of the rails. Exposed to the rain, the flame instantly went out, leaving him in complete darkness. He couldn't see it, but staring down through the slats of the deck, he sensed the frigid water seething below, and for a time he lay frozen as the wind howled around him. He must have been close to a half mile out, which meant it was as far back to shore as it was to where he imagined the train, or at least the locomotive, had to be. With that in mind, he continued on, though not on his feet. He crawled on all fours, sliding his right hand along the top of the rail, not daring to let go. It was cold—so cold that it sent a chill up his arm. He was beginning to shiver, and he thought of the locomotive. Whether or not the rest of the train had gone over, it had to be out there, and with it the warmth of its boiler.

Suddenly, his hand slipped from the rail, and his chin cracked down hard against the deck. His head was spinning as he groped in the darkness for the rail. It was as if it had disappeared, and when he found it, he understood why: It ended, which was the reason his hand had slipped off in the first place. There was nothing in front of him. No rails. No deck. The bridge was gone.

Chapter 41

It was after midnight when Darrs was awakened by a loud knocking at the front door. He'd been in a deep sleep, and he struggled to put on his bathrobe before going downstairs.

"Sir Stewart?"

"I am Sir Stewart," Darrs replied. He bent down. Matilda, the dog, had followed him from the bedroom, and he blocked her from going outside into the rain.

"Sir, I'm with the British Northern. There's been an accident."

"An accident?"

"Yes, sir. I don't know how to tell you this, but the Fee Bridge is down."

"Down!" Darrs exclaimed, straightening up.

"Yes, sir. And it's believed there may have been a train on it when it fell."

Darrs turned white as the blood drained from his cheeks. "When?"

"Sometime early this evening. Other than that, I cannot say."

Darrs was clearly shaken by the news, and for a moment, the man said nothing more. He then gestured toward the street, where a cab waited at the curb.

"Company officials are gathering at the station as we speak. They're planning to leave for Feeport within the hour. I was sent to get you."

Darrs glanced at the waiting cab and then back at the man. "Yes, of course. I just have to dress. And please, come inside. There's no reason to stand in the rain."

"Thank you, sir. That's very kind," said the man, who, in spite of the rain, had been holding his hat in his hands in deference to Darrs's recent knighting.

Darrs left the man in the foyer and made his way back upstairs. He couldn't have been gone more than three or four minutes, but when he returned to the bedroom his wife had lit the lamp on her night table.

"Stewart, what is it?"

"There's been an accident. The Fee Bridge is down," he said, as he crossed the room to dress.

Mrs. Darrs gasped, pressing her hands to her mouth.

Darrs turned to her. "And they believe there may have been a train on it when it fell."

"Oh my God, Stewart. Do they know how it happened?"

"That's all I know. A group of officials from the railroad is leaving for Feeport. They've sent a man for me. He's waiting downstairs with a cab."

Darrs removed his bathrobe and opened his wardrobe. His wife's eyes remained on him. She wanted him to say more. That, or she wanted to say something herself, but she simply watched as he put on his clothes.

When he was through, Darrs again turned to her. Even in the dim light of her lamp, she could see the ghostlike cast of his face.

"The cab is waiting. I must go," he said. "I'll send word as soon as I know more."

Mrs. Darrs watched after him as he left the room. She could hear his steps as he descended the stairs and then the sound of the front door closing behind him, at which point, she threw off the covers and ran to the window. She got there in time to see the two men climb into the cab and set off through the rain.

When Darrs arrived at the station, a number of British Northern officials were already present, including Chairman Taylor, who spotted Darrs the instant he came through the door.

"Sir Stewart," he said, moving straight for him.

"Tell me, has there been any more news?" Darrs asked.

"Both Brindee and Feeport are unreachable. The lines are down and have been since seven or eight this evening, when the wind tore off part of the roof at the Feeport station."

Darrs's eyes widened.

"As bad as it is down here, apparently we're just seeing the tail end of it."

"It would seem so," Darrs said, shaking his head.

"The stationmaster in Feeport had someone ride down to Grailton to get the word out. He said close to 300 passengers were on board."

"Three hundred!" Darrs exclaimed.

He faltered somewhat on his feet, and Taylor stepped forward.

"Sir, let me help you," he said, taking hold of Darrs's arm.

"Thank you, though I assure you I'm all right."

Taylor, however, did not let go as he guided Darrs toward a nearby bench. "Perhaps if you sat down for a moment."

"Yes, thank you. That might be best."

Three hundred was a staggering figure. It was the sort of number generally associated with the loss of a ship at sea.

"Excuse me, Mr. Taylor, but the train is ready to leave," a man said.

"Very well, have the others start boarding," Taylor replied.

Darrs started to rise, and again Taylor offered his assistance, though this time Darrs declined and the two men made their way to the waiting train.

It was approaching five o'clock in the morning when they reached the Feeport Station, where they were met on the platform by the stationmaster. Taylor was the first off the train, but before he said anything, he paused at the sight of the broken timbers and tangled telegraph wires hanging down from the side of the building.

"Yes, sir," the stationmaster said, seeing his expression, "it's quite a time of it we've had, though the last hour or so, the rain has finally begun to let up." He motioned to the sky.

"Do you know anything more about the train? Is it certain she's lost?" Taylor asked.

"I'm afraid she must be."

"But you don't know for sure?"

"The lines are down so, I've had no word from the north shore, but I do know what the lamplighter saw and also what the signalman found when he went on the bridge. You can ask them yourself. They're inside."

Taylor nodded and went into the station, followed by Darrs and the others. Inside, Berkeley and Kinney huddled by a stove behind the ticket counter, which was at the end of the building undamaged by the storm. But with a third of its roof gone, the station offered little protection from the cold.

"This is Mr. Berkeley, the signalman, and Martin Kinney, the lamplighter. They were both in the south box when the train took the baton and started onto the bridge," the stationmaster said.

"So you actually went out on the bridge," Taylor said, addressing Berkeley

"Yes, sir. I was the one who first discovered the bridge was down."

"What, exactly, did you see?" Taylor asked.

"I did not see much. I know the bridge is down because I nearly went off the end. I was sliding my hand along one of the rails when it suddenly slipped off. Beyond that there was nothing."

"Did you see anything of the train?" Taylor pressed him.

"In truth, I did not look," Berkeley said. "I had quite a fright nearly going over, so my only thought was getting back to shore. I crawled the half mile on my hands and knees."

"Half a mile," Darrs said, speaking for the first time. "That would have put you out by the inverted spans."

"Aye, sir," the young lamplighter said excitedly. "And that's where the train was when I saw the flash."

"What flash?" Taylor asked.

"I was watching the train from the signal box. I could see it on the bridge and knew it must have been a strong wind, because I could see the wheels sparking."

"Sparking?" Taylor said.

"It was not uncommon in a wind such as tonight," Berkeley confirmed, "the wheels of the coaches being forced against the rails."

Despite Berkeley's claim of commonness, it was the first Taylor had heard of it, and he turned to Darrs for some sort of explanation, but the sparking was news to Darrs as well.

Taylor turned back to Kinney. "Go on about the flash."

"As I said, I was watching the train on the bridge. I should say I was watching the taillights, because at that point they were all I could see. Suddenly, there was a flash of light. It was so bright that I lost sight of the taillights, and afterward, they were nowhere to be seen."

"So you think it was one of the inverted spans that went down," Taylor said.

Kinney did not immediately respond. He glanced at Berkeley, who in turn glanced at the stationmaster.

"Sir," the stationmaster began slowly, "it is not just one. We now believe it's all thirteen of the inverted spans that went down."

"All thirteen!" Taylor exclaimed.

"Our first inkling was when no one could make out any of the navigation lights. But with the storm raging, it was difficult to say for sure. This last hour, though, the moon has come out and you can clearly see."

He motioned toward the window and Darrs moved quickly in that direction, followed by the others, pressing up against one another to see.

"Dear God," someone said.

More than a mile away, the bridge was little more than a dark band against the sky. Even so, just as the stationmaster had said, there was plainly a long gap where the inverted spans should have stood.

Chapter 42

Charles removed the mail from the catch by the front door and carried it into the breakfast room, where Victoria sat at the table. She was glancing through a magazine and she didn't look up as he took the seat across from her. Charles also said nothing. He simply began to sort through the mail as the maid set down a plate with his breakfast.

When finished, he passed the letters for Victoria across the table, which she took from him, again with hardly a glance. In fact, there was a distinct hostility to the manner in which she snatched the correspondence from his hand, but he'd come to expect such things, so he again said nothing. He simply took a sip of tea and opened the morning paper, which had come with the mail. No sooner had he opened it, however, than he nearly spat out the contents of his mouth.

"My God, the Fee Bridge went down with a train on it!"

"A train!" Victoria exclaimed, looking up. "What does it say?"

Charles, who'd merely been scanning the headlines, began to read aloud.

"Sunday evening, just past seven o'clock, one or more of the Fee Bridge's eighty-five spans collapsed during a winter gale, taking with them the British Northern's evening train from Edinburgh, with as many as 300 passengers."

"Three hundred!"

Victoria gasped at the figure, and Charles looked up before reading on. "The bridge, designed by the celebrated and recently knighted Sir Stewart Darrs, was, until last evening, the longest bridge in the world, having been opened to universal acclaim some fourteen months ago." Suddenly, he stood. "I've got to get to the office."

Victoria looked at him, startled by his abruptness. Despite the fact that they'd barely been speaking, at that moment she wished he wouldn't leave and she followed him from the breakfast room out to the front hallway.

"What does it mean?" she asked as he pulled on his coat.

"What do you mean? The bridge went down. That's what it means."

"I know that," she said with irritation. "That's not what I meant."

"Then what did you mean?"

She shook her head. "I don't know. I guess I'm not really sure."

"Well, I left the paper," he said, going to the door. "See what else it has to say."

When Charles arrived at the firm, partners and associates were all gathered among the drafting tables in the firm's main hall. Outside of the bridge being down and the number of passengers on the train, nothing was known. Like Charles, however, no one needed any specifics to know something terrible had happened, something with particular significance for them. As engineers, it touched each of them personally.

Farlow arrived some fifteen minutes later and immediately called Charles into his office.

"I've just come from a meeting with James Dormand," Farlow said. "If you don't know, Dormand is president of the Board of Trade.

The Fee was built under an Act of Parliament. A Court of Inquiry is being formed, and they want to include someone from outside the government. Dormand contacted me at home this morning to ask if I would act as one of the judges. The other two are Richard Hathaway and Colonel William Roland. You've heard of Roland, of course."

"Chief inspector of railways," Charles said.

Farlow nodded. "Hathaway is the board's wreck commissioner. He's new to the position. I've never met him, but he'll be chairing the proceedings, so if you meet him before I do, be sure to make a good impression."

"Yes, sir. Though, may I ask what it is you want me to do?"

"I want you to go to Brindee. The Board of Trade already has inspectors on their way to the Fee. Given the loss of life and the fact that the bridge hadn't been up but fourteen months, the board wants to get the investigation under way as soon as possible. A preliminary inquest is scheduled to begin this Saturday, in Brindee. I'll be joining you in Scotland on Friday, but in the meantime, I want you to wire me with any developments."

"I understand," Charles replied.

"Now go," Farlow said. "There's an express leaving for Edinburgh within the hour. It's sure to be full, so you'd better get to the station if you hope to be on it."

Chapter 43

The appearance of the bridge in broad daylight, though not nearly so eerie as the previous night, was no less devastating. The inverted spans were completely destroyed. It was not simply the spans that had fallen, but the supports as well. In most cases, they'd been shorn clean, so all that remained were the brick foundations. In one instance, twenty feet of a support still stood, and in two others, about half that. Here and there, a few mangled beams lay atop the foundations or trailed into the water, but that was all.

It was a grim sight, though the bridge was not Taylor's only concern at that moment. It was nearing two o'clock, and he and the other board members were crammed together inside the stationmaster's office at the British Northern's Brindee station. With him were Darrs, who'd barely said a word since the previous night, and Simon Nichols, the British Northern's lead man in Brindee.

The door was closed, but Taylor could hear the crowd of relatives and reporters just outside, in the waiting room. They'd been there for hours, some since the night before, when they'd come to the station intending to meet loved ones due on the train.

There was no longer any question as to what had happened or whether there might be survivors. The exact location of the train had yet to be determined, but a few minutes before, a man appeared with news that bodies had been sighted as far away as Broughty, more than five miles downstream. The report had yet to be confirmed, but as people realized some of the victims might never be found, there was an outpouring of grief unlike anything Taylor had ever heard.

Taylor had been in the waiting room, describing the steps the railroad was taking to deal with the disaster. Within minutes of the man's appearance, however, Taylor found himself the focus of jeers and taunts, the viciousness of which eventually drove him into the stationmaster's office.

"From the way they act, you'd think I was personally responsible," Taylor said.

"They're distraught," Nichols replied. "They've been here for hours. Many since last night."

"That's no excuse. What do they think, the bridge simply keeled over on its own? Listening to them, you'd never even know there was a storm. Do they know the Feeport Station lost its roof or that the wind blew a line of loaded freight cars 200 yards down a siding? You heard the stationmaster."

Nichols shifted anxiously. He was already on tenuous ground with the chairman, since it turned out there were nowhere near 300 passengers on the train. In the confusion, the Feeport stationmaster counted all the ticket stubs in his box, not simply those for the train that was lost. It was the first estimate, however, on which Nichols based his statement to the newspapers, and while the stationmaster's confusion was perhaps forgivable under the circumstances, Nichols's was not—at least so far as Taylor was concerned. Had Nichols taken even a moment to think about it, he would have realized the train could not possibly have been carrying anywhere near 300 passengers. At most, the through trains from Edinburgh carried 150 passengers.

On a Sunday night, even the last Sunday night of the year, it was unlikely to be carrying even half that many, but as it stood, every paper in the country had led with a headline placing the number at 300.

"They may know about the Feeport station," Nichols replied, "but I don't think anyone has told them about the freight cars."

"Well, maybe someone should." Taylor replied sharply, though he understood their feelings. They were in pain, so they lashed out. Their loved ones had been on the train—husbands, wives, children—and were lost to them forever. But he, too, was devastated. His railroad lay in ruins. Taking the ferry from Feeport that morning was like sailing through the remnants of a shipwreck. The Fee was littered with cracked and shattered boards from what had been the bridge's deck. They thumped and squealed against the hull the entire crossing. He had not lost anyone dear to him, but the sickness he felt permeated his entire being.

Chapter 44

"Stewart, is there anything I can get for you? A cup of tea or something to eat?" Mrs. Darrs asked, leaning her head inside the door to her husband's study. "Mary made up a lovely pot of soup, and you hardly had any breakfast."

Darrs looked at her for some time, but without answering, glanced back at the plans on his desk.

"Stewart," Mrs. Darrs said again, this time stepping fully into the room.

Darrs shook his head, as if clearing his mind. "I'm sorry, my dear, what did you say?"

"I asked if I could get you anything. Mary made up some soup, and you should eat something; you hardly had any breakfast."

Even now, however, Darrs did not answer. It was Friday morning, five days since the bridge had fallen. She knew he could sometimes become so engrossed in his work that it was difficult to get him to answer even the simplest question. But this was different. His expression was one not so much of concentration as of distance, as it had been since he returned home from Brindee the previous night.

Darrs leaned down to pet the dog, which had followed his wife into the room. "There's a good girl," he said softly.

"Stewart," Mrs. Darrs said once more, this time in a slightly stronger tone.

Darrs glanced up, though he continued to pet the dog. "Forgive me, my dear. As you can imagine, I'm a bit preoccupied."

"Even so, you have to eat."

"There's no reason to concern yourself. I'm just not very hungry."

"But you have to eat, if only to keep up your strength."

Darrs sat up straight in his chair. "Very well, then. A cup of tea."

"A cup of tea. Is that all?"

"Please, my dear. Mr. Stevens will be here this afternoon, and I have quite a lot to get through before he arrives."

"All right, then, a cup of tea. But you must promise me you'll eat dinner."

Darrs watched her leave and for several moments continued to gaze at the door, which she'd closed behind her. Eventually, however, he turned back to the plans on his desk, which were for the inverted spans. When first told the bridge was down, he didn't know what to think. He thought perhaps a ship had collided with one of the supports in the storm. Even when he first saw the bridge, he couldn't imagine what had happened. It wasn't until two days later, reading the accounts of eyewitnesses in the newspaper, that he understood.

There were several people who had seen the train on the bridge, including the sailor on watch aboard the *Apollo*, one of the gunboats stationed at the naval base to the west of the bridge. He actually saw the train enter the inverted spans. He also saw what looked to be two luminous columns rising directly from the firth to a height of one or two hundred feet. They were headed straight for the bridge moments before it fell, but just as they reached it, a blast of wind forced the sailor to look away. When he turned back, the lights of the train were gone.

Darrs had heard of waterspouts, tornado-like formations of spray, but rarely so tall, and never on that part of the firth. Still, if nothing else, they were a testament to the strength of the storm, and given the timing, he assumed they must somehow have been involved. Like all newer rail bridges, the Fee was equipped with safety rails to prevent trains from jumping the tracks and going over the side or crashing into the bridgework. If the train had been upended by a waterspout, however, it might very well have collided with the side of the bridge, something for which Darrs had made no provision. The very opposite was true.

Unlike the rest of the bridge's spans, each of which was supported individually, the inverted spans were bolted together in three groups, two of four and one of five. It was an added precaution he'd implemented following his discussions with Sir George Larsen, the Royal Astronomer. The idea was to spread the force over an even greater area, but it meant that if one of the spans fell, it would bring down that entire section, and possibly the other two as well. Darrs shuddered at the thought of the impact radiating through the structure.

Even now, bodies continued to wash up all along the firth. The British Northern was paying a reward of five pounds apiece for their return, which had people combing the banks on both shores. As of the previous day, forty-seven had been recovered. Including the crew, it was now estimated there had been seventy to seventy-five people on the train, which was welcome news compared to the 300 originally reported. Still, for Brindee and Feeport, it was a disaster of the highest order as there was hardly a person on either side of the firth who didn't have a friend or relative on the train.

Chapter 45

Charles was in Scotland for the New Year, but there was little celebration along the Fee, and the damage from the storm was still apparent when Farlow arrived five days later. The streets of Brindee and Feeport had been strewn with debris—uprooted trees, shutters, chimney pots—and the remains could be seen piled in heaps along the side of the road as the two men headed from the ferry terminal to the hotel, where Charles had booked rooms.

Charles had been sending wires to London on a daily basis, and Farlow's first question had to do with the two luminous columns reported by the sailor who had been on watch aboard the *Apollo*.

"Has anyone yet corroborated the sailor's account?" Farlow asked.

"He was the only person to the west of the bridge who saw anything," Charles said. "Those to east saw nothing but a flash and the lights of the train as it fell into the water."

"What do you make of it?"

"There's no question the sailor had the best view of those who've come forward so far. There must have been something. At the very least, it would attest to the strength of the storm."

"What did he say, 100 to 200 feet high?" Farlow asked.

Charles nodded. "He also saw the train enter the inverted spans."

"Which makes me wonder why nothing was done to close the bridge to traffic when the wind was so strong. There are already battle lines being drawn. Given that the bridge was inspected by the Board of Trade less than fourteen months ago, opponents of the prime minister are pointing to this as a complete failure on the part of the government."

"Out of all proportion to its possible necessities," Charles said, quoting a line he had seen repeated in the paper dozens of times since Monday. It was how the inspector described the bridge at the time of its completion.

"Yes," Farlow said, grimacing. "It's a phrase that's coming back to haunt them, as are Sir Stewart's comments at the time."

Farlow referred to another quote the papers had been running in the days since the accident: "The purpose of having the Board of Trade inspect the work is to make the security of the public an absolute certainty, as far as design, material, and execution are concerned."

The statement seemed to underscore the extent to which the board had failed in its responsibility, and from what Farlow knew, the government was indeed going to come in for severe criticism.

"After you left on Monday, I met with William Roland, chief inspector of railways and the third member of the Court of Inquiry, in addition to Hathaway, the wreck commissioner. Roland seemed very uneasy, and I didn't know the reason, but we met again before I left for Scotland, and it became clear. He has a letter from Sir Stewart, sent prior to starting construction. Sir Stewart wrote specifically to inquire about the wind, and Roland was unequivocal in his reply. 'We do not take wind pressure into account with fixed spans of the type you propose.' It's sure to come out during the proceedings, but while Roland is worried for himself, I'm more concerned about what it's going to do to the entire profession," Farlow said.

"How do you mean?"

"What was Roland's response based on?" Farlow responded sternly. "As we both know, current tables estimate the highest wind pressures at twelve to fifteen pounds per square foot. We discussed it at length in terms of the Forth. Since the accident, some people are suggesting the wind the night of the storm might have exceeded forty or even fifty pounds per square foot. We'll look like fools, basing our calculations on figures that don't mean a thing. Hathaway doesn't yet know about the correspondence between Roland and Sir Stewart," Farlow said. "He should be meeting us at the hotel, after which I want to go out on the bridge. From what I could see on the ferry crossing, what's standing looks solid enough."

"I'm sure you noted the spans."

"Are the connections bolted or riveted?" Farlow asked.

"Riveted, with double redundancy on the tie plates," Charles replied.

Farlow nodded in response. Charles was referring to the fact that the bridge's spans looked nearly identical to the ones Farlow had designed for the approaches to the Forth, and Farlow had taken note.

"Already the talk is about the supports," Charles added.

"Cast iron," Farlow said disapprovingly. "I was never an advocate. I've always thought it suspect. The Americans have stopped using it, and after this, I'm sure we will, too."

Charles knew that in speaking of the Americans, Farlow was thinking of the *Ashtabula*, a bridge that had gone down in the United States three years before. When it fell, the *Ashtabula* was also carrying a train. The bridge was also partially built of cast iron, though in that case the cast iron had been used in the span itself. British engineers had stopped using cast iron in spans the previous decade, restricting it to the supports, as Darrs had used it on the Fee. Since the *Ashtabula* disaster, however, the Americans had not simply restricted it to the supports; they'd outlawed its use in railroad bridges altogether.

Chapter 46

Richard Hathaway, the wreck commissioner, wanted to be thorough, and the Court of Inquiry, which convened for the first time in the Brindee Council Hall the Saturday following the accident, began by hearing testimony from just about anyone wanting to give it. For the most part, this involved family members of people lost on the train, who had little to say about the accident itself. One witness, a man from a town miles away, testified he'd had a vision of the bridge going down as it was happening.

Whatever the court's conclusions, it was clear it was going to be weeks, even months, before anything was known for sure. For Taylor and the railroad, the issue was simply to determine what should be done at that moment. To keep the line operational, Taylor had given orders to draw up a schedule based on the one in place before the bridge opened, but they'd already dismantled the adjustable ramps and moved the Fee's train ferry down to the Forth to help with the Edinburgh traffic. For the moment, they could only transport people. They had no freight capabilities whatsoever. The only thing Taylor was certain of was that the bridge would have to be rebuilt, and he took some comfort in the fact that, in spite of tragedy, many of the stories in the newspapers seemed to agree. In the short time it had been up, the vast majority of the people in both Brindee and Feeport had grown extremely fond of their bridge and wanted its return as much as Taylor did.

Two weeks after the accident, however, events took a dramatic turn.

"Who is this MacVincent, anyway?" Taylor demanded, looking across his desk at Robert Kendall, the railroad's treasurer.

"He's an engineer from Glasgow."

"That much I know. I saw it in the paper," Taylor said. "I meant, who is he that he should be so interested in the bridge?"

"From what I've been able to find, he's a friend and colleague of one of the engineers whose proposal for the Forth was rejected."

"What has that to do with anything?" Taylor asked.

"It was actually the Forth that was the focus of his address," Kendall replied. "He believed his friend's design superior to that of Sir Stewart and was simply using the Fee for introductory purposes."

"Given that the Fee was also designed by Sir Stewart," Taylor said, finishing Kendall's thought. "This changes everything,"

Kendall made a face. "I don't see how."

"As soon as people realize his intentions, they'll know they can't believe everything he says. Bolts turned to rust," the chairman sneered. "It's preposterous. The bridge was just painted. I doubt this MacVincent has even been to Brindee. He's simply looking to make a name for himself at our expense."

Kendall appeared less than convinced. "It's not simply rusted bolts he talked about. He also mentioned broken lugs and flanges on the main columns."

It was Monday morning. The previous Friday evening, a man named John MacVincent had given a talk before the Glasgow Institute of Engineers and Shipbuilders, during which he'd blamed the bridge's collapse not on the storm but on the gross negligence of those who'd built and maintained it. It was not the sort of thing generally reported in the regular press, but under the circumstances, it made for sensational copy, and after appearing in the Glasgow papers over the weekend, the story was picked up across the country.

"If what he says is true, the bridge never would have passed inspection." Taylor said.

"The inspection was more than a year ago. Since then, twenty-five to thirty trains a day have crossed the bridge."

Kendall's expression had hardened. Taylor even sensed something accusatory. Six months before, the board had dismissed half the bridge staff and reduced the number of inspections. In addition, ever since the accident, there had been murmurings about the speed of the trains, and reading the account of MacVincent's address, Taylor couldn't help but recall a meeting in which Darrs's assistant called into question the quality of the iron being used in the supports. It had taken place several years before, but Taylor distinctly remembered questions about the lugs and flanges.

Still, the savings from the dismissal of the inspection staff was, if not at Kendall's direct urging, in response to his desire to reduce costs. He had nothing to be accusatory about, but before Taylor could say anything, Kendall went on.

"I hope as much as you do that what this MacVincent says isn't true. But it almost doesn't matter. The damage is done. The Board of Trade is under as much pressure over this as we are, which means they are going to have men crawling over the bridge. They're bound to find faults, and even if they're not the sort that would have brought it down, we're bound to be held liable."

Again, Taylor did not immediately respond. A moment before he'd been ready to answer the treasurer with an attack of his own, but what Kendall said now was true. It almost didn't matter. The damage was already done.

There was a knock at the door.

"What is it?" Taylor asked as his secretary stuck his head into the room.

"Excuse me, sir, but there's another reporter downstairs. This one is from the *Times of London* so I thought you might want to speak to him."

"Well, I don't. Tell him what I had you tell the others. Given the Board of Trade's approval, the railroad never had any reason to doubt the integrity of the bridge, either in its workmanship or its design."

Chapter 47

Charles sat in the hotel lobby, waiting for Farlow. After reading the news of MacVincent's address, Hathaway canceled testimony for the day and spent the morning meeting with Farlow and Roland. For his part, Charles had spent the morning at the harbor. He'd already spoken with the stationmaster and rail crews about the speed of the trains, and had gone down to the waterfront to speak with the harbormaster and ferry crews as well.

It was shortly after noon when Farlow arrived, and he and Charles went into the hotel dining room, where Farlow promptly ordered a drink, gesturing for the waiter to bring one for Charles as well.

"Hathaway actually wants to make MacVincent an adviser to the court."

"Can he even do that?" Charles asked.

"He can do as he likes. The Board of Trade has given him free rein," Farlow replied scornfully.

"Nevertheless, MacVincent is hardly an objective party. I'm sure Colonel Roland . . ." Charles started to say, but Farlow cut him off.

"Roland told Hathaway about his correspondence with Sir Stewart and offered to disqualify himself, but Hathaway wouldn't hear of it.

He doesn't want to call more attention to the board, thinking he's found a way to absolve it altogether."

"How would this absolve the board? They still performed the inspection," Charles said, as the waiter returned with their drinks.

Farlow thanked the man with a nod and took a long sip of his drink before answering.

"The board won't be held responsible for shortcomings deliberately hidden from its view," he said, looking directly at Charles. "That's Hathaway's stance and, given public opinion, the railroads make an easy target. When I left him, he was on his way to wire London to engage Finch & Stanton to perform an independent evaluation of the bridge."

"Well, the bridge did fall," Charles said, after taking a sip of his drink.

"I have no problem with his bringing in Stanton," Farlow replied forcefully. "What I have a problem with is his turning this into a circus. He's going to adjourn the inquest while the inspection is being performed. They'll still be taking testimony, but the hearings won't resume until April, at which point Hathaway plans to hold them in Parliament itself."

"I went down to the harbor this morning," Charles said after a pause.

"Did you speak to the harbormaster?" Farlow asked.

"He said the northbound shuttles would often reach thirty-five or forty miles per hour. It could even have been faster, but he didn't know that kind of speed. He is a sailor."

Farlow huffed a laugh. "And the wagering?"

"I did not find anyone who saw significant sums being exchanged. There were definitely wagers being made, but it was for drinks at the pub."

"Between the drivers and the ferry captains?" Farlow asked.

"No one would say for sure, but I also heard from a dockhand there had been wagering among the ferry captains before the bridge ever opened."

Farlow finished his drink and gestured for another. "Was that before or after you spoke with the harbormaster?"

"Before," Charles said. "The harbormaster knew nothing about wagering."

"Even if he did, he wouldn't admit to it" Farlow said.

"But he did say he'd heard talk of someone who timed the trains and actually kept records."

Farlow's eyes widened.

"If the speed limit was being ignored, that goes straight to the railroad," Charles said.

"And the board, too," Farlow replied, "if it's a question of enforcement. Hathaway didn't like it when I said that. He also didn't like it when I told him that, from an engineering standpoint, all that was going to change from that point going forward was that no one was going to use cast iron in a railroad bridge, or likely any bridge, ever again."

"As you've said, the Americans have already stopped using it," Charles agreed.

"Still, as far as Hathaway is concerned, if that's the case, it simply adds to the government's culpability."

"In allowing it at all."

Farlow nodded, reaching for his second drink.

Charles looked at Farlow, though he did not say anything. By the time Charles left for Birmingham, he was already thinking in terms of wrought iron and steel. Cast iron never entered his thoughts, except perhaps for decorative purposes. Farlow's experience was much different. It was only during the last decade that cast iron had been restricted to use in supports. Prior to that, Brunel, Stephenson, and almost every engineer in the world were looking for a way to replace stone and brick with cast iron. Indeed, thinking about it, Charles suddenly found it quite telling that Farlow's initial tunnel for the London Underground was built entirely of brick. Given the timing, he could easily have used some combination of of wrought and cast iron.

Chapter 48

Stanton arrived from London the next afternoon, and Farlow was there with Hathaway to meet him. Farlow made it clear that in matters having strictly to do with engineering, he, Farlow, was to have equal access to anything Stanton might discover in the course of his work. Stanton agreed, and to ensure it, Farlow offered Charles's assistance. Farlow, returned to London the following day but was kept informed by Charles, who sent daily telegrams.

Stanton began by dragging the riverbed. The cast-iron towers had literally gone to pieces. The bed of the Fee was strewn with beams, bracing bars, and thousands of nuts and bolts, all of which were intact, except for the beams; though many of them were also relatively whole, a substantial portion had shattered. MacVincent was plainly exaggerating when he spoke of rust, but just looking at some of the remnants, Charles could see anomalies. In some cases, the cement cores had not been properly aligned. The iron was thicker on one side than the other, and in some instances the difference was half an inch or more.

Within a few days, Stanton had several tons of ironwork piled on a wharf in the Brindee harbor, which is where Charles was, looking over a collection of pieces Stanton had set aside for closer inspection, when a steamer arrived, towing a pair of enormous pontoons. They were from Queensferry. Darrs had designed them to support a floating construction platform for the new bridge on the Forth, but he'd given orders for them to be brought to the Fee.

Stanton's dredging work was strictly concerned with the supports. The spans, however, had to be raised as well. Lying where they did, they blocked the main shipping channel, and as chief engineer, Darrs was the one charged with raising them. It was something he intended to do in the same way he'd originally launched them, using the tides, but first the spans had to be separated. Bolted together as they were, they were too heavy. The lower portion of the spans was also now buried beneath two to three feet of sediment, and Darrs had procured a supply of dynamite for the job of uncovering them.

Dynamite was a closely regulated substance, and Darrs made sure to go through the proper channels, but when Hathaway got word of it, he immediately went to the Brindee City Council to block its use, attacking Sir Stewart and the British Northern as criminals who, having murdered seventy-five people, were now looking to destroy the evidence.

Once more the bridge made headlines across the country, and Charles was in the council chamber the next morning when Darrs appeared to challenge the charges in person. Darrs began by explaining that his first thought had been to unbolt the fallen spans where they lay, with the hope of possibly reusing them. Given the currents, however, and knowing the spans were already buried beneath several feet of sediment, he was also aware such a plan could take months to complete, if it could be done at all. At the same time, the fallen spans formed a damn in the middle of the firth, and there was considerable desire on the part of shipping concerns to have a route open as soon as possible. It was for that reason alone that Darrs had secured the dynamite, as it was clearly the most expeditious course.

Darrs was so straightforward in his explanation that it was difficult to see him as a criminal; Charles and Stanton had themselves talked about the need for dynamite. For a moment, the packed council chamber was silent.

"Most expeditious for someone looking to destroy evidence of his guilt!"

It was Hathaway who broke the silence, but once broken, others in the audience joined in—the victims' relatives and friends, who continued to follow events on a daily basis.

"At this point, can we really trust the railroad to say what can and cannot be done? Can we really trust the railroad for anything at all?"

For many in the audience, it was no longer grief they felt, but anger. Darrs had no illusions about his role in the matter, but the ferocity of jeers caused him to start. Only the year before, he'd received the Freedom of the Burgh award in this very room, but when he turned to face his accusers, there was only fury.

The council chairman silenced the room with his gavel. "I am inclined to agree with Mr. Hathaway. The use of dynamite will be forbidden until the council has had a chance to properly review the matter," he declared sternly.

The crowd roared its approval, and for a moment Darrs seemed to falter on his feet, though he steadied himself. He'd brought a set of drawings showing the position of the fallen spans and the depth of the sediment at various points. He delivered these to the council secretary and then left the chamber without another word, his eyes focused forward, as those in the audience continued to hiss taunts and slurs as he made his way up the aisle.

Charles watched Darrs leave and then stood up to follow. He wanted to get back to the hotel to wire Farlow, and he moved quickly. In fact, though Charles left the council chamber after Darrs, he ended up directly behind him in the hallway outside the council chamber. Darrs moved slowly, but it would have been awkward to pass, so Charles simply followed, saying nothing. The two men were so close, however, that Charles found himself holding the door for Darrs on the way out of the building, and Darrs turned to thank him.

Darrs had seen Charles at the proceedings, but there was something else familiar about him.

People continued to exit the building behind them, and Charles used his arm to guide Darrs from the entrance.

"Have we met?" Darrs asked.

"My name is Charles Jenkins. I'm an engineer with Denney & Farlow."

"Yes, Benjamin Farlow, with the court. But I feel as if we've spoken before," Darrs said.

"Many years ago," Charles replied. "I submitted plans for the Fee."

"The steel cantilevers," Darrs said, remembering. "You were the one with the painting."

"That's right," Charles said.

"The cantilever plan for Queensferry—I did not make the connection."

"Yes, that was mine as well. The main spans anyway. Mr. Farlow was responsible for the approaches—the spans of which are extremely similar to yours here."

Darrs nodded. "Though, if I remember correctly, your supports for the Forth were masonry."

"As you intended here. All the supports were to be of brick, were they not?"

Again Darrs nodded, though his focus was elsewhere. "The last thing I want to do is destroy the spans," he said. "From what's been found by the divers, they appear fairly intact."

Charles nodded. "You can see the upper portion at low tide. They do appear mostly whole."

Darrs looked at Charles. "It will be impossible to salvage them now, but they have to be moved. Parliament has contacted the British Northern directly, something both the council chairman and Mr. Hathaway must know. Pythe and the other towns upstream have been clamoring to clear the channel for shipping."

"Parliament? Really," Charles said. "That I did not know."

"Yes," Darrs replied.

Darrs spoke with conviction and did not act as if he were looking to cover anything up, certainly not in this regard. Still, though Darrs worked to conceal it, Charles could see in Darrs's eyes that he was hurt by the charges.

They were just outside the door, on the step to the Brindee City Hall, and Charles asked Darrs where he was headed. Darrs was on his way to the British Northern's ferry terminal. He wanted to wire Chairman Taylor about the council's ruling, and as Charles's hotel was also in the direction of the harbor, they set off together.

Darrs continued to move slowly and Charles kept pace at his side. Charles wanted to say something encouraging but couldn't think of anything meaningful. They walked in silence, and when they reached his hotel, Charles simply took his leave, while Darrs continued on to the ferry terminal. There was a vision Darrs had been having. He'd wake to it from his sleep, picturing the passengers on the train as it plunged through the darkness. Seeing the bridge only made it worse, and when he reached the terminal, he went inside, avoiding any look in that direction.

Chapter 49

Farlow was furious when he received Charles's telegram. It was clear that the spans had nothing to do with the bridge falling. Hathaway was simply looking to cause more trouble, and Farlow immediately wired Stanton. Stanton, however, while he agreed about the spans, did not want to run afoul of Hathaway or the Board of Trade. He'd been hired to perform an independent evaluation and was not going to take any public stance until the investigation was finished.

Charles and Farlow exchanged numerous telegrams that day, and when Charles checked his messages before going to bed, there was a wire not only from London but also one from Edinburgh. It was from Darrs, who'd returned home after leaving Charles. He wanted to know whether Charles had made any specific calculations with regard to the wind when producing his plans for the Fee.

Charles wired London with the information the next morning. Given Farlow's position with the court, Charles did not want to contact Darrs without Farlow's approval, but under the circumstances, Farlow was more than happy to have Charles meet with Darrs. Charles himself was not a member of the court, nor was it he who'd initiated the contact. Indeed, Farlow very much wanted to know what Darrs had to say, and by ten o'clock that morning, Charles was boarding a ferry at the British Northern's Brindee terminal, bound for Edinburgh.

It was a cold winter day, but the sun was bright, and Charles stood outside for some time, leaning against the rail. It was high tide. There was no site of the fallen spans or really much wreckage at all. If one didn't know the circumstances, one could have thought the bridge was still under construction. Charles imagined it complete, one continuous band stretching between the shores. There was no question it was a bare-bones affair, but Charles had no doubt he would not be there now if all the spans had run at the same height under the track, as Darrs initially intended.

Charles thought of the broken beams piled on the wharf in the Brindee harbor. The jagged ends were sharp, and he'd cut himself several times handling pieces. Wrought iron and steel didn't break that way. When a beam failed, it bent, generally near the middle. When the beams on the Fee failed, it was the flanges and lugs at the end that gave way, shattering like glass.

It was nearing 10:30 a.m. when the ferry docked in Feeport and the gangway was lowered over the side. Though not nearly as crowded as during the morning and evening rush, the small ship was fairly full, and Charles got caught behind a woman with a baby carriage, who had to be helped down the gangway by two crew members. He squeezed by somewhat discourteously at the first chance and went inside the terminal to check the schedule. There was still very little coordination between the ferries and the trains, and Charles had to wait close to an hour for the next southbound train to Edinburgh.

It was roughly fifty miles between the Fee and the Forth, and the railroad followed a meandering course along the coast, which soon brought the train to St. Andrews, where Charles glanced out the window. Charles knew nothing of golf but had heard from several conductors that, since the bridge had opened, they'd taken to calling the Sunday morning train from Aberdeen the "St. Andrews Express," because of all the golfers with their bags of clubs. Spring was coming, and they were apparently quite put out over the disruption to their weekly outings.

From St. Andrews, it was another hour, with stops, before the train reached Grailton, the town on the north shore of the Forth, across from Edinburgh. There the train was loaded onto a ferry by means of one of Darrs's floating bridges. Charles had seen them before, back when submitting plans for the Fee and again when he'd first traveled to Brindee after the accident. They were likely thirty years old at this point and looked somewhat antiquated. The huge timber beams were gray with weather and age, while the massive iron bolts holding them together were covered in a coating of brown rust. Charles remembered Darrs himself speaking of replacing them, and that was nearly ten years before.

At the same time, the ferry was not large enough to carry the locomotive. The engine had to be uncoupled and removed, after which the coaches were attached to a steam winch that pulled them onto the deck. It was hardly an effortless process, but looking out the window at the overlapping leaves of the ramp, Charles was impressed by the design. There were iron rollers inset at the end of each leaf to allow for the rising and falling of the tides. Though common enough in harbor works, keeping the rail connections between the leaves required considerable subtlety, as did the connection with the ferry itself.

The ramp led to a large drawbridge that, when lowered, locked to the rear of the ferry. It was here that the enormous timbers stood, positioned triangularly on either side with another massive beam connecting them overhead. Charles glanced at them through the window of the coach. There was no question they looked old, but again Charles thought of the pieces of broken cast iron piled on the wharf in Brindee. Just as he had no doubt the bridge would still be standing if all the spans had been underneath the track, he also had no doubt it would still be standing if all the supports had been built of brick like the first fifteen on the south end of the bridge. Now, though, he was thinking the bridge would likely have been better if the supports had been built of wood. Wood bent and flexed; it did not shatter like cast iron.

It was nearing three o'clock when Charles finally reached the Edinburgh terminal, where he hired a cab to take him to Darrs's office, which turned out to be only a few blocks from the harbor. Had he known, he would have walked, though he noticed that it had gotten rather cold.

The building looked as if it were a private residence. There were three mailboxes, but it was only the one for Darrs & Associates that bore the name of a firm. It also bore the number three. Charles went inside and climbed the stairs to the third floor, where he rang the bell.

He was met at the door by two people—the company receptionist and Stevens, who introduced himself as Sir Stewart's chief assistant and resident engineer of the Fee Bridge. It was a fairly large room, with a bank of windows facing the Forth, and there was also a third man at one of three drafting tables arranged along the windows.

"Mr. Jenkins, thank you so much for coming," Stevens said. "I must apologize. Sir Stewart was called away about an hour ago, but he assured me he would be back as soon as possible. I know he is anxious to speak with you."

"That's quite all right," Charles said, as the receptionist, a young man, helped Charles with his coat. He nodded his thanks and turned back to Stevens. "In his wire, Sir Stewart asked about the wind."

"Yes," Stevens replied. "There are actually two questions he is interested in. The first has to do with your own plans for the Fee. But he's also very interested in determining the strength of the wind the night of the accident. Since Mr. MacVincent's made his accusations, there have been people claiming it was barely a gale. Nothing close to one of the worst storms in twenty years, as first reported."

Charles nodded. "I've heard similar talk. What do you think? Where were you that night?"

"Here in Edinburgh," Stevens replied, "and it was quite a storm. Next morning, the streets were strewn with chimney pots and branches."

"Did you lose any trees?"

Stevens did not immediately respond. He did not know the answer, though he thought it a meaningful question.

"According to reports, a number of large trees went down in both Feeport and Brindee," Charles added.

"I have not inquired, but I will," Stevens replied.

"What about the waterspouts reported by the sailor? From what I've heard, that was certainly an unusual event," Charles said.

"They are known to occur, but generally downstream, where the firth opens to the sea. The same is true here on the Forth."

"Given their height, they could have played a role."

"That is Sir Stewart's belief. He is convinced the bridge would not have fallen if not for the train. By my calculations, the bridge should have been able to withstand at least thirty pounds of pressure per square foot, something unlikely even in the worst storm. But if the train was involved, if it was blown from the rails into the side of the bridge, the force could have been two or three times that."

"Where does the thirty pounds per square foot come from?" Charles asked.

Stevens led Charles across the room to the drafting table closest to the door leading to Darrs's private office. There was a set of linens opened on the table, and Stevens turned to a sheet showing one of the supports for the inverted spans.

"The bearing load for the beams in the supports was nearly sixty-five tons. In terms of dead weight, they should have been more than capable of withstanding thirty pounds per square foot of lateral force. For the bridge to fall, that figure had to be exceeded."

Charles looked down at the plans on which there were several calculations scribbled in black ink. "I can see you've been going over the figures."

Stevens sighed. "When we made the change to iron, I did dozens of calculations. Sir Stewart wanted to be able to think of the bridge just as if it stood on brick. He had me assure him the new supports would be as strong or stronger than the ones they replaced in every way. I thought they would be."

"The calculations you speak of, does that include the extra bracing used to bolt the spans together?"

Stevens shook his head. "The additional bracing was an added precaution. It would have increased the figure, but I did not include it in my calculations."

"Not imagining the possibility of a train colliding with the side of the bridge," Charles said.

Stevens nodded and lowered his eyes. Like Darrs, Stevens did not need to be reminded of what was already on his mind, and Charles thought to change the subject.

"What do you know of burned-on lugs and flanges?" he asked.

"You're referring to Mr. MacVincent's charges about the connection points?" Stevens asked, looking up.

Charles nodded.

"I know Sir Stewart gave Mr. Pike explicit orders not to use any beams with burned-on lugs or flanges in the supports for the inverted spans."

"Mr. Pike, the contractor?" Charles asked.

Stevens nodded.

"It's mainly been a gathering process to this point, but given MacVincent's charges, we've been on the lookout for burned-on lugs and flanges," Charles said.

"And?" Stevens asked.

"There is no evidence of it. And no evidence of rust," Charles said, as the door opened and Darrs stepped in.

"Mr. Jenkins, thank you for coming. I see you've met Mr. Stevens."

The secretary helped Darrs with his coat, after which Darrs crossed to shake hands with Charles.

"Come, let's go into my office," he said, gesturing to the nearby door.

Stevens gathered the linens from his drafting table and followed Charles and Darrs into the other room, where Darrs made his way around the desk to his chair. Charles watched Darrs as he took a deep breath. He could see Darrs had been hurrying to get back to the office and was still a bit winded.

"I apologize for keeping you."

"That's quite all right, sir." Charles said.

"I also know your relationship with Mr. Farlow, and I can assure you that I am not hoping to acquire any special influence with the court. My interest is in establishing an estimate for the force of the wind the night of the accident. I did not think of it until after we parted, but you've designed bridges for both the Fee and Forth, as have I. You know the issues involved."

"When we were speaking before you arrived," Stevens said, "Mr. Jenkins mentioned the fact that trees were reported down in both Feeport and Brindee the night of the accident."

Darrs looked at Charles, who nodded in concurrence.

Like Stevens, Darrs found the information significant, though not simply as an indicator of the wind.

"Most of the supports broke above the bases, but in two instances, several tiers of masonry were torn out as well," he said.

"The footings came out whole," Charles said. "I saw that."

The footings were cast-iron plates set beneath two courses of large capping stones. Thinking in terms of dead weight, as Darrs had when designing them, they were strictly for positioning purposes. As it now occurred to him, they were also the roots for eighty feet of trunk.

"Sir," Charles said, "when we were speaking yesterday, I mentioned the similarity between your spans on the Fee and the approach spans Mr. Farlow and I designed for the Forth."

Darrs nodded. "Yes, but as I said, your approaches on the Forth had masonry supports."

"That is my question. I know about the issues with the original survey and that weight became a concern. I'm sure Mr. Farlow and I went over many of the same questions with regard to the Forth, the bed of which, though deeper down, is of similar composition to the Fee."

"Indeed," Darrs replied. "Five years before I ever started work on the Fee, I was engaged to conduct a survey of the Forth as part of a study for a bridge. Eventually, the railroad opted for my ferry system, but for a time they were considering a permanent crossing, and I made a number of tests involving a large cast-iron cylinder, similar in size to the ones we used on the Fee. The cylinder was lowered to the riverbed and then gradually filled with scrap iron and lead. At the end of three months, it was exerting a force of more than five tons per square foot without any measurable sinkage."

"Mr. Farlow and I used five tons as well, but, even so, we settled on masonry. The difference seemed negligible, assuming the supports were going to be stone or brick beneath the water."

Charles was looking at Darrs, but it was Stevens who responded.

"Mr. Jenkins, Sir Stewart is unlikely to say anything himself, but the truth is, my concerns are what led to the change."

Charles turned to Stevens, but before he could say anything more, Darrs intervened.

"Mr. Stevens, that is not the case."

"It is," Stevens replied, looking at Darrs. "I was the one who said we shouldn't take any chance of the supports sinking." He turned back to Charles. "There being so many of them.

"Mr. Stevens, I appreciate your feelings, but your concerns alone did not lead to the change." Darrs turned to Charles. "There were a number of factors. The initial choice of brick was strictly for maintenance purposes; I didn't want to paint the supports every few years. But there is no question that metal supports are faster to construct. At that point, the project was already substantially behind schedule, and when I mentioned the possibility to Mr. de Forge, he jumped at the opportunity, thinking he could save not only time but also money by casting the beams himself on site."

"Mr. de Forge?" Charles questioned.

"The original contractor," Stevens replied.

"I thought Hodges & Pike was the contractor," Charles said.

"Mr. de Forge died two years into the project," Darrs said. "He had been sick for some time, and the financial strain of the delays were too much for him."

Charles had heard the name Hodges & Pike numerous times over the past two months, but it was the first he was hearing of de Forge. "That's when Hodges & Pike took over," he said.

Darrs nodded. "Yes. And like de Forge before him, when Mr. Pike came on, he wanted the chance to cast the beams himself. I don't imagine you are familiar with it, but Mr. Pike was responsible for building the Birkendale viaduct."

Charles shook his head.

"Sixteen spans—wrought-iron trusses on cast-iron supports," Darrs said. "The project went extremely well, and we thought to repeat our success. Clearly, we have not had the same results, but by no means should Mr. Stevens assume the blame for what happened."

"I'm sure you are aware there have been questions as to the quality of the iron," Charles said. "I've looked at some of the pieces and, in certain instances, there are significant flaws."

Darrs lowered his eyes before again looking at Charles. "I have heard. The molders never cared for the iron Pike was sending them. They complained of its brittleness under the drill, preferring their own Scottish iron. Nevertheless, as you are no doubt aware from the work of Stephenson and others, there are many fine bridges constructed of Clevelandham iron."

"But that was the reason you gave the order not to use any burned-on lugs or flanges?"

Again Darrs nodded.

"What is Mr. Pike's response to all this? I assume you've spoken with him," Charles said.

"Mr. Pike and I have not spoken in more than a year."

Charles waited, expecting Darrs to say something more, but it was Stevens who spoke next. "Hodges & Pike declared bankruptcy within months of the bridge opening."

Chapter 50

Charles spent the rest of the day with Darrs, who invited him to stay the night. Charles declined and stayed at a nearby hotel, but Darrs insisted on walking with him when Charles left the office late that afternoon, and they ended up dining together at the hotel. Although no mathematician himself, Darrs was familiar with the type of calculations then being done, and over dinner he discussed with Charles ways to determine the strength of the wind the night of the accident.

It was something Charles had already been working on in his mind, and he was happy to help. At the same time, they were not the only ones speaking of Pike. When Charles wired London the next morning, Farlow immediately wired back. The court prosecutor was interviewing Pike the following day, and Farlow wanted Charles there as well. So instead of returning to Brindee, Charles headed south to Clevelandham, where he met James Turner, the man Hathaway had appointed as chief prosecutor for the court.

Pike was now doing business in a shedlike structure not far from the city's London & North Eastern rail yard. The sign read Clevelandham Iron and Engine Works, and it was there Turner and Charles went to interview Pike. When they entered, Pike was standing before the forge; because he was expecting them, he was quick to approach when he saw them. He wore a leather apron, which he removed before shaking hands.

"Welcome, gentleman. Welcome."

Pike hung his apron on a hook near the door and gestured for the others to do the same with their coats before leading them to the wall farthest from the forge, where there were two old desks and several chairs. Pike gestured to the chairs and took a seat himself at one of the desks.

Turner began by asking about Hodges & Pike and the company's bankruptcy. His tone was sympathetic, and it was clear from his responses that Pike did not seem to think that he himself was in any direct danger from the court. Contrary to what was being written, he contended the iron that went into the bridge was of the "best" quality. He also corroborated the fact that Darrs had given orders not to use any beams with burned-on connection points in the supports for the high spans, and Pike complied. Pike pointed to the Board of Trade's inspection of the bridge prior to its opening. He blamed any flaws discovered since the accident on the speed of the trains and the poor maintenance on the part of the railroad.

Upon leaving, Turner said he was very glad to have spoken with Pike. "Our conversation has removed many clouds of suspicion from my mind." It was a comment that surprised Charles, especially given the way Pike emphasized the word "best." As Charles had discussed with Turner on the way to the interview, after arriving in Clevelandham the previous day, he'd spent several hours visiting some of the city's supply houses. Like Pike's shop, they were clustered around the London & North Eastern rail yard, and in more than one case, the iron for sale came in three grades: Best, Best Best, and Best

Best Best. For his part, Charles was extremely suspicious, and his suspicions only increased when he returned to Brindee.

Stanton had begun to examine the broken parts in detail. It was true they had not found any burned-on lugs or flanges, but Stanton discovered that a good number of the bolt holes were misshapen. They were smaller on one end than the other, and though not immediately apparent to the naked eye, it was instantly apparent when he went to reassemble the parts. There were two different size bolts, one that fit and one that didn't, something Charles immediately tied to Darrs's order not to use any burned-on connection points. Rather than take the chance of breaking them with a drill, Pike simply used smaller bolts.

Moreover, given the questions about the iron's quality, Stanton had literally put it to the test, stressing it to the point of failure. As Darrs's assistant had said to Charles, the cast iron used in the beams should have been capable of sustaining close to sixty-five tons of force, the lugs and flanges included. In most cases they were, but several of the connection points broke at about forty-five to fifty tons, and a few broke at only twenty-two tons of force, something for which neither Stanton nor Charles had an explanation. The misshapen bolts holes and ill-fitting bolts were a significant issue; it meant that even when fully tightened, the beams could still shift back and forth, but it should have had nothing to do with the strength of the metal itself.

Chapter 51

"Father, have you thought about it? May I go with you when you return to Scotland? I'm a big girl now. I won't be any trouble."

Charles looked at his daughter, Anne, who sat between Victoria and him in a hansom cab.

Until he returned a few days before, Charles had not been home since leaving for Scotland, and it was clear how much Frederick, who was at home with his nurse, had grown in the three months. This, however, was the first time he recognized the difference in his duaghter.

"You are a big girl. I don't think I realized it before, but having been away, I can see you've become quite a grown up lady."

"Then may I go with you? I so want to see the bridge," Anne said.

"You have seen it, in pictures. And I don't think I'll be going back to Scotland just now."

"It must have been awful for the people on the train."

She was looking straight up at Charles, and he looked back, surprised by the maturity of the comment. She was only six.

"I imagine so," he replied.

"I told Mother that if you had built the bridge, it wouldn't have fallen."

"And what did your mother say to that?" Charles asked, glancing at Victoria.

"Mother agreed, of course."

Victoria was gazing out the window, and Charles looked at her, thinking she might turn. Their relationship had actually improved over the past few months. They had been corresponding regularly, and though the letters were mainly about household matters, they were at least cordial. Charles waited several moments for her response, but as Victoria continued to look away, he glanced back at his daughter.

"I appreciate your faith in me—and your mother's, too," he added with some emphasis.

Victoria heard what he said and knew it was meant for her benefit, but she felt no need to respond. Having been gone so long, Charles seemed to think everything should have returned to the way it had been. She did not at all feel the same, especially right then.

They were on their way to the home of Charles's sister and brother-in-law, neither of whom Victoria had seen in nearly two years. The few times Charles had seen them was without her. Nor was Victoria looking to encourage Charles when it came to the purpose of the visit. Their nephew, Oliver, who was the same age as Anne, had been reenacting the fall of the bridge with his toy trains, and though Charles laughed when he'd heard about it, Victoria could see that he was flattered as well—just as he was by the fact that his parents continued to read everything there was to find on the bridge. They, too, would be there, and within the family at least, Charles had become quite the celebrity.

The cab came to a stop and Charles got out. He turned to help Anne, but she quickly climbed down by herself. He held out his hand for Victoria, who took hold of it as she descended to the curb.

Charles paid the driver and they started up the steps to the house, where Anne rang the bell. A moment later the door opened, and they were greeted by most of the family.

"Welcome, welcome," said Arthur, Charles's brother-in-law. "Victoria, it's such a pleasure to see you. It's been some time, and we've missed you. And Anne, what a big girl you've become."

"Arthur, good to see you," Charles said, as the butler helped him with their coats.

"Charles, I must tell you, I have been waiting for this moment ever since we got word you were back in town. You simply must tell us all that you know."

"Arthur, at least let Charles take off his coat. He's only just arrived," Celia said.

Charles glanced at his sister, who was standing with his mother and father, just behind Arthur.

"Uncle Charles, Uncle Charles."

In front of Charles, Oliver charged down the stairs.

"Oliver, you come back here this instant," the child's nanny called after him.

"Ollie, you know you're not supposed to come down the stairs like that," Celia said as he reached the bottom.

"But I want to show Uncle Charles my bridge."

"I heard about your bridge. It's the reason I'm here," Charles replied with great enthusiasm.

"He does a very good job of it," Charles's father added. "Especially the sound of the train plunging into the water."

"That part I could do without," Charles's mother said, giving Charles a hug. "The first time I heard it . . ."

"Mother nearly fell out of her chair," his sister laughed.

"Uncle Charles, you must come and see."

"I want to see, too," Anne said.

"That's a good idea," Celia said. "Ollie, why don't you take Anne upstairs to show her your bridge? The rest of us will come up in a little while."

Oliver was disappointed, but when Anne started up the stairs, he followed, and Charles, who had been watching the children, turned to Arthur.

"I am at your disposal," he said.

Chapter 52

"I'm impressed with much of the work," Farlow said, pausing from his paces to relight his pipe. "Especially the manner in which he documented his findings. I simply don't agree with his conclusions."

Charles sat across the desk from Farlow, holding a copy of Stanton's report on his lap. The report ran more than 400 pages and had been delivered to the Court of Inquiry the previous day. The majority comprised photographs, drawings, and statistical analysis, most of which Charles was privy to and had shared with Farlow prior to publication. The report, however, began with twenty pages of text, in which Stanton provided both an outline of the causes leading to the bridge's collapse and an explanation for its ultimate failure on the night of the storm.

"I don't see how he can cite insufficient bracing as the primary cause for the bridge's collapse," Farlow said.

"I think he was surprised to find there was no interior bracing, as was I, given the height," Charles said. "If for no other reason than redundancy."

"Even at that height, the supports were only insufficiently braced if one knew there were beams that were going to break at twenty-two tons of force. That's putting the cart before the horse," Farlow said.

Charles looked at him, not understanding, and Farlow took his pipe from his mouth.

"Sir Stewart designed the bridge assuming the beams would support sixty-five tons of force. They didn't. In my mind, that makes the primary cause the failure of the beams. Insufficient bracing," Farlow scoffed. "It's absurd. In every instance it was the beam that gave way, not the bracing bar."

What Farlow said was true. Charles had examined the parts, and in many cases there were still pieces of the lugs and flanges attached to the ends of the bracing bars.

Charles leaned forward and placed the report on Farlow's desk. "I disagree with the wording. I would have said insufficient rigidity, but the point is the same, in that the additional bracing would have added rigidity."

"Just properly fitting bolts would have," Farlow countered, "which again goes to the beams and the fact that they were cast iron."

"Pike's not wanting to risk putting a drill to them," Charles said.

"Exactly," Farlow nodded sharply. "And what of Stanton's comments regarding the design of the flanges and lugs? You yourself said you disagreed with him there."

"I think he's trying to explain why some of the lugs and flanges broke at sixty-five tons of force as expected, while others broke at forty-five tons and others at only twenty-two tons of force. I've been thinking about it, and I admit I still don't have a good explanation, but what Stanton says doesn't make sense."

"That the combination of the beams' design and the casting flaws put all the force on one edge of the connections?" Farlow asked in clarification.

"Even if all the force was on one edge, that wouldn't have affected the strength of the metal. If the stress was unequal, it was because the beams were shifting back and forth," Charles replied.

"Because the contractor made the decision to use smaller bolts," Farlow said. "There's a lesson for you. We may design it, but others are going to build it."

"Do you agree the bridge was likely close to specification when it opened?" Charles ask.

"It's one of Stanton's conclusions I do agree with. Nothing had moved. After that, it was a disaster in the making," Farlow added, shaking his head.

"I told you it was Sir Stewart's assistant, Stevens, who was the one concerned with the weight of the supports."

"You said that when Stevens first started the job, Sir Stewart was in the midst of shoring up the supports of a bridge that was sinking into the riverbed."

"Yes," Charles said. "Darrs eventually had to replace the bridge altogether, and Stevens was concerned about what would happen if the supports started to sink on the Fee, with more than eighty spans to deal with."

"Still, there's no question at this point they would have been better to stick with brick," Farlow replied.

"Stevens told me that Sir Stewart wanted to be able to think of the bridge just as if it stood on solid brick, but the fact is the supports were neither solid nor brick," Charles said. "Cast iron, wrought iron—like the spans, they were trusses, metal cages with joints."

"Tell me again what Sir Stewart thinks about the second-class carriage," Farlow said.

Charles looked at him, not understanding.

"That it was the first coach to be upended," Farlow clarified.

Divers had now fully explored the fallen spans, and the train was mostly intact. The locomotive and the first four coaches lay within the fifth of the inverted high spans, relatively whole, while the last two cars were jammed together in what had been the fourth of the inverted spans.

"The second-class carriage was the next to last coach on the train," Charles said. "It was also the lightest, and Sir Stewart believes it canted over in such a way that the corner struck the bridge; then, a moment later, it was crushed from behind by the last car, a heavy van loaded with luggage and freight."

"Which would explain why they became separated," Farlow said.

Charles nodded, thinking of the fact that Darrs had made the spans continuous for additional strength. "I'm sure bolting the spans together into three groups is a decision Sir Stewart regrets now," he said.

"At the very least, having spans individually supported would minimize the damage in situations like this," Farlow said.

"I was thinking of the force. If Sir Stewart is right, the blow from the train would have radiated down the entire section."

"You're right, but in terms of the bridge's collapse, that, like everything else, brings us back to the supports and the fact that it was the cast-iron beams that failed."

"The reason the beams failed and not the bracing bars is because the bracing bars were wrought iron," Charles said.

"And if the beams had been wrought iron as well," Farlow agreed, "we wouldn't be talking about it now."

Chapter 53

The Court of Inquiry reconvened the first week of April in a parliamentary conference hall overflowing for the occasion. There were reporters from as far away as Paris, Berlin, and New York. The first witness to take the stand was the inspector, Henry Markum, who explained how, for the past year, he had been one of only two men permanently employed on the bridge. He also described the cracked beams he had strapped with collars and said there were a fair number of chattering bracing bars he had been packing with washers and other bits of metal to quiet them, without Sir Stewart's knowledge. James Turner, the court's lead counsel, was quick to point out how, rather than improve the situation, this left the bracing bars in a permanently distorted position—just as he was quick to point out that Markum was, in fact, a masonry expert who, prior to the Fee, had no experience at all working with iron.

Markum's testimony took up the entire morning, and he was followed to the stand that afternoon by Edgar Pike, who was completely unprepared when Turner, the same man who had interviewed him in Clevelandham, produced a two-foot section of iron from one of the beams that supported the spans that fell. He asked Pike to measure the thickness of the metal on opposite sides of its cement core, giving him a caliper for the purpose. Turner did this with three separate pieces from the beam, and each time Pike was forced to admit that the thickness of the metal varied by more than half an inch. He also produced pieces in which putty had been used to conceal major flaws in the metal. Though a common practice in the trade, it was designed to fill minor imperfections, not lengthy gaps like the ones found in the sections Turner presented to Pike. And Turner had only begun. He spent most the afternoon questioning Pike about the misshapen flanges and lugs and his decision to use smaller bolts.

Once again, the newspapers were filled with stories condemning the bridge and all involved, and it only got worse when the court heard from three experts on the subject of the wind. The first was the Royal Astronomer, Sir George Larsen, to whom Darrs had written about the Forth. Larsen repeated his view that, while localized gusts might exert a force of forty or even fifty pounds per square foot, the greatest wind pressure a bridge would be subject to on its whole was only ten pounds per square foot. No one present knew precisely what that meant, and Larsen went on to make an even bigger fool of himself when he noted that at the height of the storm the night of the accident, the wind had registered only ten pounds per square foot at his home in Greenwich, 400 miles away. He was followed by an Oxford professor of natural science, who was followed by the secretary for the Scottish Meteorological Council, both of whom agreed that winds in the region were known to exceed forty pounds of pressure per square foot. One of the men suggested that particular gusts could even exert themselves across a broad front, as much as 200 to 300 feet.

Darrs was in Brindee, working with the salvage crew to bring up sections from the spans in which the train was found, but he followed events closely through wires from Stevens. There were also the newspapers, which, though written in a markedly different tone, contained much the same information, and Darrs, too, was stunned by some of what he read. Pike's decision to use smaller bolts came as a complete shock. Darrs knew that he had given the order not to use any burned-on lugs or flanges on the supports for the inverted spans, but he never imagined it would lead to Pike using smaller bolts. And Markum, not telling him of the loose bracing bars—Darrs had spoken to him specifically about noises, rattles, and chattering.

Regardless, not every beam was flawed. Between the cracks, the off-centered cores, and the misshapen bolt holes, Darrs estimated some five percent of the beams supporting the inverted spans were likely defective to one degree or another. It was a substantial number, and plainly more than he would have liked, but Darrs did not believe that was the reason the bridge fell. Even with its flaws, Darrs was certain the bridge would still be standing if the train had not struck the side, and he'd been working hard to find evidence in support of his theory. It was the reason he'd stayed behind in Brindee and sent Stevens ahead to London. The Brindee City Council eventually approved the plan to use dynamite to separate the spans, but Hathaway insisted the train was evidence and demanded its preservation. Darrs, therefore, started with the spans farthest from the train while determining the size of the charges, and by the time the salvage crew got to the span in which the last two coaches were found, he was due to testify. He left Brindee before any portion of the span was raised, but two days later, the night before he was scheduled to take the stand, Darrs received a telegram from the foreman of the salvage crew. "Lifted one large section, and I am convinced the rear of the train must have been dragged along the span. There are distinct marks on the east side of the span, and there are pieces of timber from the coaches still stuck between the tie plates. Taking photographs and will send them along."

Darrs arrived at Parliament just before ten the next morning, escorted by his wife and Stevens as well as his attorney, Edward Bidder. A few of the reporters attempted to question Darrs as he passed, but he said nothing in response. Even so, he met their looks with a firm glance of his own. The foreman's telegram gave him some hope, and Bidder, who was allowed to speak first, used the new information to great effect. He began by recounting for the court the highlights of Darrs's more than thirty-year career. He mentioned how, at the age of twenty-eight, Darrs had been been appointed chief engineer of the Edinburgh & Brindee Railway, one of the lines that would eventually become part of the present British Northern. He described the ingenious rail ferries Darrs had designed for the Fee and the Forth and cited examples from his long list of bridges, including the Birkendale viaduct. Nor was his expertise limited to bridges and ferries. He'd designed entire rail lines—the St. Andrews line, the South Durham, the Darlington and Blackhill line—nearly 300 miles in all. In spite of all that had been written, it was obvious that no man who had achieved so much would have allowed the sort of negligence and disregard alleged on the Fee. Like many of the newspapers, Bidder quoted Darrs from the time of General Hudson's inspection: "The purpose of having the Board of Trade inspect the work is to make the security of the public an absolute certainty, as far as design, material, and execution are concerned." Bidder concluded by saying, "Surely those were not the words of a man with something to hide."

It was at that point that Darrs took the stand, and though weary from all he'd been through over the last four months, he remained a distinguished figure, with his white hair and beard.

"Sir Stewart," Bidder said, "I want to begin with the many allegations that have been made in the months since the accident. As you know, they are quite serious."

"Yes."

"And given some of the evidence the court has heard so far, it would seem impossible to deny that everything that has been claimed to this point is untrue."

"No, I don't say it is untrue. But I do believe most of what has been said has been greatly exaggerated or viewed out of context."

"How do you mean?"

"In the months since the accident, the bridge has undergone intense scrutiny, which is only natural. There is no denying that it was an immense tragedy for the families and loved ones of those who died. As a result, great attention has been paid to each and every defect that has been discovered. However large or small, the significance of each has been magnified, whether or not any one of them caused or even contributed to the bridge's collapse. On the whole, I believe the bridge's construction to have been of a high quality, a fact attested to by the praise it received at the time it was first inspected by the Board of Trade. I do not mean to say it was perfect. With regard to the supports in particular, which have received most of the criticism, thousands of beams had to be manufactured and assembled under what were, at times, the most severe conditions. If a portion of them has been found to be in some measure less than perfect—and I believe that it is, in fact, only a portion we are discussing—it would not be surprising. To believe, however, this implies a general carelessness or disregard is entirely unjustified. Despite what has been said to the contrary, Hodges & Pike is . . . was," Darrs corrected himself, "an extremely reputable firm, with a long history of achievements."

Darrs spoke earnestly. It was clear he recognized the enormity of the disaster. Given the stories in the press and what had been said, his comments about Pike were also quite striking. The fact that he would have anything positive to say about the bridge's construction was unexpected, and his attorney highlighted the point.

"You are speaking now of the contractor, Mr. Edgar Pike," Bidder said.

"Yes," Darrs replied. "And the men working for him. I would be remiss if I did not mention that I have the highest regard for those who took part in the building of the bridge. In the main, I found them to be men of both ability and character, who showed great perseverance under the most trying circumstances."

"You say this even knowing all that has since been said?"

"I do. Unequivocally," Darrs said.

The supports were the focus of the criticism, and Bidder had Darrs recount the events leading to their redesign. Darrs described how, when the bridge was initially designed, it was thought it would stand on bedrock, but the original survey of the riverbed had been wrong. Much of the bridge was founded on nothing but mud and clay, so something had to be done to lighten the load, and Darrs explained how he enlarged the size of the foundations, nearly doubling them to spread the weight over a larger area. He also explained that while the supports remained brick beneath the water line, he'd replaced the portion above with cast iron to further reduce the weight.

"And did this give you any cause for concern?" Bidder asked. "After all, you had originally designed the bridge to have brick columns, and you were now changing your plans, literally midstream?"

"Naturally, given the choice, I would have stayed with the original plan. But no, it did not cause me undue concern, as my initial reasons for using brick had more to do with maintenance than anything structural. I did not believe the changes would in any way compromise the integrity of the bridge."

"And isn't it also true that it is common practice to build bridges such as the Fee using cast-iron supports?"

"It is."

"So even in making this change, something that at first glance might appear quite radical, you were acting entirely within the bounds of accepted practice?"

"Absolutely."

At that point, Bidder shifted to the night of the accident and, in direct contrast to all the court had heard to that point, painted a picture of the bridge standing firm against the storm, unaffected by the great winds raging through the spans and supports. Then, suddenly, as the train was passing through the high spans, a gust of exceptional force took hold of the last two cars. It uplifted them, battering them against the side of the span, the impact of which was transmitted along the entire length of the bridge. It was only then that the high spans, already under extraordinary strain from the storm, were toppled from their supports and thrown into the firth below. As proof, Bidder described the pieces of timber, still lodged in the girders, and the marks on the span found by the salvage crew, assuring the court that even more evidence would be found when the whole of the span was recovered.

Outside of Darrs's immediate group, what his lawyer said was news to everyone present, and there was considerable stirring throughout the conference hall. As a witness, Darrs made a very good impression. It was clear he had no intention of blaming anyone and was in fact so obviously a gentleman, it was difficult not to feel at least some sympathy for him. At least that was true while he was being questioned by his own lawyer. It was different once Turner took over.

"Sir Stewart, how long was the Fee Bridge?"

"How long?" Darrs repeated.

"Yes, how long?"

"From abutment to abutment, just over 10,000 feet," Darrs said, surprised that was the first question.

"Almost two miles?"

"Yes."

"And how high was it?"

"It varied," Darrs said.

"At its highest point," Turner replied, "where the inverted spans stood."

"Approximately ninety feet."

"And how wide was it?"

"The deck is fifteen feet wide," Darrs replied, using the present tense.

"Ninety feet high, two miles long, and fifteen feet wide. I am not an engineer, but that does seem rather narrow."

Darrs looked at Turner. "You must keep in mind that the bridge was designed to carry a single track. The average rail car is no more than eight or nine feet across. The width is quite sufficient for that."

"Eight or nine feet—that would leave two or three feet extra per side."

"Yes."

"Not much room if you happened to be standing on the bridge when a train came along."

"It can be done." Darrs said. "I was on the bridge numerous times when trains crossed."

"Then you are a braver man than I. Ninety feet in the air, and only two to three feet between you and a racing locomotive. I know I wouldn't want to be in that position."

"The work isn't for everyone," Darrs agreed.

"But not all bridges are so narrow, are they?" Turner asked. "Many are designed to carry two tracks."

"That is true."

"In fact, many of your own bridges are not nearly so narrow as the Fee's was, are they? The Birkendale Viaduct for instance, which Mr. Bidder mentioned in his opening remarks. That is a two-tracked bridge, is it not?"

"It is."

"Designed by you and constructed by Hodges & Pike."

"Yes," Darrs replied.

"And how long is it?"

"Just over a thousand feet."

"About a tenth of the Fee."

"Yes."

"And how wide is it?

"How wide?"

"Yes, how wide?" Turner repeated somewhat impatiently.

"I don't recall precisely. It has been several years since it was completed."

"Roughly. There's no reason to be precise."

"Approximately twenty-five feet."

"So then the Birkendale Viaduct, at just over a thousand feet long is twenty-five feet wide, while the Fee, which was some two miles long, was a mere fifteen feet wide. One can't help but wonder which was the sturdier of the two," Turner said.

"With regard to stability, or sturdiness as you say, it is not the width of the deck that is the critical factor, but that of the supports. The deck of the Fee is fifteen feet wide, but the supports were more than twenty feet wide."

"Twenty-two feet to be precise," Turner repeated.

"Twenty-two at the base. They were tapered for additional stability, so that they were twenty-one at top."

"Still, even at twenty-two feet, that's narrower than the deck at Birkendale—and I imagine that for the sake of stability, the supports at Birkendale are also broader at the base."

"Yes," Darrs concurred.

"How much broader?" Turner asked.

Darrs hesitated. "As I said, it has been some time."

"Roughly," Turner said, more sternly.

"Perhaps another five feet," Darrs said.

"So then, the width of the decks aside, at Birkendale the supports are nearly thirty feet at the base, while on the Fee the supports were only twenty-two feet."

"But again, the Fee carried only a single track," Darrs said.

"And why is that?"

"Why? Because of its length. That and the fact that it crosses water and not a dry valley."

"What difference does that make? If anything, I would think one would give even more thought to stability when building over water, especially given a site as exposed as the Fee."

"Given the cost of construction, it is simply not possible to build over water in the same manner as over land," Darrs said.

"Cost," Turner replied in astonishment. "Do I understand correctly? You are prepared to state before this court that the difference in width between the Fee and the Birkendale bridge's was the result of cost considerations?"

"Naturally, one does what one can where it does not add appreciably to the cost of a project. To widen the structure to two tracks over land, all one has to do is enlarge the supports. Over water, the foundations have to be enlarged as well, which is the most difficult part of the job."

As Darrs spoke, those in the audience stirred noticeably, as he was openly admitting to the fact that economy had played a role in his thinking.

"But I take it that had time and cost not been considerations, you would have made the supports wider?" Turner asked.

Darrs did not immediately respond.

"How much wider?" Turner asked. "Two feet? Four feet? In fact, if money were no object, you undoubtedly would have designed the bridge to carry two tracks as you did at Birkendale. As it was, though, you were thinking not of how wide you might have liked to make them but of how narrow you could make them. Isn't that right?"

Darrs tightened his fist. He realized what Turner was doing, but before he said anything, Turner went on.

"Isn't it true that, right from the start, it was your aim to build the cheapest bridge possible?"

"Economy is always a consideration," Darrs said. "But not as you imagine. Given enough time and money, it is likely that anything can be built, at least in the way of a bridge or railroad. The question is whether it is economical to do so. Or whether, by some application or design, it can be made so."

"Sir Stewart, as was mentioned, during the course of your career you have been responsible for designing not simply bridges and viaducts, but entire rail lines."

"That is correct."

"In fact, in his remarks your lawyer mentioned a number of them by name—the St. Andrews line, the South Durham, the Darlington and Blackhill, to name but a few."

Darrs tilted his head. "That is so," he agreed warily.

"Indeed, there are a great many more that could be added to the list, are there not?"

"Quite a few, yes," Darrs said, still suspicious.

"And what is it that distinguishes these lines? That is, what would you say they all have in common?"

"I don't know what you are asking?"

"Sir Stewart, is it true that almost from the start of your career, you developed a reputation for your ability to build railroads at substantially reduced costs?"

"It is true I have always done my best to build economically," Darrs replied.

"You say economically, but isn't it true you have actually made a career of building as cheaply as possible, producing works at prices no other engineer would even attempt?"

"As I said, I have always done my best to limit costs."

"Sir Stewart, didn't you once design a bridge for the Darlington line that was submitted for a second opinion to none other than the late Sir Robert Stephenson."

"I did."

"And isn't it true that Sir Robert found your design lacking and therefore made a number of changes?"

"It is not unusual for a consulting engineer to suggest changes. That is the reason the engineer is consulted," Darrs said.

"But in this instance, didn't Sir Robert describe your design as unstable, specifically with regard to the supports, which he believed required additional buttressing?"

"The episode you mention took place many years ago, but if I recall correctly, at the time Sir Robert was called upon to consult on my plans, one of his own bridges had recently collapsed—an accident, like this one, that involved the loss of a train and its passengers.

The fact that he would be particularly cautious at that moment is understandable."

"Sir Stewart, when building the St. Andrews line, didn't you boast that you could build it for one-fifth of what was then the going rate for a rail line?"

"Not that I could build it, that I could design it. It merely had to do with my own fees. The St. Andrews Company, like many of those by which I was employed, had limited resources. I endeavored to work at prices they could afford."

"You say design it, but isn't it true that you also made every effort to lower the actual costs of construction—reducing, for instance, the number of cross-ties, having them placed every four feet instead of the usual three."

"The St. Andrews is a branch line, as are the others you mentioned. They are not trunk lines like those of the Great Western and the London & North Eastern. They are not required to carry main-line loads, so it was not necessary to build them to the same standards. But in every case, I made it plain to the operators that only light locomotives were to be used, and that even then they were to be run at moderate speeds. I only practiced economy insofar as it was consistent with obtaining safety. And aside from the Fee, which I fully admit was a tragedy of the highest order, the safety records of my lines are no worse than those of others."

"But are they any better? Is it possible that, until now, you were merely the beneficiary of good fortune? Until now, your practice of forever pushing the limits of what was required, reducing everything to the barest minimum, was never before put to the test as it was on the Fee?"

Turner went to the prosecution table and pulled a newspaper clipping from his files. "I have here an editorial that appeared in the

Scottish Railway News in February of 1872. I quote: 'The width needed for a double line would strengthen the architectural security of the undertaking, a consideration having special force with reference to a bridge spanning a river which is tidal, liable to enormous floods, and open to blasts of wind from two directions that are without the least mercy in their fury.'"

Turner looked at Darrs, the newspaper clipping still in his hand. "Sir Stewart, at this point there are two primary theories about the accident. Either the bridge was so poorly designed and built that it simply blew down; or, as you and some others contend, the wind blew the train into the side of the bridge, causing it to fall. Assuming you are correct, wouldn't that mean that, from the very moment that it opened, the bridge was in danger every time the wind picked up and a train was crossing?"

"I must admit that prior to the bridge falling, it is not something I gave consideration to," Darrs said. "As stipulated by the board's own regulations, the bridge was equipped with safety rails, the specific purpose of which is to keep trains from derailing on the bridge."

"Not something to which you gave consideration! How did the *Railway News* put it?" Turner asked, again glancing at the newspaper clipping in his hand. "'Open to blasts of wind from two directions that are merciless in their fury.'"

"I am well aware that storms on the Fee can be quite violent. It is one of the main reasons I chose the design I did. With trusses of the type used on the Fee, it is assumed that if the bridge is capable of supporting itself and its load, it is more than capable of withstanding any forces posed by the wind, and the Fee was designed to support a load more than twice that required by even the heaviest locomotives."

"It is assumed," Turner repeated, "And why is that?"

"Given their open design, the wind simply passes through."

"Pass through the beams to the train inside, should one happen to be crossing. Sir Stewart, the truth is, in your design, you gave no special consideration to the wind, even to close the bridge to traffic when the wind reached a certain force?"

Darrs glanced down before once more raising his eyes to Turner. "The truth is, until the bridge fell, I never imagined it was in any danger."

Chapter 54

"I would strongly advise the railroad to begin taking steps to settle with the families of the dead as soon as possible. If you go to the claimants now, you may get off easier than after the court issues its conclusions—particularly as no one of high position lost his life."

"How fortunate for us," Chairman Taylor said sarcastically.

Sitting across from him was Adam Johnstone, the British Northern's chief legal counsel, who looked at the chairman with a somber expression. "Harsh as it sounds, it does mean the claims are likely to be small."

"You suggest we simply admit our guilt?" Taylor asked.

"I am not suggesting the railroad admit anything. I'm merely saying that the railroad should take steps to settle with potential claimants now."

"Doesn't that amount to the same thing?" asked Kendall, the railroad's treasurer, who was also present.

"I am still not convinced the question of liability is as clear as you think," Taylor said.

"You are referring to the fact that the bridge was inspected by the Board of Trade," the lawyer said.

Taylor nodded sharply.

"As I've said, the board has already stated that it can't be held accountable for shortcomings deliberately hidden from its view."

"And you think that will stand up?"

"Mr. Chairman, ultimately the question is one of money. Someone will have to pay, and as no one can sue the Board of Trade, that leaves the railroad."

Taylor grimaced, but the lawyer went on, undeterred.

"Mr. Chairman, the British Northern is due to present its plans for restoring the bridge next month, and as things stand, there is no chance at all of getting a bill through either of Parliament's houses."

The plans to which the lawyer referred were those Darrs had submitted, based on the 50,000 pounds the railroad had allocated for repairs. They called for reducing the bridge's height by dispensing with the inverted spans altogether. Beyond that, however, the bridge was to remain as it was.

"I would think our chances are better now than after the court renders its judgment," Taylor said.

"The members will not even consider passing an act to restore the bridge until the court comes back with its findings. I have sat through the proceedings every day for the past month, and I can tell you that it is not merely the members of the Board of Trade who have been in attendance. With all the attention being paid by the press, many members of the government have taken an interest as well, and the truth is, there is not even a hope of getting an act through, so long as Sir Stewart's name is in any way attached to the plans. Indeed, I have given the matter a great deal of thought, and if the railroad ever hopes to get a bill through Parliament, I think it would do well to engage Benjamin Farlow as Sir Stewart's replacement. His credentials are impeccable. He is the sitting president of the Royal Society of

Engineers, and given that the Board of Trade itself chose him to sit on the court, it will almost have to approve his selection."

Taylor sighed. What the lawyer said made sense, and Taylor himself had been thinking along similar lines. Still, it seemed the greatest cruelty not to at least give Darrs the opportunity to redeem himself. He'd given years to the bridge and never made a penny on the project. There never would have been a bridge if not for him.

Chapter 55

We therefore conclude the bridge was badly designed, badly constructed, and badly maintained. Furthermore, for these defects, it is our opinion that Sir Stewart Darrs is primarily to blame. For the faults in design, he is entirely to blame. For those of construction, he is principally to blame, having failed to exercise the supervision that would have enabled him to detect the faults and apply remedy. And for the faults of maintenance, he is also principally if not entirely to blame, having neglected to maintain such inspection over the structure as its character so imperatively demanded.

So ended the opening paragraph of Hathaway's official report to Parliament, at which point Charles glanced up at Farlow, who paced behind his desk.

"We!" Farlow said, taking his pipe from his mouth. "Roland and I didn't sign it. We couldn't, the way it was." Farlow had come to a stop, and he glanced down at Charles. "'For the faults in design, he is entirely to blame.' That's a blatant lie, given Sir Stewart's correspondence with Roland."

Charles understood Farlow's point but was not entirely convinced. "When Sir Stewart sent his plans to Roland, the inverted spans were 200 feet. As eventually built, some of them were 245 feet. That's a difference of more than twenty percent."

Farlow returned his pipe to his mouth. There was no question, twenty percent was a substantial figure. It was something he'd already been considering on his own, and he again began to pace behind his desk. "Assuming the supports were sound, would it have made a difference?"

"Assuming the supports were sound. But they weren't," Charles replied.

"But if the problem was simply that the supports were built of cast iron, you can hardly blame that on Sir Stewart."

"Maybe not, but he did know there were problems with the castings."

"And he gave orders not to use any beams with burned-on flanges or lugs on the inverted spans."

"Which only made the problem worse," Charles said.

"Because of the contractor," Farlow said, again coming to a stop. "There's no indication Sir Stewart knew about the smaller bolts. There's a lesson for you: You can design something, but someone else is going to build it."

"Best. Best Best."

"Best Best Best," Farlow finished Charles's thought. "Precisely."

"But he did know of the loose bracing bars. He specifically gave Pike orders to have them tightened before the bridge opened," Charles said.

"Which Pike did. It's not Sir Stewart's fault that the drivers were racing over the bridge. That's the railroad's fault. And if there had been three or four men assigned to the bridge, making sure it was secure, it's likely it would still be standing today. Again, that's a matter that goes to the railroad."

"No doubt," Charles agreed.

"The fact is, Hathaway is using Sir Stewart to cover for the board itself, and obviously, under the circumstances, the railroad is happy to go along." Again Farlow looked at Charles. "As I told you at the very beginning, all that's going to come of this is that cast iron will never again be used in a railroad bridge. We should have stopped using it ten to fifteen years ago. Enough bridges had gone down by then. As Sir Stewart mentioned, Stephenson lost a bridge fall, and even then we didn't stop using it—which you know from personal experience has as much to do with politics and business as with engineering. There's no question the bridge could have been better. That's not what I'm saying. I'm saying that right now there are hundreds of bridges across the country of the same design."

"Thousands, if you count all the footbridges built in the last ten years," Charles said.

"Do you think the Board of Trade wants to take responsibility for that? If this becomes a discussion about cast iron, the government will have a nightmare on its hands. It won't even be just bridges. It will be Crystal Palace and the Great Western's new train shed. That's the reason Hathaway is so intent on blaming the entire disaster on Sir Stewart. So far as he's concerned, this has to be about one man and one bridge."

Chapter 56

Following Hathaway's report, the Board of Trade officially absolved itself of any blame.

"Given the findings of the Court of Inquiry, it is clear that Major General Hudson cannot be held responsible for faults in the material and workmanship that were not visible after the work was already finished and painted, and still less for defects that did not exist until after his inspection."

Only days later, *Engineering*, the oldest and most prestigious industry journal in the country, weighed in with its assessment, approving the straightforward and manly way in which Hathaway had dealt with the matter. He was described as a "fearless and outspoken judge who has cleared the whole body of British engineers in the minds of not only the British public but also their French and German brethren, who have not hesitated in their criticism regarding the state of British engineering."

Mrs. Darrs sat at the breakfast table looking across at her husband. She never expected him in any way to deny his own responsibility, but she also never imagined that he would become the object of such vilification.

Since the end of the hearings, she'd read stories in the press that claimed the storm the night of the accident was nothing out of the ordinary, but merely a typical winter storm. Another writer turned Darrs's contribution to the relief fund against him, suggesting it had been made not out of concern or generosity but because of guilt. Mrs. Darrs knew her husband as well as she knew herself. Never once in all their years together had he ever done anything to cause her to question her estimation of him, and he was nothing if not an honorable man.

The doorbell rang.

"That must be Albert," she said, setting her cup down.

Darrs glanced at the clock on the wall, which read five after nine. "He isn't due until ten."

"Who, then?"

Darrs shook his head.

"Sir, a telegram for you," the maid said, coming into the room.

Darrs opened the envelope and removed the thin sheet of paper folded inside.

"Who is it from?" Mrs. Darrs asked.

"Chairman Taylor," Darrs said, as he unfolded it.

He didn't look up, but Mrs. Darrs could see through the paper it was not very long.

"What does he say?" she asked.

Darrs did not immediately respond. His eyes remained focused on the telegram, as if he were re-reading it.

"Stewart, what is it?" she asked anxiously.

He looked at her, hesitating before answering, and she felt her heart break even before he said anything.

"The bridge. They've taken it away from me."

Chapter 57

Shortly after wiring Darrs, Taylor contacted Farlow, and by the end of the week, Charles was once again in Brindee, where he spent much of the next two months. From everything that was known, there was nothing wrong with either the spans or the foundations. In terms of the seventy-two spans that were still standing, even the cast-iron supports appeared sound. They were also ten feet shorter than the ones that fell and were supporting spans of only half the length.

Given the mood in Parliament, however, the government was not going to approve a plan that simply repaired the existing bridge. Even if the spans were going to be reused, the government was going to require all new supports that were not only wider but lower, as the navy had already reduced its height requirement in view of the accident. It took Charles most of the summer, but by the middle of August, he'd developed a fairly detailed plan for using the existing bridge as a staging platform for its replacement. The new supports would be built directly in line with the existing supports; once complete, the spans would be transferred from the old supports to the new.

Charles presented his plan when he returned to London, and Farlow was satisfied enough to give him a few days off, during which he joined Victoria and the children at a lake house her parents rented each summer, outside the city. It was there that Charles sat with his father by a small deck extending from the shore of the lake.

"I read in the paper a new bill is scheduled to be read when Parliament reconvenes next month," his father said.

Charles nodded. "Yes, but no one is thinking it will pass," he said, taking a sip from a glass of whiskey. "As I'm sure you've also read, there is a great deal of opposition to the bridge at the moment."

"But there's no question you have the job?" his father asked.

"No, there's no doubt that when the bridge is rebuilt, Denney & Farlow will be the firm to rebuild it."

"Grandpapa, Grandpapa!"

The elder Jenkins turned as his granddaughter came running from the house in her bathing clothes.

"Let me have a look at you," he said, lifting his granddaughter onto his lap. "I've never seen you swim before."

He watched as Anne and Victoria made their way to the end the dock, where Anne put her hands together over her head and dove into the water, quickly followed by Victoria.

"It's a beautiful spot the Coopers have here," Charles's father said, taking a sip from his own glass.

"It really is," Charles agreed. "They have it through the summer but haven't been able to come, and Victoria's mother suggested that Victoria and the children use it."

"Victoria's father is quite ill, isn't he?" Charles's father asked.

Charles took another sip. "I haven't seen him, but I know he isn't getting out very much."

"It must be hard for Victoria. It's no pleasure seeing your parents get old."

Charles looked at his father. "You're not thinking of yourself?"

"I'm not getting any younger," Jenkins laughed.

"From what I can see, you and mother are still quite healthy."

"Your sister makes such a fuss whenever she sees me. Doesn't want me to exert myself."

"Well, to that extent, I have to agree. At this point there can't be any reason for you to go into the shop every morning. Tim is certainly capable of handling things."

Jenkins took another sip of whiskey. "Actually, in that regard, there is something I've been meaning to speak with you about. The truth is, I've been thinking of selling the shop."

"I think that's an excellent idea," Charles replied.

"As you know, one of the reasons I kept it this long is that I never knew exactly what your plans might be. I thought maybe you'd want it."

"I know that, and I do appreciate it, but at this point, I can't see there's any reason to hold on to it on my account."

"You're sure?"

Charles nodded, taking another sip. "Absolutely. Tell me, have you got any offers?"

"The fact is, Tim has made me an offer."

"Tim! Where in the world would he get the money?"

"The idea would be for him to buy me out over time."

"That was the offer he made?" Charles scoffed.

"It's nothing immediate. Obviously he doesn't have the money to buy it outright. But I certainly trust him. And as I don't need the money right away, I can't see that it makes any difference. You're not going to take it, and I would rather turn it over to Tim than to some stranger."

Charles said nothing in response. He simply finished off his drink and after a moment stood up. "Can I get you a little more?" he asked.

His father nodded. Charles took the glasses and started toward the house. He wasn't sure why the idea of Tim getting the shop bothered him so. What his father said made sense, and it wasn't as if Charles would ever want it. Once a bill passed to restore the bridge, he had no doubt he would be made partner. Even more important, assuming Farlow was right, events were likely to play out in their favor on the Forth as well. Given what happened to the Fee, strength was going to be more of a factor than cost, something that boded very well for their cantilever design. Indeed, it was not too much to say he was in precisely the position he'd always wanted to be.

Charles reached the house, which was quite rustic in comparison to their home in the city. Victoria's parents did not even refer to it as a house, but as a cottage. It was more than 200 years old, and the rooms did not follow a definite plan so much as ramble from one to another. The front room, which was now the main sitting room, had once been the kitchen and still retained the original fireplace, with recessed ovens on either side.

The floor was also original, an aging conglomeration of boards that were no longer entirely flat. The floor crested near the center, forming a hill over which Frederick was rolling his trains. With him on the floor was Charles's mother, who was doing her best to answer the child's questions about the name and purpose of each of the cars. Both glanced up as Charles came into the house, as did Fredrick's nursemaid, who sat in a chair in the corner of the room, allowing the boy time with his grandmother.

"Papa!"

"He knows more than you do, I'll bet," Charles said to his mother.

"I know something about steam engines," his mother protested. "Don't forget, I've been married to your father all these years."

Charles walked over to a small cabinet, where he kept the liquor, and she watched as he refilled the glasses.

"You're not getting your father drunk, are you?"

"Did you know Father was thinking of selling the shop to Tim?" Charles asked, ignoring his mother's remark.

"He mentioned it."

"Why didn't you tell me?"

"When was I supposed to tell you? You've been gone all summer."

"Do you think it's a good idea?"

"You don't want it, do you?"

"No, but I doubt he'll get what it's worth selling it to Tim."

"You may be right, but so long as Tim has it, your father can go down there and putter, which is all he really wants."

Charles shrugged but did not immediately say anything in response, and Mrs. Jenkins used his silence to change the subject.

"I was speaking with Victoria. She tells me it will be a few months before you have to return to Scotland."

"That's true, though when the project eventually gets under way, I'm sure to be there for several years. I have little doubt Mr. Farlow will want me on-site."

"Several years," his mother said with some surprise.

Charles nodded.

"Well, I can certainly understand his wanting to be cautious," his mother said. "They're still saying the most horrible things about Sir Stewart in the newspapers"

"He'll never work again," Charles said definitively.

"I'm sure you're right, but I doubt Victoria will be very happy about your having to live in Scotland. Will you be able to come home on the weekend?"

"It's a long trip to make every week."

"But what about Victoria? Two children to care for all by herself."

"Hardly by herself. There's Molly," Charles said nodding to Fredrick's nursemaid. "And don't forget Esther. Between the two of them, Victoria doesn't have to do a thing if she doesn't want to."

"But even when your father used to work so late, he came home at night."

"What would you have me do? Not go?" Charles asked.

"Of course not. But you might think of taking a house in Scotland. That way, Victoria and the children could go with you."

"That would never work. Victoria would never want to be so far away from her parents, especially with her father being so ill."

"Does she want to be so far away from you?"

"Mother, I don't know why we're even discussing it. This is an opportunity of a lifetime."

"Papa's going to Scotland to build a bridge," Frederick said.

"That's right," Charles said, looking down at his son. "I'm going to Scotland to build a bridge."

"But to be away for so long—that can't be good for any family," his mother said.

Charles glanced at his mother. "It will be all right. Now, I don't want to hear anymore about it."

Charles took the drinks and headed back outside. He knew what his mother was doing. She knew he and Victoria had been having problems. Charles didn't doubt she even believed she knew the cause, and her concern was a warning of sorts that whatever he'd done, he ought not do it again.

As far as Charles was concerned, however, it was enough already. As he alone seemed to be aware, nothing had happened, and it angered him that he still found himself under a cloud of suspicion. Of course, it wasn't his mother's suspicions that really bothered him but those of

Victoria, who, in spite of appearances, had yet to really forgive him. She continued to keep her distance, and while he'd accepted it at first, it had him thinking more and more of Elizabeth. The last time they'd seen each other, she'd made him promise to stop writing, a promise he'd kept. Still, she could hardly fault him if for some reason he had to contact her father. If Charles could convince Farlow to replace the fallen spans in steel, there might very well be reason to travel to Birmingham, and while it was plainly premature for Charles to be making any plans along these lines, Elizabeth was sure to have seen that it was Denney & Farlow who had been engaged to rebuild the bridge. That would have to mean something to her, he was thinking, as he rejoined his father by the lake.

Chapter 58

Even after his dismissal, Darrs found it difficult to dissociate himself from the Fee, especially when Parliament reconvened and the subject again came up for debate. Opposition to the project remained fierce, but Darrs had little doubt the bridge would eventually be rebuilt, and though no longer officially involved, he continued to produce drawings, thinking that, when all was said and done, his successor would want to confer with him. The fact that his successor was Denney & Farlow encouraged him in this regard, and he continued to write to Charles, offering his services in any capacity.

Charles replied politely and received numerous sets of drawings in response. As the debate drew on, however, the British Northern went to greater and greater lengths to assure the government that Darrs was in no way connected with the effort to rebuild the bridge, and it became clear that even if a bill were to pass, it would not be during that term of Parliament. It could be a year or more before reconstruction began, and with the future of the Fee in doubt, there was no reason to continue with the Forth project either—or so Taylor was informed by Blackman, who put to Parliament a Forth Bridge Abandonment bill, which was promptly granted.

For Darrs, that was the final blow. He did have a number of projects on which he was still engaged, but, as with the Fee, there was tremendous pressure to remove him. One of those was a tram project in Brindee itself, where the city council opened its meetings on the subject to the public. Once again Darrs was jeered viciously. Following that experience, he approached his work with a growing dread. He tried to carry on as usual, but he couldn't concentrate. He realized that had he been the captain of a ship, he would simply have died with the others the night of the accident. The price for whatever mistakes he had made would have been paid for there and then.

That, however, was not the case for Darrs. Since the accident he had had time to think, and he'd developed a starkly different view of the bridge from the one he'd had before it fell. It was not at all the rigid structure he imagined. The supports were in constant motion, shifting and pulling with each passing train—nothing at all like brick or stone. He also couldn't help but wonder whether the bridge would still be standing if he hadn't lengthened the spans. At the time, months had seemed to matter, but now the fact that he'd thought to base any of his decisions on Hodges & Pike securing its bonus seemed the greatest folly. The company no longer existed! Indeed, though not a superstitious man, Darrs could not help but think about the fact that in lengthening the inverted spans, he'd reduced their number from fourteen to thirteen.

Other thoughts gnawed at him as well. He remembered during his Forth presentation talking about not wanting to have two different materials in contact where the suspension chains passed over the tops of the towers. Why had he not applied the same argument to the bracing bars and beams in the supports? Even in his sleep, Darrs had a recurring dream in which he could see the lugs giving way, one after another, like the stitches of a seam. It merged with his vision of the victims' terror as they plunged through the darkness into the Fee. All of it preyed on him with increasing severity, and following one particularly hostile session in the Brindee City Council, he collapsed on the train while returning home to Edinburgh.

Afterword

Sir Stewart Darrs was laid to rest on a gray November day less than 11 months after the fall of his Fee Bridge. Following his collapse on the train, he was rushed to his home, where the family doctor recommended a period of complete rest. The doctor suggested that Darrs leave Scotland altogether, but he did not want to be seen as running away. Instead, Mrs. Darrs arranged for them to go to a small town in the hills south of Edinburgh. But Darrs never recovered. Only days after arriving, he caught a chill and developed a severe fever from which he died the very next week.

Mrs. Darrs, who was with her husband at his bedside, returned home with his body the following day and made arrangements for the funeral, a graveside service attended by some two dozen people. There was a group of men from the bridge, including Pike and Henry Markum, the inspector. Darrs's assistant, Stevens, also was there, as was Chairman Taylor. Charles and Farlow traveled to Edinburgh, as did Thomas Bass of Bass & Company, the firm that had been contracted to build Darrs's now abandoned bridge across the Forth. Though no one spoke of it, many of those present knew their own actions had contributed to Darrs's demise, and even after his remains were lowered into the ground, he was not allowed to rest in peace.

His reputation was once more savaged in obituaries throughout the country. When his last will and testament was read, it was revealed he had a fortune of more than 200,000 pounds, at which point a number of British Northern shareholders filed suit, looking to recoup their losses through his estate. The suit was ultimately dismissed, but that did little to alter the fact that Darrs, who only the year before had achieved the highest of heights, died the subject of scorn and ridicule. As for his bridge, the spans that did not fall were reused and continue to carry trains to this day.

Acknowledgments

There are many excellent books and articles on the construction and fall of the first Tay Bridge. The history in this book is based primarily on *The Tay Bridge Disaster: New Light on the 1879 Tragedy,* by John Thomas, and *The Fall of the Tay Bridge,* by David Swinfen.

CPSIA information can be obtained at www.ICGtesting.com
Printed in the USA
BVOW06*1811230616

453223BV00009B/16/P